" 'Tis a wise man who learns something from each of his lovers."

Confusion once more held sway over his thoughts before Davey dismissed it. A slow, wicked curve to his lips passed for his answer.

"I believe there have been many," she stated with a sharp tone intended to prick.

"Then you have me at a great disadvantage, my lady, for I know naught of yours."

"None," she said in a forthright manner calculated to surprise him, but instead he laughed.

"My lady, were my clan—nay, the whole of the Highlands—to give a prize for inventive seduction, you would surely claim the win. Why did you believe you needed such an elaborate ruse to get me alone?"

She came off the bed quick as a fox scenting a trap, and stood beside it. "I offered no ruse. I offer no seduction. I cannot. *You were chosen for me....*"

Magic and Mist

Theresa Michaels

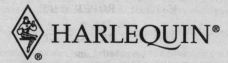

HARLEQUIN®

TORONTO • NEW YORK • LONDON
AMSTERDAM • PARIS • SYDNEY • HAMBURG
STOCKHOLM • ATHENS • TOKYO • MILAN • MADRID
PRAGUE • WARSAW • BUDAPEST • AUCKLAND

ISBN 0-373-29168-X

MAGIC AND MIST

Visit us at www.eHarlequin.com

Printed in U.S.A.

Please address questions and book requests to:
Harlequin Reader Service
U.S.: 3010 Walden Ave., P.O. Box 1325, Buffalo, NY 14269
Canadian: P.O. Box 609, Fort Erie, Ont. L2A 5X3

To Melissa Endlich,
who works her own brand of "magic."

Prologue

Scotland 1384

The young woman known as Meredith of Cambria sliced through the last bunch of tall, late summer grasses with a graceful motion that belied her uneasy thoughts.

She stopped abruptly, straightened then slid her long dagger into the sheath on her linked belt. The rich scents of heather and grass filled the air. She had cut enough to make a thick cushion for her bed this night. Her lonely bed, but then, she was always alone.

She cast aside her worries for the moment and wondered what it would be like to slip into peaceful slumber with someone she cared for lying close, arms enfolding her to keep her warm through the night.

The image of a man's face came to mind so swiftly that it startled her.

Deep-set, dark brown eyes, a straight nose, a mouth that hinted of a ready smile, the shadow of a cleft in the squarish jaw, all framed by thick, dark brown hair

falling to his shoulders. She saw the face so clearly.
It was the image of a man she could not forget.

Davey of Clan Gunn.

Far beyond the River Halladale, the setting sun
darkened the crags of Ben Griam More. Meredith
swayed where she stood in the deepening dusk, overcome with weariness. She struggled to fight the feelings of exhaustion and of being alone.

Meredith turned to look at the half circle of standing stones behind her. Not a breath of air stirred. She
could not hear the soft whispers of the spirits who
dwelled in this place.

And she, of all who visited there, would know, for
her druid training allowed her to see and hear what
others could not.

She lost time standing there, staring at what the
Highlanders called the Achavanich Standing Stones.

In this place, those Cymry who had fled their lands
hundreds of years before had settled and worshipped.
Her people had fled the swords of Romans bent on
destroying all those who refused to wear the yoke of
slaves and to turn from their sacred beliefs.

Meredith did not fully understand why the forty
standing stones were set in a U shape, with the tallest
over six feet high. She knew there was power there,
a great deal of power. The old druid priests who had
taught her the ancient ways, then sent her out into the
world, had not deemed it necessary to tell her the
meanings of the stones' placements. They had assured
her that she would always find safety within their
groupings.

Armed with such knowledge, and her gifts, she had

traversed the length of England, then Scotland, to fulfill her quest.

The time had come to reclaim all that had been stolen from her people.

A sudden chill reminded her of the lateness of the hour. She bent to gather the cut grass and heather, then carried the thick bundles to the center of the standing stones to make her bed. If she remained there until dawn, nothing could harm her.

But as she knelt to spread the bedding, the earth's power rose to her unvoiced need. Rest was forgotten as she stood and turned toward the south shore of the tiny Loch Stemster.

Without the wind to ruffle it, the surface of the water would be still and, with the rising of the moon, as clear to her as if she gazed through a precious blown-glass bowl.

Sensing the shadows gathering and hovering beside her, she walked forward unafraid. These spirits stood guard to protect those like her. She was at her most vulnerable to anyone who happened upon her when she used water to scry. Most especially to an enemy And he was not far away.

At the shore she stopped. Her voice, sweet as birdsong, lifted and fell as she chanted the ancient words.

Memories rose into her mind of the little girl, surrounded by the taller, robed and cowled priests, being taught in the sacred oak grove high in the mountair of the land the Saxons first called Wales.

She had been born for this, trained as the la her line, and she dared not fail.

Enemies were close by and hunted her. Fear took hold, powerful in its intensity.

Meredith concentrated on the moonlit water and saw again the face of Davey of Clan Gunn.

Fear ebbed.

Her heart fluttered as he appeared to stare directly up at her. His mouth curved in a grave smile, as if he knew that she watched over him, and understood what she needed from him.

The vision of Davey was wonderfully clear. The moon, at her asking, revealed more than the light of day. Everything around her was bathed in the pale radiance reflected on the water.

The vision below her faded, shimmered a few seconds, then rapidly changed to a few months past. She saw Davey, armed, mounted and fighting, saw the blows from behind that gravely wounded him. She had warned him not to go with his brother Jamie, but the warning was not heeded.

From afar she had watched over him, breathing his every labored breath, visiting his every fevered dream.

Meredith had drawn upon the most ancient and powerful healing spells of her people to keep him alive and safe.

The vision in the water clouded over, then cleared.

Davey appeared with his beloved hounds in the courtyard of Halberry Castle, stronghold of Clan Gunn.

Although she had seen this image before, she ed at the haunted look in Davey's eyes.

continued absence had put it there.

A faint whispering began, a sound no louder than the breeze ruffling the tips of the tall reeds, but it was a warning that it was time for her to leave the loch shore and seek her rest.

Meredith heeded that warning. To scry as she had done was to open the pathway for those who hunted her. At all costs she must keep herself from the hands of Owain ap Madog, for he would use her gifts for his own twisted ends. He wanted to use her to augment his own black powers.

She spun around and ran back into the circle of standing stones. She could almost feel Owain's power coiling in the dark around her.

Danger was so close, but she would not allow fear to take hold again. Davey was the answer. Her sacred oath forbade her to use her gifts to maim or kill. Davey was not bound by such an oath. He would help her, and protect her until she completed her quest.

With a bitterness she rarely allowed, Meredith understood that in the scheme of events foretold, neither her life nor Davey's truly mattered once her goal was met.

Davey had been chosen for her. She had wanted to wait until after his brother Jamie's wedding celebration to claim her warrior, but Owain's presence this close forced her to change her plan.

She rubbed her ring of silver. Longevity, continuity, eternity. The ageless symbolism of the seamless, unbroken circle and the twining endless knot.

She stood in the moonlight, tall and proud, whispering prayers. She had only to convince Davey leave behind his home, his family and all else he cared about to help her.

Despite his stubborn nature, these were small obstacles for a druid priestess to overcome.

Chapter One

"*There be none of Beauty's daughters with a magic like thee....*"

George Gordon, Lord Byron

All of Clan Gunn attended the late summer *reiteach* to celebrate the wedding of Jamie Gunn to Gilliane de Verrill.

The radiant bride and handsome groom were teased unmercifully for beginning their family before taking the vows that made them man and wife. The bridal couple, seated at the center of the high table, merely laughed and cuddled the three orphaned little girls they had claimed as theirs. They still awaited the king's decree to allow the adoption.

Sunlight shafted through the tall, narrow window openings into the great hall of Halberry Cas stronghold of the clan, and made a bold play of and shadow over those who danced with wil don to the keening of the bagpipes.

Servants darted through the crowd, carryi

whose rich scents from roasted meats and fowl, pastries and breads mixed with the salt tang of the sea, for the castle occupied the headland jutting into the North Sea at Mid Clyth on the northern coast of Scotland near Caithness.

Micheil, eldest of the Gunn brothers, ruled there as chief of the clan. He had relinquished the center seat to his brother Jamie, and sat at the end of the high table with his wife, Seana, and their young son, Heth.

He waved off an offering of baked pike stuffed with chestnuts and onions and swimming in butter and cream. He raised his gem-encrusted goblet in yet another toast to the wedded pair. The rich wines from Aquitaine, heather ale and the Scotch malt of their own brewing flowed from ewers without thought of cost.

Micheil drank deep, not only for the good wishes offered to his brother and wife, but for the peace his clan would enjoy for some months to come. George, chief of Clan Keith, was dead. And his blood feud with the Gunns died with him. The Keiths were split into factions over who would be named chief. Micheil emptied his goblet with the hope they would fight among themselves without end.

He caught sight of his youngest brother, Davey, the only one yet unwed. From the look of the two lasses crowding him, that state would not last long.

Micheil rose to catch Davey's attention, and when he caught it, he motioned his brother to him.

Micheil smiled as Davey wove an unsteady path toward him. He watched him snatch up a wineskin, slake his thirst and arrive with a devilish grin curving his lips.

"'Tis time, Micheil?"

"Aye. Do it now, Davey," he whispered in his brother's ear so no one would hear him.

Davey's voice rose above the din. He shouted for Jamie to come and perform the sword dance for his bride. Micheil and others of the clan were quick to take up the chant to get the swords.

Davey laughed when he was swept up bodily by four men. Crisdean and Colin grabbed hold of his arms, while Gabhan and Marcus held his legs. They were his brothers' closest friends as well as clansmen. The four of them carried Davey toward the far wall where enemy weapons were mounted.

There was whistling, clapping and stamping of feet as Davey balanced himself on the top of a three-man-tall tower to reach the swords.

Through hundreds of years, weapons had been mounted there, and each told a tale of some enemy vanquished in battle. Swords and pikestaffs; *claidheamh mór,* the Scots great swords; daggers, dirks and English long knives of every length and description hung on the wall.

Davey's hand hovered over the most recent addition. Guy de Orbrec's sword had been claimed by Jamie after their battle to the death. Davey chose another. All weapons were true testimony to the determination of Clan Gunn to survive, surrounded as they were by larger and more powerful clans.

Davey had recently recovered from the near death wounds he had taken, along with a fever that refused to break. His balance now was an incredible feat, for the men below him were far more drunk than he.

But Davey held the advantage. While ill, he had received a gift. His perceptions of others' movements were sharpened to such a degree that he knew each sway of the men supporting him almost before it happened.

Straight, tall and steady, Davey lifted free a sword that held no recent memories for his brothers. He tossed it down to the men who waited below. The loud jests and urgings had Jamie out of his seat as the bagpipes began to wail the "Dance of the Swords." Space was cleared in the center of the hall for Jamie to lay the first sword in place.

Once more Davey started to reach for a sword, but found himself hesitating, and again chose another. But the one he'd passed drew his hand, and he found himself lifting it free.

Just as his hand closed over the hilt, he glanced toward the archway where the massive doors had been wedged open with large blocks of stone to allow free passage between hall and courtyard. A cloaked woman stood there, her face in shadow from the drape of her hood.

Davey knew who she was. He knew her name and the sound of her voice. Micheil had sent men ranging far and wide to find her. All the weeks of anger and frustration that came with no word of her burned away. A sizzling awareness in his body bore the truth of who she was.

Davey held tight to the sword he had lifted free.

The music and voices faded until he could hear them no longer.

His gaze targeted her still figure sure that she looked up at him and no other. He barely concealed the shock of seeing his two massive hounds, Junnet and Cudgel, suddenly appear at her side. The dogs did not bare their teeth, nor did either one release the deep-throated growls that warned of a stranger.

"Lower me down," he demanded, unable to stop staring at the woman. Nor could he bear to delay being with her. Still grasping the sword, he waited until the first man bent to his knees, the others being steadied by those around them. Davey made a leap for the floor then, hitting the stone surface in a crouch.

He did not spare a glance toward where Jamie still danced. Davey stood up and made his way around the fringe of the crowd. He wanted to see her face. He knew her voice, was haunted by the musical sound of it, but he had never seen her face.

Davey still fretted over the single, brief meeting he had had with her not far from where they now stood. His gift, or curse, as he sometimes named the second sight, had given him a vision of a bloodied sword. He had never determined who wielded the sword or if the warning was for his brother or himself. But she had been there with him, had indeed spoken to him, then she had disappeared.

He still remembered her words, *"All things come. All things pass. All will be known when it is time."*

Now she had returned to him. He felt the strangest sensation of being drawn toward her, almost as if she had the power to compel him to her side.

If anyone called out to him, he heard naught of it. His focus was fixed upon the young woman. At least he believed her to be young. He respected as well as heeded the urgency flooding through him to be with her, to ease the yearning to hear again her voice.

At last, Davey stood before her. His height easily topped her own. The dogs swiftly left her side to come and nudge him. They wanted to be petted and praised, but he ignored them.

"I thought you would never come back," he said when she offered no greeting or word. He resisted his need to push aside her cloak's hood and view her face.

"But you *knew* I would come back to you."

He closed his eyes to better savor the sound of her voice—a true gift of melody to his ear.

"You did know of my return?" she asked. "I tried to—"

"Mayhap I only wished it to be so," he murmured, neatly avoiding having to admit or deny what she was trying to tell him. He did not want to believe her, refused to concede she had the power to visit his dreams. He looked upon her again.

"But you would have seen...." Her voice trailed off as doubt intruded. Surely she had spoken the truth. Davey would have envisioned their meeting again. He would *know,* as all those with gifts of sight did.

"You play a May game of words with me. Come on," he invited, taking gentle hold of her arm. "The dust upon your cloak bespeaks a long journey. You must be hungry and thirsty."

"I must speak with you. There is not time enough—"

"There is time," he insisted, once more interrupting her. His grip on her arm firmed. He had no intention of allowing her to disappear again. He leaned closer to whisper, "Lower the hood. I desire to see your face."

They were jostled by a group of young clansmen anxious to see the trained bears lumbering about to music in the courtyard. Davey swept her before him, using his body as a shield while he pressed her against the cool, smooth stones of the deep arch.

"The hood, lower it," he demanded.

She pushed the hood back and revealed her hair, black as the sheen of a raven's wing. It was then that Davey realized he still held on to the sword, for he lifted that hand to cup her chin and raise it to fully view her face.

"The sword," she whispered, somewhat bewildered that she, too, had forgotten that he held it. "I was right. You did know that I was coming to you."

"Again you whisper naught of sense," he responded with impatience. "I took down the sword for my brother's dance. Seeing you distracted me."

"Nay, 'tis not so. You never offered this one to your brother. You could not offer it to any." S' touched the hilt of the sword with her fingertips hand visibly trembled.

Davey, following her motion, stared d sword he held.

Over four and a half feet long, the peared as sharp as the day it had h wavering torchlight, he was unsure what the metal was, for it looked foreign, unfamiliar.

He blamed the drams of liquor he had drunk for the sudden thought that the sword seemed to brighten with every passing moment that he held it.

Davey continued to study the weapon, lifting it higher toward the light. Both the hilt and guard were intricately patterned. There were faint colored flecks on the thickly muscled coils of twining serpents. Davey thought they gleamed like precious gold where they wound up the handgrip, guard and hilt.

A flash of heat swept his body from his leather-shod feet upward, so that his breeks clung to his legs, hips, groin and waist. Beads of sweat broke out on his furrowed brow. His fine linen shirt with its long fitted sleeves felt confining as he drew deep breaths. The shorter, sleeveless tunic he wore belted over it had been comfortable moments before, but now he felt overwarm, though its broome-green dyed wool was as loosely spun as linen.

Davey lowered the sword just as Meredith withdrew her hand. He blocked her move to the side with a quick shift of his body, afraid that she would flee.

There was something about her, and about this sword, that sent a ripple of unease sliding down his ck.

Guard," he ordered the dogs.

ve my word that I will not leave you," she

my lady, but I willna consign that to

v honor, Davey."

"Women know naught of honor as a man sees it."

"And you know little of me to say as much."

Her calm, firm voice, as well as the words she spoke, annoyed him. "Then think on this. I might leave." His words were empty ones and he sensed that she knew it.

She stood with her head bowed, still wrapped in her dark cloak, while he once again stared at the work on the sword centered below the handgrip, almost embracing the blade.

The sunburst was unlike any he had seen. The face depicted there had pale gray moonstones for eyes. The features appeared to hold all the wisdom and sorrow in the world. Each of the curved, spreading rays flashed as if they were of gold and silver.

How had this magnificently wrought sword escaped his notice?

Davey, like his brothers and others of the clan before him, had been taught to recite the enemy, battle and final acquisition of every weapon mounted on the wall, for that was the history of their clan.

Suspicions formed. He recalled no story about this weapon. Just who had mounted it on their wall? And when?

"I've no liking for sly games, woman."

She raised her hand as if to plead, but the look on his face stopped her from uttering a sound.

Davey noticed the ring she wore. His expression wary, he studied it, then the weapon he held. The same endlessly entwined knots in the ring were worked over the guard of the sword. Each glance brought something new to light.

"Whose sword is this?" he demanded in a voice suddenly thick with fear. Then anger stirred to life. He felt as if some force toyed with him. "Is this what you seek here? Did you return to steal it? But that cannot be," he continued, without giving her a chance to answer him. "The delicate bones of your hand could not lift, much less wield, this sword."

The biting edge of his anger was unexpected. Meredith sought to deflect it. "Please, you must listen to me. Is there no place we can be private?"

"Private?" he repeated with an arched rise to one brow. A slow, wicked smile curved his lips as his eyes brightened with interest. "Surely, my lady, you can see for yourself I've no need of your healing skill. You did claim to my sister by marriage, Seana, and to my brother Jamie that you are a healer?"

"Aye. 'Tis true! I need to talk to you, to tell you—"

"Tell me? Aye, 'tis a promise I make myself that you'll be telling me all I want to know. You'll be explaining your sudden reappearance after men have been searching these many months for you with nary a word of where you had gone. That is what you intended?" Once again he gave her no opportunity to answer him. "Och, fair one, I thought your request to be private had far more pleasurable designs."

Davey was caught unaware as pain stabbed his brow. With the pain, the image of leisurely uncovering all that her cloak concealed disappeared. His grip on her arm tightened to a bruising intensity. "Cease! What are you doing to me?" he demanded.

"Naught! I swear 'tis none of my doing."

The dogs growled deeply from their massive chests, restless now, for they sensed some danger to their master, but like Davey, could not see where the danger came from.

"Tell me true!" he ordered, while fighting pain that splintered his skull like shards of broken crockery. "Tell me now what it is that you do to me or you'll find your own life in peril. Or better still, find yourself confined in the tower. A few days there and you will beg to tell me all." Then in a darker, far more sinister whisper he added, "You will find yourself, woman of mystery, willing enough to give all for your freedom."

"I swear I bring you no harm!" she cried out, for his grip tightened to a degree where she feared her bones would snap, so hard did his fingers bite into her arm. "It is your own foul thoughts that bring the pain. Cease thinking of me as a woman of the fields and yours for the taking." Meredith raised her head to look directly into his eyes. "You cannot hold me. There are forces greater than yours, Davey, that are at work here."

Davey heard her and could not deny what he was thinking about her. But he did not answer her even as the thoughts faded. He stared down at her oval face, as if he could divine what thoughts and schemes lay behind the finely textured skin with its hint of rose coloring. Thick lashes and gently curved brows of the same glossy black as her hair framed eyes deeper and more luminescent than the moonstones in the sword hilt. He found the same wisdom and sorrow within those gray depths.

He glanced briefly at the delicate, straight line of her nose, and caught the slight flare of her nostrils, as if she suddenly scented danger. But it was her lips that drew and held his attention, lush as they were with the full ripeness and color of sweet berries. He fought the temptation to lower his mouth to hers and drink deeply of the sweetness promised there.

She pressed harder against the wall, her move releasing the faint pungency of rosemary, thyme and heather.

"Fear not, maid, you willna find harm by my hands." He eased his grip upon her arm so she could slip free if she wished to. He had some satisfaction that she did not.

"Aye, Davey, I know the truth of those words."

Davey shook his head. His thoughts were muddled. He went back to what had started this. "The sword," he began.

"Aye, that sword. Do you not feel something now that you have held it within your grasp?"

He had to look away from her far too penetrating gaze. He wanted to ignore the underlying need in her question. He attempted to block the thought that her youth and beauty drew him far more than solving the mystery of the sword.

"Please," she whispered. "You must answer me. I must know."

"It is a finely wrought weapon. One of the finest swords I have ever seen or held. The sword appears heavy, but does not drag my hand with its weight. Is this what you wanted to know?"

Torchlight flared to life in both the hall and out in

the courtyard. It was only then that he realized the sun had set and true dark had fallen. Feeling somewhat dazed, he looked around, surprised that no one appeared to pay them attention. It was as if they were not present.

"Who are you?" he asked, turning to face her again. "What do you want with me and this sword?"

There were many ways to answer him, but Meredith chose the simplest one. "I am Meredith of Cambria, what you and the English call Wales. I am a healer. 'Tis true that I warned Seana that you should not accompany your brother Jamie or you would suffer near death wounds." She closed her eyes briefly, hiding the rising agony of what she had to show him, before she forced herself to continue.

"I have prayed and watched over you these many months. I could not come to you. I knew that the men of your clan searched for me, but I, too, searched, and could not allow them to find me. I have been sent to reclaim all that belongs to my people. The sword is the first.

"And I have come to claim you, Davey of Clan Gunn. You spoke the truth when you said I could not wield the sword. I have not the strength or a warrior. And...and I am forbidden by my sacred oaths to kill."

She felt pity sweep over her when she saw the stunned expression on his face. She had to force herself to harden her heart against it, just as she had been instructed to do. But it hurt. No one had warned her that it would hurt so much. His wounding was her own.

Like a blow, the horror of what she wanted from him hit Davey. He jerked his hand free of her and at the same time stepped back.

"You want me to spill men's blood for you? What manner of healer are you? One of the *Cruithneach?* One of those wanton fairies descended from those cruel, barbaric and most bloodthirsty race of Picts?"

"Are your people so different, Davey? Your people never fled in terror of their lives from those who wielded swords against them? Do the Scots not speak of the English and what horrors they bring with their unquenchable desire to conquer all within these lands?" Low and impassioned, her voice allowed him no escape.

"Those you call cruel, barbaric and bloodthirsty fled their homelands to save their lives from Romans demanding that their own beliefs, their ideas of culture and civilization, were to be crammed down gullets of folk that had no wish to sup from that dish. And if they did not, they faced slavery until death. The Romans invaded a land and a people, governing them with robbery, murder and outrages that almost destroyed a race. Those Romans desecrated a rich land, and called that making peace."

"You speak of ancient times and happenings that have no import now. And you cannot know what it does to a man to spill another's blood," Davey said.

"Cannot? I will show you." Without warning, she placed her hand upon his, the one that still held the sword.

"Look with me, Davey. Close your eyes and see what was."

He thought he saw blue, green and gold flecks swirling within her eyes before the stench of burning overcame him.

Everything he knew in this life disappeared.

Everything, that is, but the woman of Cambria.

Chapter Two

*W*ith a sickening lurch, Davey saw the mist before him lift. A wooden palisade, blackened and smoldering, lay ripped from its earthen breastwork. The stench of burning rose. All around him crackled the flames of destruction. Screams filled the air. He heard the moans of the dying. A shout and the clash of weapons had him spinning around, shocked to find that he still held the sword. A sudden spear thrust drove him to his knees. The sword was jerked from his hand. He cried out at its loss, knowing, without understanding how, that the sword was his, and his alone. Fashioned for him, blooded with his life force, and with all the power the druids commanded, his sword to keep his people safe... He groaned with the burning agony spreading from his wound. He reached out to touch the slender figure before him, with its wild tangle of raven-black hair and fierce gray eyes. He saw and felt the tremendous effort she exerted to lift his sword to slay his attackers. Yet again he cried out. The sword was cast down. He was being dragged toward the safety of the forest.

Again came that sickening lurch. Davey staggered, then quickly steadied himself when he found the support of the stone archway of Halberry Castle beneath his hand. He gulped air, his body giving a great shudder. He shook his head, wanting to refuse to believe what had just happened. The gradual swell of noise reminded him he stood within his clan's stronghold, where his brother's wedding was being celebrated.

He stared at Meredith, who stood pressed against the wall, her eyes closed, her cloak wrapped tightly around her.

Davey felt depleted of even breath to speak. This was like, and yet unlike, being assaulted with a vision, a gift of his second sight.

He had never seen that place, brief and vague as the image had been. He fought not to acknowledge the searing image left behind. But try as he would in those few moments, he could not deny that both the sword and the woman had appeared there with him, and returned.

Only now, Davey no longer held the sword. Meredith clutched it against her side.

A group of clansmen entered the wide archway from outside. Davey lifted a wineskin from one, smiling at the good-natured teasing about the woman he hid with his body. He drank deeply of the sweet Aquitaine wine as the men moved on into the hall.

He turned to face Meredith. "Your thirst must be as great as mine. Can you wait until I fetch you a cup?"

She shook her head, then tilted it back, her silk black hair falling away to expose the smooth line her throat. There was an implied trust in the gesture that touched him. He supported the wineskin with one hand as she held it up to drink, and with the other hand, he grabbed hold of the sword.

He watched as she sipped and swallowed. Lost in the intimacy of her lips touching where his own had been, he tightened his grip on the sword.

The possessiveness he felt for the weapon spread to encompass the woman. Yet Davey knew that if he believed what she had revealed to him, what belonged to him in the past did not extend to the present.

There was an undefined something about this lovely young woman of Cambria, something that warned him not to touch, not to claim or to hold.

And with that warning came the fierce, nearly over-powering desire to do those very things.

He had to look away, uncertain if he could hide his thoughts from her. The knowledge that she had powers beyond his own unsettled him as never before.

When her thirst was sated, she returned the wine-skin to him, but Davey gestured for her to hold it. He was not about to release the sword.

"You refuse to look at me," she stated in a soft voice. "Do you understand now, Davey?"

"I ken that you are all I accused you of being. And more. Much more."

"'Twas not shown to bring harm to you. Where-fore comes your anger?"

"So, I canna keep that hidden." The admission made him grind his teeth together. "Aye, 'tis true though I'm angry. Can you no' use your magic to it seethe within me until my blood heats?"

Meredith sagged against the wall in defeat. "How else was I to prove to you that I knew what it means to cause another's death? Please, I beg you yet to be private with me that I may speak freely."

Her voice grew so faint at the last that he was forced to look at her. Tiny beads of sweat formed on her smooth brow. The color was leached from her cheeks. She swayed even as he stared at her.

"This...this thing you did has weakened you. Curse me for a fool not to have known."

As Meredith earlier had moved to touch him without warning, so now did Davey move. He swept her up into his arms, ignoring the spill of wine from the dropped skin. He turned and strode into the hall. Her weight was naught to him, but he moved slowly through the crowd, watching the tumbling, juggling jongleurs perform in the center of the hall, ever aware of the naked blade he still held.

Meredith shifted so she could look up at Davey's face. He wore an expression of fierce concentration. Her warm breath, sweet with wine, feathered against the bare flesh of his neck. Innocent of the desire she stirred, she sighed deeply and marshaled her strength.

"Davey, you cannot deny who and what you are. Yet you still harbor doubts."

He barely glanced down at her hands, one covering the other, hiding the ring. He had not come to terms with anything she told him or showed him, so would not answer her.

His path brought him close to the wall, where there was less likelihood of his being stopped. Halfway to his goal of the north stairs, she repeated her words.

"Doubts?" he whispered, without breaking his steady stride. He rubbed his cheek against the sheen of her hair. The caress released an elusive, sultry scent more intoxicating than the Scotch malt he had drunk so freely.

But the liquor cloud was gone. Davey was coldly sober.

"You came into my clan's stronghold not once but twice now, and disturb me with your beauty, with this strange power that calls to my soul. You demand my sword arm for killing. You show me what must be impossible. You say I feel doubts? 'Tis more, fair maid. Try anger unlike any I've felt before. Try disbelief. Add suspicions that you play some sly, evil game with me. But utter no more words. I'll see the truth of you before this night is out."

He had taken no more than a few steps when he felt another presence close by.

"Davey, are ye stealing away for private sport? I might have known what caused you to disappear so swiftly."

The voice and the weight of the hand on his shoulder identified Micheil. Davey halted, but with a shift of his body that turned him toward a pocket of shadow. He did not face his eldest brother. Nor did Meredith wish the chief of the clan to see her, that was obvious by the way the maid buried her face against his chest.

"Davey, what ails you?"

"Naught, Micheil. You were right. 'Tis a bit of private sport I seek. An' you're keeping me from enjoying it."

"Never let that be said of me." Micheil slapped his youngest brother's back. With a laugh, he added, "Go on, be off. 'Tis a night for the Gunn brothers to pleasure their wives. Best find your own, Davey, and soon. An' mind you, no rushing."

Davey escaped as quickly as he could. He felt the heat of color rise in his cheeks at the old jest from his youth. If he was not determined to get the maid away from all company, he would have taken exception to Micheil's ill-timed jest. The fault in those days had not been his. With his clan in the midst of a war with the MacKays, he had been constantly riding with messages or leading his first raids against their enemies. There had been little time for sport. He had tumbled his fair share of willing lasses, but soon found the pleasure fleeting and empty. And far too hurried. His only mistake had been in complaining of this to his brothers. The two of them thought it a fine jest to tease him about.

Now, with times being as close to peace as he was likely to know, he had found seduction a pleasure all its own.

Abruptly shaking off his thoughts, he neared the stone stairway and looked to see that the maid nestled her head trustingly against his chest. Her eyes were closed and her breaths even. If she knew of his thoughts... But this time there was no blinding pain.

Once more his escape was interrupted.

"Davey! Save us. Peigi's sending us to bed!"

The very last thing Davey wanted was to play avenging angel to Jamie's and Gilliane's adopted daughters. The childish pleas stopped him, but he could not move forward in any case with four small arms wrapped around his long legs.

"Here now, what have you imps…" He paused. "Onora, if you dinna stop clinging so, I'll fall and crush you. Jeanne, cease your wailing or I'll be thinking Peigi's right to send you to bed."

Peigi, clearly out of breath, arrived at his side. In her arms was Ailis, the youngest. "Och, I'm growin' too old to chase after the likes of these three. Off wi' ye now. 'Tis doings you're too young to see goin' on."

"Peigi, love," Davey soothed, "you'll never grow old. As for these two wailing banshees, I'll have a word with them."

"Talk, is it? I'd be sayin' you've your own arms full with a lass in sore need of a bed."

"She's not drunk, Peigi, just overtired."

"Och, bite me tongue then. Go on wi' ye. I'll manage the little ones."

"Davey," Meredith murmured, "set me down."

"Hush now. I'll deal with them." He turned a stern look upon the two girls clinging to his legs. "See what your crying's done? The lady needs rest and quiet."

Small arms released his legs as Onora and Jeanne backed away. Davey held tight to Meredith as the mist swam up before his eyes. There was no sickening lurch, just a sweet slide into a vision of Onora grown, offered as a prize of war. And Jeanne, so blindingly lovely, fleeing from a dark-haired pursuer. Was that fey wood sprite who bowed before a king truly little Ailis?

A sigh and soft whisper ended the sight as quickly as it began.

Peigi, whose wise old eyes had seen more than she had ever told, dipped her head toward Meredith. "Thank you for letting me see what I'll no' live to know. As I live out my born days, my lady, you're smooth as a burn-tumbled stone and quick as lightning. Your power's as great as the ancient ones," she said in a voice filled with reverence. It brought a sharp look from Davey.

"Aye," he agreed, nearly choking. He barely hid his shock at Peigi's acknowledgment, and at seeing the sweet smiles and bright eyes of the three little girls. "Did they see it, too?" he asked Meredith.

"Only that they'll grow to lovely young women. They will sleep with sweet dreams this night."

Peigi glanced back once as she herded her now quiet charges up the stairs.

"She has the gift, too, your Peigi."

"Aye," Davey replied. More speech was beyond him at this moment.

He quickly climbed the uneven stone stairs to Gilliane's old room without meeting anyone else. He had chosen this chamber knowing there had been no chance to strip it clean. Inside, he placed Meredith on the bed, then went to hunker down before the hearth, where he quickly laid a fire.

Davey deliberately lingered over this chore. He shot quick glances at the sword he had set against the large, carved chair at his side. His thoughts swirled in confusion.

What had the sword to do with the visions see

Had his anger with her brought one with a sickening feeling, and the other a sweet easy slide due to his feeling more impatience and curiosity than any other emotion? He did not know the answer and that disturbed him.

From the stairway came the wild wail of the bagpipes, and from the high slit window the sound of the breakers below, along with a gentle breeze that brought the salt tang of the sea into the chamber.

Davey had delayed as long as he could. He pivoted to see that Meredith lay curled on her side, watching him.

Davey rose to his full height in a lithe motion. He stared at her. He had expected an outpouring of speech now that her wish to be alone with him had been granted. Her serious regard unnerved him. He determined he would not be the one to break the tense silence between them.

As the seconds turned to minutes he found himself disconcerted, for her gaze did not lower as a modest maiden's should, but seized and held him in a bold way. He wanted the tall branch candles lit so he could see her better, but felt any move of his would be giving in to her.

Part of him knew it was foolish to think their silence and stillness suggested a battle of wills, which he had never indulged in with any woman. Despite Micheil's earlier teasing, Davey had never lacked for female company. Girls and women came after him, and Davey rarely said no. Though before they became ~vers he warned every female that he was not look-
· for a wife.

He had to laugh at himself. This lovely young woman did not want him for a lover. She had need for a warrior to wield a sword of steel. Or so she claimed.

The thought, for some reason beyond his understanding at this moment, stung him like nettles against bare flesh. He could stand no more of her silence. He snatched up the sword. "I bid you sweet rest. None within these walls will disturb you."

"Wait!" she cried out, roused from her trancelike contemplation of this man she needed above all others. "You have not yet listened to what I must tell you."

"Your continued silence told me naught," he said, without moving toward the door, as had been his intent.

"'Tis sorry I am for that. You are far more handsome than I believed." *And far more stubborn to convince.*

The breathy intimacy of her voice recaptured his attention. The comment about his looks did not indicate a sole desire for a strong swordsman. Davey returned to the chair, angling it to face the bed before he sat down.

Meredith eyed the way his long fingers caressed the hilt of the sword. Thus would his fingers caress a woman. No man not a priest could reach Davey's age without knowing many women. She could not put a name to the conflicting emotions that raged through her. She had never thought about another man as she did Davey. She gently shook her head as if to chase away thoughts that had no place in what she must do.

"You have a great deal of patience with me," she said, drawing herself up to sit in the middle of the bed.

"I've found patience to be its own reward when dealing with women."

"'Tis a wise man who learns something from each of his lovers."

Confusion once more held sway over his thoughts before Davey dismissed it. A slow, wicked curve to his lips passed for his answer.

"I believe there have been many," she stated with a sharp tone intended to prick.

"Then you have me at a great disadvantage, my lady, for I know naught of yours."

"None," she said in a forthright manner calculated to surprise him. But Meredith herself was surprised, for he threw back his head and laughed.

"Och! My lady, were my clan—nay, the whole of the Highlands—to give a prize for inventive seduction, you would surely win it. Why did you believe you needed such an elaborate ruse to get me alone?"

She came off the bed quick as a fox scenting a trap, and stood beside it. "I offered no ruse. I offer no seduction. I cannot. You were chosen for me by my people for the help I require to reclaim the ancient gifts that were stolen from us." Seeing his closed, set expression, she lifted her hand in a pleading gesture. "You must understand, and believe. We can never be lovers, Davey Gunn. It would mean death to the dreams of others."

"Never?" That one word was a challenge. His gaze swept over her, from the loose, wild tangle of her glossy black hair, which she wore as a second cloak, to the tips of her leather slippers.

"Never," she repeated, frightened that he heard the wavering note in her voice.

Davey ignored the voice of reason that urged him to be cautious. It was her quick look seeking escape, the stance she took up, of prey held at bay, that brought him to nod in agreement. The guileless eyes and the smile that had fooled more than one lass into believing she had won some concession from him made the maid bow her head. He rose from the chair.

"I have been remiss in my duties as host. You have succeeded in intriguing me to hear the whole of your tale. Let me fetch food and drink that you may fortify yourself. This will require more than a few minutes telling?"

"Aye, that it will."

Her arm fell to her side and she looked upon him. Her shy smile smote his very guilty conscience. She truly believed he had accepted her statement that they could never be lovers.

Far from accepting it, Davey knew he could prove it for the lie it was. This woman of the Cymry, as she called herself, tempted him beyond any other. Either she was truly innocent or she played a deep, dark game with him. If what she had shown him of the past was true, she had given him an advantage. The woman who had killed to save his life had been *his*. His as only a lover could be.

And what had been once could be again. Nay, he amended his thought. Not could, but would be again.

Meredith watched him leave and did not move. She had made a terrible mistake in what she had revealed to him. How was she to guard herself against the very man she needed to protect her?

Chapter Three

Meredith stood by the unshuttered window. She stared at a night sky brilliant with stars and inhaled the sharp, clean air of the sea, while imagining the rush of waves below, battering at the rocky coast. The wail of the bagpipes provided a distracting note to the quiet she needed.

She recalled, as a child, lying in a meadow to watch the clouds drift by. In her mind she'd seen castles, great beasts or a face form in the constantly shifting shape of the clouds. She remembered the peace that filled her then, along with a sense of freedom, and longed for it now.

But that was so long ago. She found no peace anywhere these days.

Truly, she admitted, there had been no real peace since the day she had been shown Davey's face in the flames, and been told what her life's quest would be.

She glanced over her shoulder to where Davey had left the sword. She had reclaimed another of her people's great gifts.

From whence, then, came this sudden fear that she would fail?

Meredith closed her eyes. She felt as if she stood upon the edge of a great cliff. One misstep meant her death. But she knew from her teachings that death came in many forms.

Looking again at the night sky, she stood and worried her lower lip with the edge of her teeth. She could never lie to herself. She knew what caused these doubts to assail her. She had been foolish beyond reason to be so honest with Davey.

But how was she to know that he would take her truth as a challenge? If she did not deflect his thoughts he would be distracted from his purpose, and she from hers, thereby endangering both their lives.

"Davey," she whispered, unable to stop herself from savoring the sound of his name upon her lips.

She could have teased him. Lied to him. There were older, darker feminine wiles known and never used that would cloud his thoughts and senses to all but what she needed from him. A far safer choice for her to have made.

It was useless to agonize over this. The fact that she had not made that choice was hers to live with now.

Meredith turned to face the fire. In a moment she saw Davey there, his aggressive stance, his handsome face the fine work of *Danu,* and cast in shadow. Davey, tall, lithe of body, strong of will. The remembered sight of him made her heart beat faster, her breathing become erratic, her thoughts chaotic.

The physical tension that had taken hold of her did

not diminish. It merely mixed with an equally exciting sense of anticipation. The combination, however savory, was most unsettling.

She had truly believed herself protected from Davey's potent masculinity.

Were these strange stirrings that he caused the awakening of desire?

She berated herself. It could never be. Not in this lifetime. She'd been warned, and then warded against allowing this to happen.

But only Meredith knew that she had kept one secret from the ancient druid priests who had taught her. She had never told them of the whispers that came on the wind, sighing Davey's name to her.

In the oldest, most ancient tales of her people, only one's mate of heart, mind, body and soul had such great power.

This was a truth she could never speak of to Davey.

It was also the one truth she could never deny.

She turned back to her contemplation of the stars just as Davey returned, carrying a laden tray, which he set on the small table near the hearth.

"Forgive my poor manners, but I never thought to ask where you left your escort."

"There are none. I came alone to you." She took a few seconds to compose herself before she faced the fire again. She was somewhat startled to find th all the candles in the tall, twisted iron holders been lit. She had taken no interest in the ch where he left her, but now, with the spre golden glow, she noted its rich appointmer

"You came alone?" he repeated at last, unable to believe her.

"Aye. I have always traveled alone."

Davey caught her betraying regard of the drapery, chests and bed. He wondered if she tallied the cost. The short time away from her, no matter how brief, had helped to clear his mind of fanciful thoughts. Now doubts and questions filled him.

Meredith did indeed tally the cost. Her gaze lingered upon the bed with its plump pillows and embroidered cover, the costly woven cloth of the bed curtains swagged from the canopy posts, which appeared to catch and freeze the shadow that Davey cast on them. She had never lived with such richness. How would Davey bear the hard earth for his bed, when he lived surrounded by such luxury?

"Your food grows cold, my lady."

"I claim no title."

"Nor more of a name?" he goaded.

"I am known as Meredith the healer to all."

"But you are far more than that." He received neither look nor response. "None were about the cookhouse, so I stole the best of what was left from the feasting. Come, join me by the fire," he coaxed in a voice that willed her to come closer.

Meredith studied him. His hair was rich with the lights cast by the candles and hearth fire. Silkier than e thought, and longer than she remembered, his hair t back from his forehead to fall over his wide ers. His mouth had somehow changed, too. A sensuality hovered in the curve and shape of 'is eyes boldly engaged hers, brown and bright with intensity. One brow arched in a knowing expression, and Meredith was the one to look aside.

She judged both his voice and smile calculated to set her at ease. She strengthened her ward against his appeal. She had a great need for all her weapons, and the strong spirit to wield them, thus disallowing any feminine weakness that could be the death of her.

Davey merely watched and waited. He sensed a renewal of her wariness, and wondered if he had made a grave error in leaving her alone. How could he turn the advantage to himself? This sudden cynical bent surprised him. He probed delicately with his newfound gift, but discovered naught for his attempt. She shielded her thoughts from him, and now that she had looked away, he realized he could read naught in her eyes or her expression.

"I thought you in need of food. If you will not partake of what I fetched, mayhap a cup of fine heather ale will please you." He poured from the ewer, then held out the cup to her. "Come, Meredith, 'tis a rare taste I offer. Drink with me. Something needs to loosen your tongue."

"Your words are sweet and coaxing, then have a bite to them. With your absence, I have somehow managed to incur your anger." She nodded, as if satisfied by her own words, then stepped closer, but not close enough to relieve him of the cup he held out to her.

"You missay my need, Davey. I will indeed s~ but now you are not open to listen to what I sa a fine gift you have, and one I'd not enc when first we met. But heed well my war

not to match your gifts with mine. You will lose."
The flare of anger that brought forth those words was
followed by regret. Why had she flung warning and
challenge at him when she needed his help? Where
was her natural calm? It was a question that went
begging an answer, for she had none.

Davey shrugged as if her words did not matter to
him. "It appears that absence has also roused your
anger." He took the larger of the two wood chairs
before the fire. He angled his body into one corner,
his long legs extended, with his booted feet crossed
at the ankles. He eyed her as he sipped from the cup
of ale he had offered to her first.

"You are a remarkable young woman," he continued. "Your powers must be great indeed to challenge
a man in his own stronghold. Dare I believe that you
will change before my eyes into a feathered vision
small enough to seek freedom through that very narrow window?"

"You mock and threaten me!"

His brown eyes, devoid of warmth, were waiting
when she raised her gaze to his. "Aye, I do. What is
more, I make no apology for it. Have you ever longed
for something until every waking and sleeping moment is obsessed with having it? I have," he stated,
giving her no chance to reply. "For that is how you
ve haunted me."

eredith listened, and made no effort to reply to
usation. She could have explained that it was
hing over him through her scrying that
belief of being haunted. But Davey would

not listen to her, much less believe her over his own conclusions.

"You are young, but a very wise woman to hold your tongue." Again he sipped from the cup, his hard stare concentrated on her face. "Now you have returned when I am befuddled with drink, to show and tell me some wild tale."

"That is the source of your anger?"

"In part, lovely maid, only in part."

"The time of my coming to you was not of my choosing." Meredith bit her lower lip. Her denial that they could be lovers had pricked his male pride. She needed him as an ally. He was the only man who could help her. But if Davey chose to be her enemy, he would not fight her, but would not let her go, either. At all cost she had to avoid that coming to pass.

Had the old priests misread the signs? Were they, and she along with them, wrong in their judgment of Davey Gunn?

Meredith briefly closed her eyes. Knowledge beyond feminine instinct warned her that he watched her still. The attention he leveled across the room toward her had a tactile quality—another fine talent she had not been made aware of. He had her fate, and that of her people, within his hands. She would have his aid by any means necessary.

"Do you wish to destroy me?" she asked at last. The faint hesitation in her voice betrayed her wariness.

"Have I that power?"

She glared at him, unable to resist the subtle goad

in his tone. "Only a fool or madwoman would answer that with the truth."

Davey could not suppress a smile. "Och, lass, that you answer at all is answer enough."

"I..." With a flare of her cloak, she came forward to take the smaller chair opposite him. He had successfully tripped her. She longed to lay the blame on so many things, but the fault was her own. She had severely underestimated his willingness to be led where she wanted him to go.

Davey looked down into the cup he held, but did not see the ale that remained. He relived those minutes when he had picked her up in his arms. The curve of her thigh filled his hand and made his fingers want to touch her flesh. Her breast was a seductive softness against his chest. His nostrils flared as he again scented her delicate fragrance. His Cymry maid was very much a woman in his arms, and he could not get past that thought or the desire for her that warmed his blood.

A most troublesome problem.

He was uncertain if entangling his emotions was part of her ploy to gain his aid. He knew well the games to play, sensual and seductive, innocent and intimate. And there were great rewards to be had for those who played such games.

She had expressly forbidden him to pursue this path.

Therein lay an appeal all of its own, the spice lent by her admission that it was forbidden.

And, he thought, he had only her word for that.

Davey set his cup aside and reached toward the tray

of food set conveniently on the low table between the chairs.

"All this talk," he said, "has whetted my appetite." He broke one of the forfar bridies, offering half of the minced beet suet and onion pastry to Meredith. "Will you share with me? Mayhap the breaking of bread will allow us to begin anew."

Her wariness increased at his sudden shift to gracious host, but she took the half he offered, very careful not to touch his fingers. She had not forgotten those minutes when he had held her in his arms. Weak as she was from projecting the images of the past for him to see, she had no shielding from her body's betrayal at his nearness.

No one had warned of this. She had no experience with a man who stirred every sense, who quickened her breath and her heart while warnings of dangers and shivers of a strange anticipation churned through her body. She could feel the heat climb to her cheeks. Davey the man was a distraction she could not afford to indulge.

The fire spat and hissed with sap set loose, and drew Meredith's gaze to the flames that shot high. She nibbled the edge of the pastry, aware that he had finished his in three bites and now reached for one of the sweet apples.

"Are you chilled? I can set more wood on the fire."

"'Tis naught."

"I wondered why you still wore your cloak."

"The cloth comforts me."

He heard the unspoken *there is little enough here*

that does, but he no longer trusted what he sensed and felt about this woman.

"Why did you disappear if it was your intent to return here? And where did you go? My brother sent forth men to follow after Janet, but she knew very little about you. Or was that a lie?"

"She knew what I wished her to know, and no more."

Davey knew Meredith was not going to answer the other questions. He neatly sliced the apple into quarters with his eating knife. He set the sharp blade on the platter of cheese.

Davey tried another tack to get her to talk. "The few days you were here in the spring must have shown you that Micheil would have returned the sword to you had you but proved it belonged to you."

"To my people, not to me."

"Your people? You allude enough times to them. Who exactly are they? Where was that place you showed me?"

Meredith weighed her response. How much power would she hand over to Davey if she told him the whole truth now?

Hard, rapid knocking at the door saved her from that decision.

Davey quickly bid entry.

A young boy of eleven stood there with the gangly grace of a colt, his eyes wide and roving over the rich furnishings in the room.

"Rhud," Davey said to bring the boy's attention to him. "You've come for a reason?"

"Aye," he answered with a quick bob of his head.

''The laird sent me to fetch you. The bride's gone to the bower with the ladies. 'Tis time to bed the groom.''

Davey sat up. He had nearly forgotten his brother's wedding. Temptation loomed for a moment or two to tell the boy to say that he could not find him. But that would be most unfair to Jamie. The shifting simmer of Davey's emotions toward the maid told him time apart now would serve him as well as the first time.

''Tell Micheil I'll come along.'' The moment the door closed Davey rose from his chair. He took two steps nearer to where Meredith sat, still as a fawn with hunters close by. He could not resist sliding his hand over her hair. He swore he felt her breath catch.

''You will await me here,'' he ordered. ''Just to be sure you do not disappear again, I will take this with me.''

Meredith stared at his hand as it grasped the sword. She looked up and saw the warning in his eyes before he left her.

She drew her first deep, free breath since she had crossed onto Gunn lands. She gasped and turned in her seat. There was no mistaking the sound of the key in the lock.

Davey had locked her in the chamber. He dared to think a locked door would hold her! He dared!

Chapter Four

Davey could not cross the hall unnoticed this time. He smiled and laughed at the jests about his turn for marriage coming next. Moments later, if asked, he could not repeat what he had answered. He guessed the words right by the great bursts of laughter he left behind.

The stairs winding to Jamie's tower room held a few stragglers. Davey took the well-worn steps quickly, anxious to get back to the maid. Before the last turning, he was forced against the wall by clans-women making their descent.

"Best hurry, Davey, or you'll be too late to give your well wishes."

"Aye," another woman said. "Jamie's fair nettled with impatience to see everyone gone."

"Davey, lad!" Crisdean called out, beckoning him forward from the doorway with a wave of his hand. "Where were ye hiding? I broached a cask an' couldn't find ye to finish it with me."

Davey smiled, slapped his older brother's dearest friend on the back, but did not answer. He exchanged sallies with the others still there: Marcus and Gabhan, with their young wives; Colin, who stood to the left of the door. These men had grown to manhood with the Gunn brothers, and shared a bond beyond that of clansmen.

Davey entered the bridal chamber, which seemed filled with flowers. His sister by marriage, Seana, had stripped her garden of flowers and herbs to scent the bower for the wedded pair. The floor and the coverlet were strewn with flower petals. None were a match for the flush on the bride's cheeks. Both she and Jamie were in bed, Gilliane clutching the sheet to her chin, her lovely face turned in profile to Jamie.

"So, they finally found you," Jamie said when he first saw his younger brother hovering by the door. "Come in. Wish us well and fruitful this night, then leave."

"Aye, hurry, Davey, say it quick, for his impatience grows by the second."

"But Micheil, they have always had well wishes from me."

"Find the lad a drink," Jamie ordered. "Our little brother is too sober by far."

Micheil, in no condition to judge, cast a quick look at Davey. He could tell nothing from Davey's expression. Silently he handed over his own goblet of gold set with precious gems, the traditional laird's c since the time of the Crusades.

A few more jests flew thick and fast, the as quick to top one sally with another as None were crude nor of salacious innuend eil made a love match with Seana, so had Jamie with Gilliane.

Davey watched the others leave, and raised the goblet. ''Love each other well, be happy and live long. Lastly, may the king's degree making the three lasses truly yours come before Gilliane's rocking a wee bairn in her arms.'' He drained the cup and handed it back to Micheil, sharing a knowing look with him. Micheil had sent a hefty bribe to bring the adoption about before the lasses were full grown.

Davey stole two of the rare and costly oranges from a silver bowl filled with fruit and nuts, and left before his older brother could stop him.

At the base of the stairs he paused to mark a path for himself to avoid those revelers still drinking and singing in the hall. Keeping to the shadows as candles burned down and torches sputtered their last, Davey reached the tower stairs on the other side of the hall. He glanced up, not overly alarmed that all appeared dark, though he had not been gone long enough for the torches to burn themselves out.

He gave no thought to taking another light from the hall. He began his climb, and before the second turning of the stairs he stopped to reach up toward the iron bracket mounted on the stone wall.

His long, nimble fingers did not encounter the sword he had hidden there. No one had a reason to me up these stairs at this hour. Who then had taken word?

maid... He dismissed the thought before it med. He had locked her securely inside the

A faint sound at the turning above caught his ear. With his long legs he took the steps two and three at a time.

Alarm spurred him. His heart pounded as he raced upward. Fear sent his blood speeding through his body. Every instinct warned him of danger ahead.

Davey was unaware that he had drawn his eating knife, a poor blade to fight with, but he had worn no weapons, in honor of his brother's wedding. He longed for the strong steel of his sword—his newly acquired one. The depth of that longing barely surprised him, for all that it went beyond the want and need for a worthy weapon. With *his* sword he could protect his maid.

Protect his maid. The rightness of the thought fit him like the cut of the deerhide boots made to his foot's measure.

The same boots that slowed, then paused before the last turning of the stairs. He listened, hardly daring to breathe.

A great well of silence filled the space ahead. Even the noises of the castle itself had disappeared.

Davey hugged the wall without making a sound as he quickly took the last few steps. All was darkness above him. Dread washed through him.

Use your gifts, Davey.

In his mind he heard the sweet melody of Meredith's voice. He held dread at bay with cold, calculating fury. He would shed blood and rend limb from limb of any who dared to harm her.

Davey took a deep breath and released it. He used his gift to probe the shadows. He knew, without truly seeing, that the door, that stout, oak-planked, iron-bound door that he had locked, now stood open.

And he sensed that death awaited him within the black maw.

His breathing slowed. His body attuned itself for battle. He opened his senses to the blackness beyond. One threatened.

One dead man, he promised himself as he eased down into a crouch. The thud of metal hitting the stone behind him made him duck, roll and rise inside the room with a smooth, continuous motion. Davey surmised it was a knife thrown at him, and that his death was sought, for had he foolishly walked into the room, the blade would have struck his chest.

A quick look showed that the fire had been doused. But Davey still had the advantage of knowing every foot and piece of furniture within the chamber. Hardly daring to breathe, he listened for a sound that would reveal the intruder's presence. He spared a thought to where the maid was, but it never entered his mind that it might be she who threw the knife at him.

In the far corner, below the high slit window, a silvery flash came and was gone in seconds. Davey thought it was the maid showing him she had the sword.

His sword. But she was forbidden to kill.

Thoughts of her and why she did not cry out were distractions he could ill afford to indulge. Her lack of movement puzzled him. Unless she was injured, or tied and gagged?

With his sharpened perceptions he sensed the throw of a second knife before the air close to his cheek stirred from the blade's passing. A quick jerk of his head saved him from having his flesh cut.

Davey pivoted slightly, probing the dark to find the man. And it was a man, he was sure. A rank smell of horse, sweat and filth came strongest from the far corner of the bed, opposite where he believed the maid to be.

He barely controlled his icy fury that this man had dared attack him in his home. Davey had to count on his strength to overcome him rather than count on the eating knife. Although well honed, the short blade would not penetrate deeply enough to kill.

Davey still had his wits about him. He used a trick from childhood that drove his brothers mad. He shouted, "Halt!" and with a dip and sway of his body, lowered his voice to throw the word out again, and again, until it was impossible to tell where the cry came from within the room, or if only one man shouted it.

It was minutes before he circled his prey and closed in from the side. He heard the man's labored breathing, and the strong smell of fear told him his ruse had worked.

Davey pressed against the wall, holding his breath. He sensed the man's crouched position and felt the stir of air as he made a half circle with his body, seeking whoever hunted him in the dark.

Davey reached out for the tall, twisted iron candleholder. He sheathed his knife and took hold of the heavy metal with both hands. He swung as the man turned and identified the danger.

Sparks flew when steel hit iron.

Davey wielded the candleholder like a thick staff, landing a blow to the man's legs, swiftly countering with one higher. His reward was the fall of the sword and howls of pain. He struck again.

"Bastard!"

Davey launched a blow toward the voice that cursed him, but he was too late. He heard the man flee. He started after him, then dropped the candleholder. He needed light to see what had befallen the maid.

By touch he located the crockery bowl holding pieces of hard quartz, and struck a piece with his knife, hoping to cause a spark. Impatience was not rewarding. Spilled ale over the hearth and kindling made the attempt to restart the fire useless. With a curse Davey rose to find a candle that had fallen free. He had hold of one in minutes and was quick to bring its wick to light.

"Sweet saints!" he cried out.

Meredith was in the corner below the window, just as he had thought. She was bound hand and foot, and gagged. But a devil's mind had added a deadly twist to keeping her still.

The hilt of the sword was tied to her hands, with the blade up, so that the sharp edge rested against her bared neck.

As he neared, he saw the cost she had paid to warn him, for a small cut still bled. Icy fury fled under the red-hot rage that consumed him. His vision blurred; his hands trembled so much that the candle flame made light and shadow a wild dance on the stone walls. This paralysis lasted only a few minutes. He hurried to light other candles and rid himself of the one he held.

With his hands free, he used his knife with delicate care to slice through the foul rags that tied her to the sword. Davey had no care for the precious blade as he tossed it to the floor. He cut through the gag. His eyes were nearly black when he saw the bruise on her cheek. He touched the reddened swelling with his fingertips, vowing silently that the one who had done this would pay with his life. Davey then knelt before her to free the bindings around her knees and ankles.

As he stood up, she swayed into his arms, and he held her close. The violent trembling that beset her made him tighten his grip around her. He wanted to whisper that she was safe now, but that lie was beyond him. All words were. Silence helped him to contain his rage.

Davey pressed Meredith's head against his shoulder. He had avoided looking into her eyes, wanted to avoid that at all cost. He could not bear to see within those swirling gray eyes the accusation that he was to blame for this. He had locked her in here, leaving her helpless.

"No."

The hoarse whisper was hers. Resentment flared that she dared read his thoughts so easily. He stifled the resentment and swept her up off her feet. He held her so tightly that she gasped with pain. He muttered an apology as he fought to ignore the sweet, heated weight of her arm curling over his shoulder and her broken breaths touching his skin. He set her on the bed, gently releasing her body before he wrapped the thick, feather-stuffed quilt around her.

"Lie still," he ordered. "I'll fetch someone to stay with you. And I swear to you that this time you will be safe here."

Meredith clutched his arm. "Wait. Beware, Davey. You know not what you chase."

"Aye, I do." He jerked his arm free. "A man and no more. Still your fanciful tongue and draw me no nightmare visions. How came he to tie you?"

"I had fallen asleep," she whispered.

"'Tis well to try that remedy now." Davey's words were as abrupt as his departure. He did not trust himself to say another word to her, lest his wrath over what had happened spill over to her. He could not trust himself to stay with her another minute, for the need to hold and comfort her threatened his need to hunt down that foul assassin.

Davey took the steps by leaps and bounds. He had to rouse Micheil and his clansmen. There was no hope of keeping the maid's tale to himself for a while; Micheil would have the whole of it from her before dawn.

Meanwhile, Meredith struggled to go after Davey. A few feet from the bed she tripped over the sword. Catching it up, she pressed the hilt to her lips.

"Beware, Davey, beware," she whispered, knowing it was Owain ap Madog's minion that Davey hunted. She chanted a spell for protection, but knew how weak she was from her ordeal. She shook with the trembling that beset her, unable to stop herself from reliving those minutes she had stood bound and gagged with the blade at her throat.

Meredith's memories were interrupted by the tramp of feet coming up the stairs. She saw that Davey had sent the laird's lady to tend her.

Ordering the two armed clansmen who followed to remain outside the door, Seana entered the chamber, and there was no warm welcome in her eyes.

"I am to stay with you until my husband and his brother return. Pray you that neither one comes to harm."

Meredith did not defend herself. She bowed her head and, still holding the sword, returned to the bed to wait.

Chapter Five

The men sent to search went with a burning rage that their laird's brother had been attacked in their stronghold. Hours later, they returned and gathered in the hall, having found no trace of where or even who had fled so successfully from the castle and immediate grounds.

"The man could not have flown from these walls!" Davey shouted at them, more out of his own frustration for not finding a sign of the intruder. "The lot of you are still blinded by drink. A bairn could slip in front of you an' none would see!"

"Gently, Davey, go gently," Micheil cautioned. He could not have said if the warning was meant for his brother or his own aching head. "Seek your beds," he ordered his men. "Naught will be accomplished now. At first light we will search for a trail."

Davey, somewhat soothed by his brother's calm voice of reason, nodded in agreement. He started to turn toward the tower where he had left the maid, but Micheil drew him aside.

"Bide a moment with me, Davey. How did all this come about?"

Briefly then, Davey told Micheil of Meredith coming to claim the sword. He did not tell him about the vision, nor could he mention his attraction to the young woman.

"She claims that the sword belongs to her people, and I believe her," Davey concluded.

"I swear if it were not for my aching head I would seek to hear the whole of her tale now."

"Follow your own orders, Micheil. I will hear what else she has to tell. Go on. Find your bed."

"Before I do that, I'll reclaim my wife. I sent her to your maid." Laying a hand on his brother's shoulder, Micheil walked alongside him. "I'm thankful that Jamie did not wake."

"I sent word to him that we had all well in hand. I, no more than you, had no wish to tear him from what he has long desired to have. Nor did I wish to greet my new sister by marriage after her newly wedded husband had been torn from her bed."

"Aye, Davey, a woman's wrath is no light thing to scorn."

The companionable silence with which Davey and Micheil mounted the stairs and then entered the chamber disappeared with Meredith's first anxious question.

"Did you find him?"

"You have naught more to fear," Micheil quickly said to reassure her.

But Davey saw that her attention and question were all for him, and that raised a suspicion that she feared this very thing. "Neither hide nor hair of him was found," he snapped. Unknown to Meredith, her grateful sigh and easy return to her perch on the edge of the bed only compounded Davey's unease. He became aware then of the tense silence that Seana maintained. He looked again at the two men who guarded the door, and had cause to wonder if they kept the maid safe or ensured Micheil's orders that she not escape.

Rubbing the back of his neck to dispel his own tension and wariness, he realized how wrong he was to be suspicious of Meredith. Had she wished to steal the sword and escape there would have been no need of the ruse to tie her like a stuffed goose for roasting. Unless his death was tied to her being able to possess the sword?

Knowing these suppositions would only drive him mad, Davey broke the silence. "There'll be no sleep for me this night. 'Tis best to hear the whole of your tale, most especially if you shed light on who attacked you."

"Aye, I've a need to hear it, too," Micheil said as he chose the chair beside his wife.

"Micheil, love, 'tis late," Seana protested. "Can't this wait until morning?"

"Micheil is free to seek his rest. I told him as much, but I will hear the whole tale now." Davey stood against the wall opposite from where Meredith sat on the bed. "I've already told my brother," he began, addressing the maid, "that you claim the sword beside you belongs to your people from ancient times. I also explained to him about your earlier visit and your intent to ask for the return of the sword until you found out our aunt was held for ransom. Micheil understands that you did not wish to distract him from the matters under consideration at that time."

Meredith understood quickly enough that Davey was giving her a warning about what he had not told Micheil. She looked away from him, but could not look at Seana, for there was distrust in her eyes. Micheil sat with his own eyes closed.

"What Davey told you is true," Meredith said. "I know the sword was taken as a prize of war hundreds of years ago, but it has special meaning to my people and I have come to ask for its return."

"'Tis strange to give this errand to a maid," Micheil remarked without opening his eyes.

"I am the last of my family. The sword was first given into our keeping, and then stolen. It has been our charge, since, to reclaim it."

Davey caught her gaze upon him and perfectly understood the significance of her soft-voiced statement. If what she had shown him of the past was truth and not some sorcerer's trick, then was he, too, laid with the charge of recovering the sword? Again he found himself rubbing the back of his neck to ease the tension that refused to leave him. She explained one thing and that only led to more questions.

"I truly understand what a burden a charge can be, but it sits ill with me that you come alone into our stronghold," Micheil stated.

"It was not intended to alarm you."

Davey glanced from Meredith to Micheil. What was his brother after?

"Mayhap. The fact remains that you were assaulted and my brother attacked."

"That's the meat of it, Micheil," Davey said. "What was he after? There was time enough to steal the sword. Or kill you," he added deliberately to Meredith, when she gazed at him with such calm. "Did he come seeking my death?"

"Aye," Meredith whispered.

That made Micheil open his eyes and sit forward. "Why would he seek my brother's death? What has Davey to do with you and that sword?"

She glanced from Micheil's glacial blue eyes to Davey's brown ones. There was a strong facial resemblance between the brothers. They shared suspicion of her, too. Davey stood with his arms folded, his face painted with the flicker of candlelight. She found no warmth within his eyes. She took her own courage in hand to continue her tale.

"From the *awenyddion,* as soothsayers are called in our tongue, there comes a prophecy. To my people in ancient times came four gifts to help them overcome the evil that swept through their land. 'Tis always the choice of those who hear of this to believe or disbelieve," Meredith said. "The gifts were given to save the innocent who died, to cease the burnings of our great forests and meadows, to still the slaughter of animals and stop the taking of free men, women and children as slaves to the Romans." Her voice wavered as she felt the memories rise. She clasped her hands together, as if that would give her strength to continue.

"To our priests were the gifts given, and it was for

them to find those among our people to wield them well and wisely. But the Romans came in hordes, numbers without end, and at the last they overwhelmed us. There were many who escaped and came to these northern lands, and with them they brought the ancient beliefs. Our gifts were all lost, stolen as booty from the wars. This sword is the first of the gifts claimed, for without it, none of the others will be had.'' There was no change in her voice as she spoke this small lie.

"I was sent alone,'' she added for Micheil's benefit, since it concerned him the most. "Aye, I came here alone, but I know I was followed. I was chosen to reclaim the sword first, to complete my quest, but I have need of a warrior who alone can wield that weapon.''

"And the others?'' Davey asked quickly, unwilling to allow Micheil to question her. "What are the other gifts you claim?''

Meredith looked at him and found his thoughts well hidden behind a shield. She frowned as she thought over her answer.

"Are we not to know?'' Davey demanded.

"The sword you hold is the Sword of Justice. Made for one special man who will never fail in any battle with that blade in hand,'' she answered in a forthright manner. "There is a Cup of Truth. Sweet water, fine wine or coarse ale, the liquid matters not. Whosoever drinks from the cup cannot lie to any question put to him. There is the *crwth*, a harp to make music so sweetly soothing that all sleep upon hearing it played.''

She paused, wondering how much more to tell them about the harp, for in hands unskilled, without the spell to release its magic, it was simply a harp, nothing more. Nay, she decided quickly. 'Twas not for them to know.

"And the last?" Davey prodded.

"There is a ring," she replied in a softer voice, "a ring that protects its wearer from all harm."

Meredith could not seem to stop herself from rubbing the endlessly entwined knot on her own silver ring, given to her by the priests, with a spell for her own protection. Unfortunately, the ring was useless against another druid or someone ensorcelled by one.

"You speak of ancient times and ancient gifts," Micheil stated, his voice as icy as his glacial blue eyes. "Why is it now that you come seeking them?"

Meredith looked at him and saw the suspicion and doubt in his eyes. She glanced at Davey, but he stared at the sword. Seana looked away before their gazes met.

"Well, have you no reason?" Micheil asked.

"'Tis the first time in centuries that all the gifts have been found," Meredith replied, once more staring down at her hands.

"And this warrior you need, I suspect 'tis my own young brother Davey that you'd be wanting."

"Aye, 'tis your brother chosen."

"Chosen?" Micheil looked at his brother. "You're aware of this and said naught to me?"

"There was no time, Micheil."

Meredith looked at Davey as he spoke, and she felt a measure of his pain at lying to his brother. No matter that he had not spoken the lie aloud, his omission was a lie. She was amazed by the depth of Davey's turmoil.

"Surely I misheard you, Davey. You could not have agreed to this?"

"I did not agree or disagree with any of what she told you, Micheil. I, too, wanted to hear what she had to say. I can wield this sword. 'Tis a fit for my hand alone."

Davey lifted the weapon and took a few steps nearer his brother. "Go on. See for yourself. This is a weapon for a man, Brother."

But when Micheil reached to take the sword, Davey's grip tightened upon its hilt.

"You can examine it well enough without taking it from my hand."

Micheil gritted his teeth, the move clenching his strong jaw. He studied the intricate design. Davey's refusal to let him take the weapon frustrated him. That frustration sharpened his voice.

"You claim you did not agree or disagree with this maid and her need for a warrior, Davey. Yet by your own hand you have already claimed the sword yours. Do not shroud your answer in obscurity and expect me to meekly accept it, Brother."

"When I want to hear a sermon, Micheil, I'll fetch a priest," Davey snapped.

"Look you, Micheil," Seana said. "Look to the woman as you speak of meek acceptance," she directed. Her hands gripped the arms of the chair as if to stop herself from attacking Meredith. "Meek indeed is her manner while she sets you against each other.''

''Not true!'' Meredith cried out. Her eyes widened as she stared at Seana incredulously. Then her gray eyes closed for a moment. She felt herself suddenly shaken with a rising surge of anger, which threatened to shatter her control. All the years of terror, hunting and being hunted, the terrible toll of loneliness, the endless doubts consuming each hour, all surfaced in those moments.

She looked again upon Seana. ''You dare? You dare to accuse me of dividing them? That was your game from the first, my lady.'' Meredith nearly choked with the knowledge she had. ''You seduced Davey to betray his brother. Aye, 'tis a love match now, but not then. And I mean no harm to any. I told Davey the truth of the sword. The charge to recover these gifts was laid to my family since they were lost. I want naught of you and yours but what belongs to my people.''

Davey caught the significance of her words. *Her family.* And if the vision was true... It was, and he could not deny it.

Micheil half rose from his chair, but Seana's hand gripping his arm prevented him from standing. Davey looked at Meredith. She stood with her hands raised before her in fists, to defend herself or attack should Micheil go near her, he knew not. It took him a few seconds to understand that she was unaware of her stance. Anger flushed her lovely skin and brought a darkness to her eyes. He saw the rapid rise and fall of her breasts now that the cloak was parted. He glimpsed something else above the curved cut of her gown: a blue curlicue.

"Enough of this!" Micheil's voice, far from rising with anger of his own that this unknown maid dared to speak so to him and his lady wife, had softened. But it was of such softness that Davey moved to stand between Meredith and his brother.

"Hold, Micheil. You'll not harm her. Nor will you or Seana accuse her of wishing to bring harm here."

"You'll stand against me, Davey? Are you forgetting—"

"I forget naught of you and who you are to me— laird, brother and friend. But this I say—I stand as protector for her in our castle and on our lands."

Micheil eyed his younger brother standing before him proud as Lucifer. "Davey," he said, lifting one hand to aid his plea, "be not so firm with your words. You do not know this woman. And I've no wish to have you against me."

"Aye," Seana hastily agreed. "Speak not in anger. 'Tis late, far too late to discuss this with any calm. Please, Davey," she added when she saw he would not be moved by her request. "I spoke too quickly." It was as close to an apology as she would make.

Micheil rose from his chair and offered his hand to his wife. "Morning is time enough to talk of what is to be done."

Davey felt Meredith's hand on his arm. He looked down at where she touched him, and with a weary nod, he bade his brother and wife go. When the door closed behind them, he shook his head as if rousing himself from a trance.

"Davey, come sit by the fire. I tell you true, I never meant to come between you and your brother."

"It was not the first time, nor will it be the last," he replied, taking a seat and stretching out his long legs. "Micheil's carried a heavy burden since our father's death. But I do not wish to speak of my brother. Rather, tell me who attacked you."

Meredith busied herself by pouring wine, handing him a cup and then sipping her own. "His name is Owain ap Madog. A man obsessed with having these four gifts for his own ends. 'Twas not he here, but one of the minions he has gathered to him with promises of riches and powers beyond their reckoning."

"There's more to tell," he shrewdly surmised when she looked away from him.

"Aye. Owain was raised high in the midst of the few druid priests that remain to my people. But when they saw the greed and blackness within him, he was cast out. I tried to tell them it was too late, and that he should not be set free, but there were those who refused to listen. He knows the charge laid upon me, and is determined to retrieve each gift for his own use. He also wants me, for I must confess to you that there is a keying to be done to render the gifts of use, and that alone is mine to do."

"Keying?" Davey asked.

"Aye. 'Tis a spell to release the magic."

"You heard what I said before my brother and his wife. I said I will stand as protector for you. I'll not take back my word now."

"Davey—"

"Nay," he said, holding up his free hand. "Allow

me to finish. I know not if you have ensorcelled me or I make this offer freely, but I stand by my word. There is within me a need to say this, and follow through wherever it may lead."

"I swear to you I use nothing to compell you!"

He stared at her and smiled, but at the same time studied her. Her fairness was lure itself. And her voice enchantment that excited and soothed him both. But it was more than her loveliness that drew forth the protective surge he felt. He knew he responded, too, to her sense of purpose in the face of great odds. He did not discount the desire she raised in him, but for the moment he was content to keep those fires banked. She had been his, she would be again. He knew that without question.

"Micheil and Seana had the right of it." Davey rose, set the goblet aside and took her hand. "Seek what rest you can this night. And know that when you are ready to venture forth on your quest, you will not ride alone."

"You risk your life," Meredith warned.

He raised her from the chair, then lifted her fingertips to his lips. All the while his dark gaze held her own as if he sought truth from lie within those gray depths.

"No life worth living is without its risks. And for you I would risk all."

Before she could stop him, before she surmised his intent, his strong fingers cupped her face with an upward tilt that brought his lips upon her own. Gentle cherishing was the first thing she felt, and her senses seemed to stretch and heighten. She felt the warm, faint touch of his breath upon her skin, and caught the waft of a tangy scent—a masculine scent that seemed new and familiar at the same time. Her breathing refused to settle.

With a low moan, more like pain than pleasure, his mouth closed hard on hers, demanding yet gentle, cruel but tender. A confusion of sensations enfolded her. His punishing need forced her head back, and yet his arms were there to hold her, to cradle and caress her body against his own.

He kissed her mouth, her eyes, her temples, and then her lips again were his until darkness swam before her. Like the wine they had drunk, he tasted of an intoxicating sweetness, with an underlying dark passion that could destroy her.

Her gifts deserted her. She had no will before his own. Only the danger remained, and with it grew a need to stop him.

"Curse you for struggling now," he breathed, with his mouth moving in a rough path over her exposed throat. "You've haunted me. You and those bewitching eyes and voice." His teeth closed on the soft skin of her throat and heat bloomed in the center of her body. "I'll risk all to have you mine again," he whispered, urgently grasping her hips against his.

Meredith wanted this, but she fought this closeness and found she had to fight the treacherous response of her own body, which softened against the hardness of his.

"I beg you," she pleaded, gripping his shoulders in an effort to push him away. "Think Davey! Think what you would do!" she cried out, struggling in earnest now against his greater strength. "Would you destroy me and my people? You have that power!"

He lifted his head, his harsh breaths filling the air. His hand slid to the nape of her neck, and with a quick move, he trapped her cheek against his shoulder. He held her tight and hard against him, so tight that she felt the faint tremor in his hands and heard the thundering of his heart, which nearly matched her own.

"Davey, Davey," she whispered against the cloth of his shirt. "'Tis not too late. Save yourself. Come not with me. If you cannot or will not control this desire you will kill all hopes that give meaning to my life."

"You claimed you needed me to wield that sword!"

"I told no lie."

He set her away from him, his hands tight upon her arms, but she did not lift her head to look at him. "I'll have a sworn promise from you, Meredith. I will come and help you, but at the end, when all is recovered and set before your people, you will be mine."

She withdrew into herself seeking an answer. A day ago, even an hour, up to the very moment he'd touched his lips to hers, she would have known what to say. But she held the taste of him on her lips and felt the heat of him and the strength of his arms around her. He would render her gifts useless were she to give in. But he asked for a promise far in the future. Could she deny him?

"I'll have your answer or not be responsible for what goes forth this night."

There was passion thickening his voice, and a warning of danger, too. She lifted her head to look upon his features, as well known now as her own.

"Aye, I'll give you my promise that when all gifts are laid before the priests to fulfill the prophecy, I will be as you wish. I pray you, Davey, that in turn you promise me this...tempt me not. Without my gifts I will reclaim naught of what is needed. And on your head will rest the destruction of my people's dreams to unite our land as it was meant to be. I will not be with you then, only against you. And do not discount my powers, Davey, for they will destroy you or any that stand in my way."

There appeared within his dark eyes a gleam of recklessness that she could not counter.

"I want you, Meredith," he replied, his voice suddenly husky because a sense of his own power seemed to flow through him from her nearness. "Aye, maid, I want you as I have never wanted another woman. They say all the Gunn men are alike in that. When they sight the one woman for them, naught will gainsay them from having their heart's desire. I want you with my mind as well as with my body." He stopped and drew a deep breath, grinding his teeth in an effort to retain at least the external appearance of control. "I have heard all that you said. So be it," he intoned in solemn oath.

"Aye, then, so be it upon your head, Davey," she agreed.

"Come then, a kiss of peace to seal these vows of honor, sweet maid."

And he took that, along with her breath and her

will, for long, lasting moments, until he released her and left her shaken where she stood.

She had what she had come for—a warrior to protect and help her. But he had taken with him that precious sword. And she knew that for all his fine words, Davey did not trust her.

Chapter Six

"Micheil's right!" Jamie's voice thundered in frustration. "It is daft to hope, lunacy to believe and disastrous to trust her. Aye, I know," he added with a swing of his arm, "you've got your senses to guide and aid you in this decision. But think, Brother, think. You know not the truth of her tale. She could be the death of you, Davey."

"Are ye done with calling me a fool and too young to know my own mind?" Davey asked from where he stood, staring out at the courtyard. The deep window embrasure almost cut him off from the rest of the room behind the great hall, for it was as thick as the castle wall. He had dreaded this, and yet done naught to evade his brothers this morning. He had even broken his fast with them, as evidenced by the littered remains on the table.

"I swear our little brother does this to be contrary and give me trouble," Micheil remarked from where he sat, slicing an apple into ever smaller pieces.

His remark made Davey turn. "Is that how you see me still? As only your little brother?"

"He meant no insult, Davey," Jamie was quick to say. He had been attempting to make peace between his brothers since the maid this morning had let slip news of the hunt that had roused most if not all of the castle last eve. Jamie chafed that none had thought to fetch him. As clan tanist, all matters of security for their stronghold and their lands rested upon his shoulders. Gilliane would have understood. He had made no secret of his standing within the clan and his intent to keep his place as war leader.

"It matters not if he did. I am not going to change my mind. The orders are given to have one horse saddled with provisions, and my own stallion. I will not take Jennet and Cudgel. She's breeding and I want those pups safe."

"Micheil's right! You are a bletherin' fool!" All out of patience, Jamie threw himself into his chair and poured himself ale. He drank it quickly to keep from shouting at Davey. Not that shouting had done him any good. Nor had reason. He shared a look with Micheil, who appeared as lost as he over what to do. Neither of them wanted Davey to ride off with this unknown maid, no matter his desire to do so.

"Perhaps not," Micheil mused. "Mayhap Davey knows more than he shares with us."

Jamie eyed Davey with bright speculation. "Like what?"

"Think about what he said. And what I myself added. You agree with me, Jamie, that we know too little. Davey does not agree. I have no doubt that he told us the truth, even if he won't swear to it, but I fear that Davey tells us half the truth, with the important parts left out.''

Davey flushed upon hearing Micheil's judgment of him, for his remarks had hit home. He turned toward where his brothers sat. ''What more would you have me say? I leave to help her as I swore to do. Would you have me offer some surety that naught of ill will befall me?''

''I never thought to need the blacksmith's pincers to get information from my brother.''

''Och, Micheil, you're sounding like Da.''

''Aye, Davey, he is, but he made a valid point. You are hiding something from us.''

''What more do you want?'' Davey asked irritably, his voice loud with the building frustration he felt at his brothers' interference. ''I have told you everything I know myself. Do you now want me to make up some tales for you?''

''Never lie, Davey. I ask that of no man,'' Micheil said.

''Nor do I,'' Jamie added, motioning for Davey to join them.

Davey at last relaxed enough to sigh heavily. He hated to be at odds with his brothers, especially after all they had been through together. He realized that his hands had been clenched into fists for so long that his fingers were growing numb. He forced his hands open and flexed them.

''All my life,'' Davey said as he walked toward the table, ''I have lived beneath both your shadows. We have fought and argued, but always, Micheil, you as laird had final say. And you, Jamie, as our tanist, were the last word in matters of war. There is no special place held by me. I wish to do this. I *will* do it. Are we clear on that?''

There was a new hardness to his eyes and a firmness in his voice as he stood before Jamie and Micheil. Davey poured ale for himself and raised the cup.

''Well, will you drink to my success? Or is this to be a bitter parting?''

''Let me send a few men with you,'' Jamie began, only to see Davey shaking his head.

''I told you. The maid and I go alone.''

''And what of the danger this Owain ap Madog presents? If he would dare send someone into my stronghold to capture the maid and sword, his attempts may end your life once off our lands.''

''I know, Micheil. But have you both so little faith in what you have taught to me? Am I not a fine swordsman, Jamie? Can I not ride the most mettlesome stallions? Have I served you ill in any task either of you have set before me? But you still look upon me as a little brother, one to be protected at all costs. I want free of this burden you so easily place upon me. Can either of you understand?''

Uneasily, his brothers nodded.

Davey smiled at them. ''Then wish me God's speed.'' He drank from his cup slowly and saw above the rim that Micheil first, then Jamie, drank with him.

''A last caution, Davey,'' Micheil said, in so neutral a voice that both his brothers stared at him. ''Can you not wait a day or so? Jamie's newly wed. 'Tis most unfair to forgo the other planned celebrations for him and Gilliane. Surely, if the reclaiming of thes gifts this maid spoke of has waited so long, a few days more cannot matter.''

"Her name is Meredith, Micheil. As for my leaving this day, the sooner done, the sooner I can return.''

"Where comes this certainty that you will return?'' Micheil cried out in a passionate voice, all thoughts of soothing and reasoning gone from his mind. "Damn you, Davey, if I order you as your laird not to go, you will not!''

"Do you so order me?''

"Micheil,'' Jamie cautioned now, thinking back to times past when Micheil had ordered Davey gone from his sight, and nearly cost Davey his life.

Micheil bent his head and shielded his eyes with one hand across his brow. Always he managed to prick Davey's pride, when his only desire was to keep him safe. He gave thought to Davey being vulnerable when the visions of second sight assailed him. Who would protect him then? That frail maid? How could Micheil reason with a brother, with a man so set on going his own way without let or hinderance from him?

"Micheil?'' Jamie said, laying his hand upon his brother's arm.

"Well?'' Davey prodded with an ugly laugh, "what more will you order, demand or offer as bribe to keep me here?'' Very carefully he set down his empty cup. "There are only the three of us here, Micheil, so none other will know how you chaffer with your own brother to see your will done.''

"Nothing more, Davey,'' Micheil answered at last.

"I will say no more. I wish you Godspeed and will look for your return."

Far from elation that Micheil had capitulated, Davey felt remorse, but not enough to cajole Micheil into a better mood. He could not say himself why he was so insistent on leaving this day. A sense he could put no name to hovered in his mind, and that sense urged him to go quickly, alone with Meredith. He was not unaware of the danger Owain ap Madog presented, nor reckless with thought of his own finely honed skills should they be set upon. The need was there and must be heeded. Guilt was there, too. He should have shared with his brothers the vision that Meredith had shown him. He knew it would prove him right in what he did, but Davey knew his brothers too well. They would somehow find a way to twist that and claim again that Meredith had bewitched him.

He was done, more exhausted by the last hour than he cared to admit. Better he should take his leave and trust to time and success that he'd made the right decision.

"Davey, have Ciotach saddled for yourself. He's been long in training to kill enemies," Micheil said.

"You'd give me Breac's near twin to ride?"

"I want you well mounted, and none of your own stallions match him."

"I'll take him gladly." Davey clasped his broth arm, silently thanking Micheil for his offer. He t and did the same to Jamie. "Keep your lasse

"And you," both brothers said together turned to leave them.

He had not gone far before he was stopped by the appearance of Seana with Gilliane in tow. He eyed the two and, with a long-suffering sigh, stood and waited for them to join him.

"You are set on going?" Seana asked.

"Davey," Gilliane said, "wait a day more. Surely you will give us all time to know the truth of what this woman claims. Please, you are not so long from your bed."

Seeing the stubborn set of his mouth, Seana moved in front of him with her hands on her hips. "Davey, have some sense," she scolded. "This is no time for you to be so proud. 'Tis your life you risk," she cried, her voice sharp with fear and exasperation. "You're precious to those who love you. Dinna go. I beg you."

"If I risk my life, Sisters, then 'tis in God's hands."

"You fool! Were the wounds you took that laid you so close to death's door enough to addle your wits?" Gilliane grasped his hand, adding her plea. "Dinna go with her."

"Gilliane has the right of it, Davey," Seana said. "God sometimes needs help. Man has free will, but your will seems bent on destroying yourself."

"I believe," he replied with cool calm, "that you ᵒth have husbands and children to tend. Leave me ᵈecide my own fate without your meddling."

"ᵈinna ye see," Seana challenged him, "none of ᵛes this is by your own will. 'Tis all her do-

" Davey strove for patience, but found he

"Give us a kiss, Peigi, and dinna worry about food. If you packed all with your own hands, I'll no' go hungry. Keep us in your prayers. If the good Lord's listening, I know He'll hear yours."

Davey turned from her then, unwilling to allow her to see the doubt besetting him. But the words she had spoken as coming from his mother haunted him. How could it be? What more would he find on this journey with Meredith?

He started to tuck the folded cloth into his sporran, the plain softened leather already heavy with coin, but found his hand moved to tuck the small packet inside his shirt, against his skin and below his heart. A faint warmth spread from where the cloth touched him, but he paid little heed to it as he once more glanced around his chamber to be sure he had not forgotten what he wanted with him.

He looked with regret at the hauberk of finely linked mail with its attached coif. 'Twas far too heavy to remove alone, and he did not relish spending days or weeks wearing it. Davey slipped the padded gambeson on, made of two thicknesses of linen, padded with wool, and quilted like an eiderdown to keep the stuffing in place. It would resist sword cuts quite well, or at least deaden the force of a blow. Instead of the hauberk, he chose leather armour, known as *cuir bouilli*. The leather was boiled, then hardened by soaking it in hot wax, and was strong enough to withstand and even deflect blows from a lance or sword. Its most precious attribute was its lightness, which would leave him unencumbered for combat. Over this he wore a soft wool tunic, its dark brown color unrelieved by any embroidery or device. He strapped on his sword belt, added his dirk, and placed the newly honed *sgian-dubh* into his boot. He spared a thought to taking a second boot knife, as Micheil always had, and thought it worth the added protection. He took up his own sword, knowing the other one was already wrapped and bound behind his saddle, as he had ordered.

He had been tempted to carry the Cymry sword, but as it was temptation to him, so it would be to any man who saw it. His unremarkable dress would allow him to seek shelter and food in any keep and castle, yet the lack of trappings should allow their safety from thieves and outlaws.

Davey hurried down to the bailey, where Meredith awaited him to begin their journey. His brothers, he thought, would surely cry bewitchment and lock him away if they knew that he did not know where he would be riding with Meredith. But for the prize he would claim at the end, he would follow the maid into the very jaws of hell itself.

He paused on the steps, a warrior true, bathed in the summer sun's morning light. He sent a skimming glance over all he held most dear. He heard his hounds howling in the kennels where they had been locked away, and there they would stay, for to loose them would have the dogs seeking his trail no matter how long he was gone from home.

No one lingered close. Davey vaulted onto Ciotach's back, and without looking directly at Meredith, seated on her young mare, he led the way out of the gates.

For good or ill he was hers to command.

Chapter Seven

In a small hidden hollow south of Halberry Castle at dawn on the same morning, Owain ap Madog spelled a fire for conjuring. He was slender, fair, handsome and, some were wont to say, as quick as a fox, with all of a fox's charm and cunning, and a voracious appetite, too. He never disputed this, for he had an appetite for power, and was bound and determined that all the ancient gifts of the most powerful druids would be his to command.

The mist-laden air surrounding him bothered him not a wit, but caused his three minions to huddle together for warmth far from his fire. What he did was magic, turning the golden-red flames to blues and greens and, at their heart, white fire for him to see. What he viewed within the flames at last appeased his rage over the bungled opportunity to have the Sword of Justice in his grasp.

The fault for last eve was his own, not that he would ever make that admission to anyone. He had been far too anxious and greedy. And it was his curse that, though he could foresee in fire what was to come, his vision never extended for more than a few hours into the future. But it was enough this time to make his plans.

And when he had the gifts, he would have the maid, for he had waited for her to become a woman, waited for her own special arts and talents to mature. All the days of the years he had waited, and watched her with possessive pride, knowing that she would be his mate, truly the only choice the old priests could make.

Owain understood very early, as few others had, that his destiny was with her. He had also understood that it would require every fiber of cunning to win her away from the teachings of the old priests.

The flames before him turned nearly black as his rage slipped its tightly held leash. Mutterings from the three he had chosen to follow him finally reached him and roused him from thoughts of what had passed to foil his plans.

He calmed himself and allowed the fire to die. He turned then to stare northward, from whence she would ride forth. And with her, a new weapon for him to use. She had chosen another to wield the sword, but his life would be forfeit. Owain smiled then and lifted his maimed, clawlike right hand to smooth back his wheat-blond hair. He stared at his hand, payment exacted for his transgressions. He could look at it now without flinching, without re-membering the searing agony as they'd held his arm out into the fire, using spells from the very book he had stolen and refused to return to mark and maim him. But he had sworn to have his revenge for this loss, too.

"Bring the boy," he ordered.

In moments a lad of no more than twelve summers knelt in the dirt before him. The dazed, slightly glassy look in his eyes brought a smile to Owain's face. He lifted his arms so the loose sleeves of the stolen friar's robe fell back to reveal twin, wide, rune-incised gold bands that covered him from wrists to midforearms.

"See you these?" he asked in a soft, almost melodious voice. The boy had drunk the wine he had prepared and could barely nod. "These mark who I am."

"Aye," the boy mouthed, rather than spoke.

A dagger appeared in Owain's hand and he dipped the blade into the fire. The blade and hilt turned black, but not from smoke.

"You know what you are to do with this. You know where you are to go. Know then that I will be waiting to reward you well for serving me." He knew there was no true understanding in the boy, but he smiled to show his approval at his attempt to agree. "Cei, get his horse. Pwyll, help him to stand and mount. Go, my son. You have the power and the need to obey me." Owain placed the dagger securely in its sheath on the boy's new belt, then turned away.

Well after he heard the horse depart, he ordered the fourth of his party, David, to break camp. "We will ride within the hour."

Seana, with Gilliane hot on her heels, burst into Micheil's private solar. "How dare you let him ride away alone with that woman!'' Seana demanded of her husband.

"Aye, Jamie, how could you?" Gilliane asked of her newly wed husband.

"Would you see your brother perish because he's lost all sense to a pair of pretty eyes? Could you not send men after him to keep him safe?" Seana faced her husband with her hands on her hips, the color high in her cheeks and her eyes promising fury.

"What ails you both?" Gilliane asked, as smiles closer to smirks appeared on both Micheil's and Jamie's lips.

"I should take grave insult, wife, and from you also, sister by marriage, for your questioning me so. I am still laird here," Micheil intoned in a stern voice. "But I am in a generous mood and will forgive you."

"Forgive me!" Seana sputtered. "Micheil, 'tis naught to jest about. Davey's in danger with her, I tell you! Why do you sit like a lackwit and do naught?"

"Seana, love, calm yourself. Do you truly believe I care so little for my brother that I would do naught to protect him from the very devil himself? For shame, wife, I thought you had more faith in me. Even now," he hurried to say, as he realized she was truly overwrought, "my men ride to follow him. At a distance they ride, with a promise to me that they would not approach him unless he was in danger of being overwhelmed."

"Och, Micheil," she cried, coming forward to hug him. "I knew you would to something."

"Well, you did not sound as if you trusted me," he complained, hugging his wife tightly. A quick look showed him that Jamie had risen and held his own wife within his arms.

"We worried so," Seana murmured against his chest.

"Aye," Gilliane said. "Davey refused to listen to us. He was like a blind man seeing naught but that woman. I fear for him."

"As do I, Micheil."

"I've done all I can. Any more an' Davey's sure to hate me. He's a man, not a boy any longer, as he took great pains to prove to me this morn. Truth be told, neither Jamie nor I would have had his patience with the way he's been held close all these years. It was time, love, to let him go."

"I trust her not," Seana whispered.

"Nor I," Gilliane seconded, pressing tight within her Jamie's arms.

"Then trust that Davey knows what he's about," Jamie said, sharing a look with Micheil over their wives' heads to show they were of the same mind. They had to believe that Davey knew what he was doing or they would both ride out after him, and thereby destroy all their brother's love and respect for them. As it stood now, Jamie thought, their parting this morn had left a great deal unsaid of love and loyalty owed to their clan, if not the family itself.

"Aye, listen well to Jamie's words," Micheil said, in such a stern voice that everyone knew the matter was not to be spoken of again. "He has the right of it. We all will trust to Davey to know what he is about."

Had they but known, Davey silently spoke similar words to his horse as true night blanketed the land on the shore of Loch Shin in the shadow of Ben More. It had taken him nearly three hours of hard riding before he had asked Meredith where they rode. South they had come, then west into the lands of Ross and Cromart. And he wondered again at the woman's powers, for they had seen naught of another soul.

To the keep at Torridon they would go, then south into England. But she had refused to tell him which gift they would be reclaiming or the how of it. She could not think to ride as she had into Halberry and bemuse another man. Or could she?

Meredith dreamed. Darkness, such black, black dark, and yet within its heart there were moving shadows. She struggled to see them as they shifted and changed, now growing large, then receding until there was nothing. She felt the threat of the dark. Something or someone reached for her. She sensed need, a need so great it would consume her were she to give in. Danger was all around her. And with it came an evil she could feel and taste.

It smothered her. She ran in her dream, tripped and fell, only to rise and run again. She had to be free of this. Besieged by darkness, she ran blindly. She could scarcely breathe. Her heart pounded until blood roared in her ears.

She was chased. As she fled, only once did she turn to see what she could. No form of man nor beast was there, just the sense of a presence reaching out to grasp hold of her. She was sickened by the stench of destruction and gore. The odor pressed in on her and she cried out, for there was no light, no safety to be found.

With a wrenching sob she pushed on, knowing that to stop was to die. The loss of something held dear beset her and nearly brought her to her knees. The scream rose in her throat, unbearable grief torn free from her lips. And then she could not stop the cries that poured forth.

She felt herself seized and held tight, no matter how she struggled, how she fought. This was how it would end, with no strength left to fight, no words or breath left to save herself.

"Gently, lass, gently now. You've naught to fear."

She opened her eyes to find that Davey held her in his arms. His soft voice was as soothing a comfort as any she had ever heard.

"Safe, Meredith. You are safe with me."

She trembled against him, another scream dying. She pressed her cheek to the steady beat of his heart, her fingers clutching his arms. All her senses were muddled, still held in thrall to the terror she dreamed. As did his voice, his gentle hold brought warmth and strength creeping into her, and her terror abated.

"You gave me a fright, crying out as you did. I thought us beset." Davey eased back a little, his gaze keen with both speculation and concern. "Can you speak of the dream?"

Meredith did not answer him. She could not. How to put name to the faceless, formless terror that assaulted her? She made a feeble attempt to push away from him, but he held her fast.

"You've naught to fear now. I'll hold you till you cease trembling." Davey settled her on his lap. He spread his cloak over them both. He knew what it was to wake from sleep, shaken by dreams that could not be put into words.

The night was sweet with the scents of summer. The quarter moon held a pearlized sheen; the stars shone with hard brilliance in the inky sky. No breeze stirred to ruffle the thick leaves of the trees or bend the tall grasses, but a faint trickle of water tumbling over stones could be heard in the night's silence.

The fire had died to ashes. Davey thought to stir it to life, for Meredith yet shivered in his arms, but he was reluctant to release her even for a few moments.

Desire awakened within him, proving that his struggle during the day to hold passion at bay had done him little good. Her trembling increased as if she sensed him weakening, and he quickly banked the embers flaring to life with the reminder that her need was to be held and feel safe.

Her head rested trustingly on his shoulder, her hands tucked close to his chest. The fragrance of thyme, heather and rosemary teased him with every breath he drew. He shot a quick look to where the horses were hobbled, and saw naught to alarm him. Fully awake now, he sensed something out there in the dark that watched them.

He would not chance a wrong decision, if there was true danger or not. His sword lay beside him, for he had snatched it up at the first sound of her distressed cry, thinking they were attacked. He had no wish to stir her fear anew. Cradling her close with one arm, he freed the other from the folds of the cloak so his hand could easily grip his sword. His own desire now was to search out what he sensed, but he feared to leave Meredith alone.

There was no way for him to judge the time that passed before he felt the tension ease from her body. Her breaths were deep and even. He wished his own were.

Mayhap, he thought, it was only the terror of her dream and rough awakening that spread its unease to him. But Davey knew better. There was someone out there. Or something...

Davey felt a chill crawl up his spine and raise the hair on his neck. Once more he checked the horses, but they stood calmly.

Very gently, he tucked the cloak tighter about the maid, glad she slept. He would forgo his rest this night and hold her while he kept watch.

Meredith did not truly sleep. His warmth heated her terror-chilled flesh and eased the tension from her body. Davey's solid presence was a refuge, and one she was most happy to have. She cautioned herself to do nothing to arouse his desire. It took all her will-power not to react when his body tensed. She knew what he sensed. She stayed as she was, believing her faith in his vow to protect her would outweigh his need to discover who watched them.

But round and round her thoughts scrambled, for it was not right that she should feel safe within the arms of the very man who threatened far more than any dream.

She barely stifled a cry when his lips brushed her temple. It was all she could do to lie still against him. Heat spread from his lips to her skin. What was he doing? Did he no longer sense they were being watched? Or did his passion rule him?

All through the day, his continued silence had troubled her. She'd wanted to ask him what concerned him, but could not. There was a forbidding air about him, one that she respected. She thought the lack of his brothers' presence to see them off might have something to do with it. Just as she was sure that both Micheil and Jamie had argued long and hard against Davey coming with her.

She felt his lips again, the kiss light and warm. It only turned her thoughts to the feel of his lips against her own, her first kiss, her first taste of passion. The remembrance brought once more those same waves of sensation that had washed through her.

Meredith exerted every bit of her will to keep her breathing steady as if she truly slept, but her body betrayed her. Her stomach knotted, her breasts swelled and between her legs she felt hot and wet. What power did Davey possess to arouse her when she ordered her body not to react to him? Danu, *sweet goddess, help me!*

But it was not the goddess whose voice she heard in answer to her plea...it was Davey's.

"Sleep, lass," he whispered. "I'll let no one harm you, as I vowed. Sleep now."

Her sigh was heartfelt as his crooning voice continued murmuring of safety and vows and promises to be kept. In her mind she offered thanks to the goddess for hearing and answering her plea. His lips no longer kissed her flesh, and he guarded her well through the night.

Chapter Eight

Dawn had not yet chased the last of the black cobwebs from the sky when Davey and Meredith broke their fast with bread and cheese. She told him then how little time they had to reclaim the three remaining gifts and make the journey to her people.

"Now is the time of Lughnasa, a long celebration lasting to mid-August. We celebrate the commemoration of Lugh, the oak god Bran. It is a time to remember the dead, to solemnize a new king, to give thanks for women and to celebrate marriage. If the sky is clear tonight, I will show you the shape of the stars that form *Lleu Llaw Gyffes.*"

He tried hard to sound the words as she had, but ended with a muttered oath when he could not.

From the rock above Davey, who sat on the blanket, Meredith smiled at him. "My tongue is not easy for those not born speaking it. The words mean 'lion with the steady hand.' And you will see the shape of the she-bear. Morrigan, the great queen who shared Bran's totem animal, the raven, often appears in the guise of a she-bear. We set a great store by animals,

Davey. Then when summer flees, and autumn passes, in early November comes Samhain. I must return by then or all will be lost for more years than I will see on this earth in this life.''

"You never told me why you must have all four gifts back.''

She looked away rather than answer, listening as the birds began their morning ritual of darting about as they chirped and sang. The morning star sparkled between barely visible wisps of clouds. In the meadow below, the night creatures would be returning to their burrows, and those of the day would begin to roam in the dewy grasses. A peaceful place this, she thought.

"Meredith, why do you not answer?''

She debated with herself how much she needed to tell him. Would he understand the yoke of oppression that had wearied her people for centuries untold? And how much would he believe?

"Meredith,'' he called, impatient now.

"The signs and portents read by the priests tell of a birth, of a prince who will reunite my people and lands as never before. The gifts I reclaim are to be his to use. Time is of the essence for me. The priests need to cleanse with ritual each gift, then they must rebless them to bring forth the truest form of their ancient powers.''

"What are you saying? Did you lie to me and my brother when you spoke of these gifts you seek to reclaim?''

"If omission is a lie, then aye, I did. But I told you the truth, Davey. As they are now, that is the extent

of the ancient powers that remain to them, but only
if I awaken them. The sword never called to you before I came. But these gifts are more, much more.''
She did look at him then, holding his gaze with her
eyes wide, willing him to know what she said without
words spoken.

"More?" he repeated. "Much more... Are you
telling me that the sword I held gives more than the
right of justice to the man who wields it?"

There was no way to turn aside his question. She
was slow to nod, wishing he would leave it all be.

"And the Cup of Truth? You said that no matter
what liquid was drunk from it, no lie could be spoken.
What more could..." The darkening of her eyes made
him halt. "What more power could a cup deliver?"
he asked in a soft voice suddenly holding menace.

"I violate the trust put in me to speak of these
things with you."

"Tell me!"

Only her need of him kept her voice calm in face
of his command. "The cup will hold the power of
life or death for any who drink from it."

He rose from his place with a swift, fluid grace.
"So the sword—"

"Makes the wielder invincible, Davey. There is no
known substance that its blade cannot cleave, from
stone to the thickest metal. 'Tis said that the blade
was fashioned in some secret method. I know naught
more of it."

"And the harp, or whatever you named it?"

She inwardly shrank from the fierce light in his
eyes and the rough command of his voice. "The

crwth will lull to sleep, as I said. Death is a form of endless sleep, too.''

"Sweet merciful saints!" he muttered, raking his hand through his hair. "And the ring that you spoke of protecting its wearer? I suppose that is an instrument of death, too?"

"Only to one who steals it, Davey. But now each is no more than what appears to the eye. They have no powers."

"'Tis you who will awaken them."

He accused and condemned with those few words, and she had no defense. How could she defend the truth he spoke?

"What else haven't you told me? What more do you do than return these...these things to your people?" He could do nothing about the anger that rolled from his tongue, for he was greatly disturbed by her reticence.

He stared at her, and found that she was the one who looked away. She took her time about answering him, too.

"Among my people women have greater freedom than they do elsewhere. None of us is a man's slave. We take our fate into our own hands and choose for ourselves a husband or not, but the man must accept our conditions. We are honored for our talents and gifts, unlike the English or the Normans, who curse women like me as witches. There is more acceptance of us in Scotland, mostly in the Highlands, where our people had settled. But despite this greater independence, there are those among us who are born bound by ancient laws and oaths."

"And you are one of those. But you skirt my questions like a most practiced—"

"I am trying to answer you with truth, Davey!"

"Aye, truth colored by your need to keep your secrets. My word is my honor. I gave it freely...or did I?"

"I did naught to your will. It was, still is and will remain your own."

"Then answer the simple question, Meredith. What more is expected of you after you return? And think well before you speak, for I remember the promise you made me."

She lowered her head. "I have not been told of the role, if any, I will play. Ask me no more, Davey, for there is, in truth, naught else I can say."

She was lying to him. This time he knew it for sure. Her skill outshone his. He could probe her mind with his new sense till night fell, and still she would be shielded against him. He nodded as she finally lifted her head and gazed upon him once more. He was certain that he conveyed the belief that he would ask no more of her. But he knew he was not yet done.

He paced before her, where she sat on her rock, his gaze keen on the awakening land. "Last night," he said, "I sensed danger around us."

"As I did."

"Yet naught came near. The horses remained calm, as if safe within Halberry's stables. I wished I could have done the same."

Meredith toyed nervously with the folds of her cloak. "What is it that you wished to know?"

"Before you settled to sleep, you walked about. What did you do?"

She concentrated on brushing the crumbs of bread from her lap. She listened for a few moments to the swift change, then abrupt silence of the birdsong, all the while wondering how much to explain to him.

"Meredith, this time you will not put me off. I demand to know how much or how little I am truly needed."

"Much," she whispered, still reluctant to look up at him. "I was given power to keep me safe because I journey alone. I told you only a little of Owain. He…" She stopped, twisting her body around, with her head tilted toward the loch. "Davey, if you value my wisdom, we cannot linger here. Ask no more of me. And make haste. We must ride hard this day and the next, or I will lose my chance to recover the cup."

He longed to argue, to keep her here and ask all the questions that had formed and plagued him through the long night. He needed to have his doubts laid to rest.

But Meredith was moving swiftly to pack, as if she cared not whether he attend her warning to make haste. He was sure, from her hurried movements, that she would leave without him.

Hers to command. His own thought from yesterday came to mind as he ran to tie their bundles on the packhorse. He noted then the oiled wrapping on some long, narrow object, and would have asked her about it, but when he turned toward her, she was already settled in her saddle.

The sun glinted on the sheen of her hair, for her

hood was thrown back. "Haste, Davey. To linger longer is too dangerous. I swear to you that Owain is near. He must not have the sword."

Within minutes Davey swung himself onto his own saddle, and another doubt added itself to the mental tally he kept. Was there true danger from Owain being near or was this a convenient way to end his probing?

From the first Meredith set a hard pace. She rode well, all fluid grace, with a firm but gentle grip on the reins. Davey rode alongside her, constantly watching the land for signs that they were being followed. It crossed his mind that she knew the land well, for there was always water when they needed a short rest, the easiest of trails skirting all dwellings and those who inhabited them, or a path not visible to his eyes when the forests of oak and alder and thick fir blocked the way.

When they stopped to rest the horses for the second time, he reminded her that they would need to turn west to avoid the falls that spilled from Loch Shin and, farther south, those of the Oykel River.

It was from there that Davey felt he rode with an arrow poised at the middle of his back. No matter how many times he turned to look, there was never a sign of riders following. He laid his unease on the fact that the lands they rode across belonged to Clan Sutherland, sometime enemies of his clan, but never called friends even when truce stood between them.

Meredith slowed her pace, and Davey did likewise. He held his silence as she gazed ahead. His notice of her lovely profile nettled him, for he should be alert only to danger. But the sunlight lent a glow to her cheek.

"What do you sense, Davey?"

"I've felt an arrow poised to fly at my back," he snarled softly. "Sutherlands have no liking for strangers riding their lands, though it's not all that long ago that Hugh of Moray received this grant from the king. There are still Norsemen about, the lands having been theirs first." He glanced over his shoulder at the woods, dappled in a few places with sunlight, dark as pitch in others. He saw nothing to alarm him, yet the feeling persisted. "Why do you now linger here? You were quick enough to silence my questions with the need to ride hard and away."

"I linger to see who rides behind us, Davey. But I do not believe that is where your feeling comes from."

She unsettled him, and he wondered if she meant to do so. They continued at a walk, he in surly silence and she with studied calm.

"I heard rumors that Robert, Earl of Clan Sutherland, would marry the daughter of the Wolf of Badenoch."

"You hear strange things that few know about," he said. "A fine mating if the daughter is half as ferocious as her father. And if she has half the conceit of her groom there will be hell to pay. Likely she'll be wanting to have him build another Dunrobin, only named for her."

"Named for her?"

"Aye, Robert built Dunrobin, which means Robin's Castle."

"Ah, Dunrobin."

"You sound as if you know the castle."

She glanced at him, to see the mistrust audible in his voice glaring in his dark eyes. "I know where he built it. The site he chose was close by a Pict broch. I told you my people had settled here long before yours or the Norsemen. There was a dry-stone tower near where he built Dunrobin. And Davey, you have naught to fear from the Sutherlands. The earl's grandmother was Cymry. There are those who watch, but they will allow us to pass unharmed. I am certain those who ride behind us mean no harm. There is no taint of the darkness that Owain leaves with all that he touches. As for your feeling of an arrow poised at your back, I wonder if it comes from the nearness of my longbow." She gestured toward the long, narrow, oiled wrapped bundle tied to her saddle.

"A Welsh longbow? I've heard there are none so skilled as Welsh archers. The English used them against us in battle. But why have you one? I thought you were forbidden to kill."

"I am. Stop trying to trap me in lies, Davey. I carry the bow for an arrow can serve to warn off those who trespass too close to me."

She set her heels to her mare before he could ask any more questions. He sped after her with every intent of taking hold of her reins and leading her, along with the packhorse. But when Ciotach's long, ground-eating strides brought Davey to her side, she laughed with all the gay abandon of a maid on a pleasure ride, and once more leaned over her mare's neck, urging her to greater speed. Davey allowed her the lead, be-

mused by the swift changing of her mood. If she told
him the truth, and her own people watched...och, but
these doubts would addle what wits he had left. There
was naught else to do but ride after her.

The path led through a meadow, and he heard the
old gaffer of the woods, a capullcoille, and thought
what fine eating the black grouse would make roasted
over a fire. A good half dozen might fill his belly.
But the sight ahead of open meadow and no maid
sent Davey racing on into the wood. No one could
have been more surprised to find a wide track a short
distance later. At the curve of the track, he saw, Meredith had stopped, and he hurried to catch up with
her.

The words of anger, of recriminations, died on his
lips, for he knew well what the stench was. Ciotach
jerked at the reins, whinnying loudly enough to drown
out the same sounds from Meredith's mare and the
packhorse. The stallion attempted to rear, and Davey
tightened his grip until the animal settled.

From the great oaks lining the edge of the wood
hung the remains of four bodies. The odor of rot hung
in the air, too foul to breathe.

"Meredith, come away."

"Why, Davey, why? How can a man order this
done?"

"They were likely outlaws. Hanging is a fitting
punishment for the crimes they committed." He
watched her turn to look at him, her lovely gray eyes
filled with tears. "Dinna—"

"No man should die like this," she whispered.

"There are those who would argue days with you

over the rightness of this, but not I. Far better to have a quick, clean death. Now, come away. There's naught to do but pray for their souls.''

She bowed her head, and made no protest when he grabbed hold of the mare's bridle to lead her away. He kept the horses at a slow trot and made no attempt to speak to her, sensing that she needed time to herself.

Less than an hour later the track widened as it rose up a hill, and when Davey reached the top, he saw spread below a small village. He drew the horses to a halt and looked at Meredith.

Her mien was somber. He called her name twice before she looked up to answer him.

''Do you wish to seek out an alehouse or camp alone?'' He gazed again upon the huddle of thatched roofs. ''At best we might find a clean hayloft to sleep the night.'' All day he had avoided touching her, but he released the mare's bridle and reached back to touch her hands. ''Meredith, you are cold. Come, my lady, we will find warm food at least.''

''Davey, I do not think we should ride down there.'' At his frown, she struggled to put her feelings into words. ''I never finished telling you about Owain. He would do anything to possess—''

''Aye, I am well aware of how far he will go. If you canna tell me for sure that he rests below, we will go.''

Meredith said no more, and once again allowed him to take the bridle of her mare to lead her. Her feelings were still disturbed. The truth of Davey awakening desire within her was not one she wished to face. She had been so sure of her purpose, but his questions raised doubts as to what would be her fate when she returned with the reclaimed gifts. If she succeeded in thwarting Owain and lived to return… She also admitted to herself that she had been false with Davey in not telling him the truth of what he faced. At the time it appeared the best course, but now…uncertainty plagued her.

A fresh wind blew in from the Minch off the west coast, bringing with it the smell of fish and the sea. But Meredith paid little attention to where they rode. Deep in thought, she saw nothing of the ripening fields or the flocks of sheep. Were there charms and spells to protect her, to ward off a man like Davey? With his fine blend of honor, kindness and strength, he undermined her pledge to remain untouched. Her own desire to have done, and think of a true future with him, weakened her. She called upon her gods, struggled to regain inner fortitude, and vowed to force personal thoughts of him from her mind.

Aid came unexpectedly by the appearance of a young lad stepping out from the deep shade of an oak tree onto the track on Davey's side. The horse he led appeared to be lame. Meredith judged him more finely dressed than a crofter's child, but not so fine that dust and a few rips seemed amiss on his clothes.

As Meredith studied the face, which was close to angelic in beauty, she thought it strange to see the boy's mouth move as if he spoke, but to hear no sound. She shook her head, thinking the fault her own, her gaze targeting a face of delicate features, shoulder-length golden hair and eyes of serene blue. Nay, there was something amiss here.

She nudged her mare closer to Davey, about to warn him. He chose that moment to lean down as the boy approached. She called out to Davey, but he was deaf to her voice.

Owain! She knew he had sent the boy. She had no chance to stop the upward flight of the dagger that flew from the innocent-looking boy's hand. Her intent to reach Davey crowded her mare against Ciotach's side and pushed rider and horse from the dagger's path. The black blade missed Davey's heart, but lodged deeply in her own shoulder.

He cried her name as, stunned by the power of the weapon, she tumbled from her horse.

Chapter Nine

Davey drew his sword, ready to strike the boy, who had collapsed on the track the moment the dagger left his hand. He did not know if the boy was dead, nor did he care. It was the sight of Meredith sprawled on the earth that commanded his attention.

He had failed to protect her! He dismounted with a wary eye on the wood, afraid that they would be attacked before he could get Meredith to safety.

With a word to Ciotach to guard them, he knelt beside her. Just as he reached for the dagger—a foul, obscene thing protruding from her shoulder—she whispered to him not to touch it with his bare hand.

Faint, already weak, she instructed him. "Wrap my cloak around it. Pull...pull it out."

"Let me get you—"

"No time. 'Tis spellbound...Davey...hurry."

Somewhere in his chest his breath caught and lodged tightly. He leaned over her, the edge of her cloak gripped in his hands. Her breathing was shallow, but she lived. The trembling seized him then, just as he seized hold of the black dagger. This was no time for gentleness, yet he ached with the pain he caused as he yanked the blade free with a mighty pull.

The blood ran and soaked the cloth. From somewhere Davey summoned the thought that it was best to let the blood clean the wound. He could not care for her there in the dust of the track. He needed to find a safe place. He gave no thought to going into the village. God alone knew what more he would find waiting for them there. He lifted Meredith in his arms and set her on Ciotach's back. He barely spared a glance at the boy sprawled on the ground. How Davey controlled his killing rage was beyond him, mayhap because the maid needed him more.

"Do not leave him," she whispered.

Davey lifted his sword, more than willing to end the lad's life, if that was what she wanted.

"Take him. He's a pawn, no more."

He glanced at her, hunched over with white-knuckled hands wrapped in Ciotach's mane, and then at his sword point, poised over the boy's chest. He would do her bidding in this, he decided, sheathing his sword. Lifting the lad, he tossed him over the mare's saddle, then quickly looped the reins of the lame horse to the packhorse's rope and mounted behind Meredith. He turned back the way they had come, racking his mind for a safe place to camp.

He cut into the woods, listening for sounds of pursuit. He allowed Ciotach his head, knowing the horse would find water faster than he. The horse did not disappoint him, for within the hour he led them to where a stream fell over tumbled rocks into a pool. Across the way Davey spied a great grandfather oak uprooted, and thought it would make a suitable and, more important, a defensible camp.

He hurried to settle Meredith on the blanket he laid over the thick moss. Once a fire was lit, he saw to the boy she'd insisted he bring along. He had not roused, but his breathing was steady, and tied like a roast for the spit, he would not be going anywhere.

Meredith begged for her pack, and when Davey brought it to her, asked him to heat water in the small iron kettle.

"There are herbs here to steep for a tea against fever," she added. She struggled to find a healing salve, each movement causing more pain.

"Meredith, the wound still bleeds. Once I wash it, I..." Davey stopped as she looked up at him. He felt helpless under her fearful gaze, but prayed she could not read the desperation he felt to sear the wound closed. The longer he waited, the more blood she lost and the weaker she became. The chance of fever was high, but even more, he worried over her claim that the dagger had been spellbound.

She looked away. "Do as you must."

He watched her set aside the salve, her movements slow, her gaze unfocused as she tried to unfasten her cloak.

His fingers brushed hers aside and he made quick work of it. With one hand he cupped the back of her head, and with the other he supported her until she lay down.

"The dagger..."

"Tucked away. Save your breath and questions and let me tend you."

He dared not build the fire higher, for he knew not whose lands these were. The water, each time he tested it, remained cold, as if to thwart his need of heat. He brought the horses to water, then tied them close by. They would be his sentries. He resettled the blanket over Meredith, knowing little enough about the tending of wounds. He cursed his own obstinacy for refusing to take at least one man with him. Someone he could send down to that village for a healing woman, or at least warm broth for Meredith.

He checked on the boy, who still had not come around. If the dagger was spellbound, it stood to reason the boy was, too. Davey had sensed naught of evil intent when the boy had drawn near him. That would show him to be so blasted arrogant over his new gift of perception that he'd believed added to their protection. He worried, too, over his easy acceptance of the boy being ensorcelled to kill. What manner of man was Owain ap Madog? Davey knew he was no coward, but if the man fought with more than steel... He had to put his thoughts aside. Meredith needed him

The water was at last lukewarm. Davey searched her pack and found one clean shift and another woolen gown, its weave fine, though the garment was as plain as the one she now wore. He fetched one of his linen shirts to cut for binding strips.

"Boil, damn you!" he urged the water, knowing it was a foolish order. But he truly felt helpless. He set a pinch of the herbs from her packet into a cup, then carefully refolded the parchment and tucked it where he could easily find it again.

She lay still as his glance was split between her and the small iron kettle. He paced, then stopped to stare up at the sky with a wisp of cloud barely visible beyond the thick canopy of summer leaves. The rhythmic fall of the water into the pool annoyed him, for it distorted his hearing. All out of patience, he knelt before the fire and, taking one of his cloths in hand, dipped it into the pot.

Meredith did not make a sound as he carefully washed her wound. Davey found it awkward to push aside the wide strap of her shift and lower the edge of her round-necked gown. The afternoon light was fading and a cooling breeze sprang up. He should undress her to more easily treat her wound, but found himself reluctant to chance her catching a chill.

Or so he told himself, holding a folded cloth to the cut and seeing the spreading stain that made his first judgment of what needed doing appear to be the right one. Sweet merciful saints! He did not want to mar her flesh with a searing scar.

She moaned when he lifted her head for her to sip the tea. He held her cradled against him until she emptied the cup.

And still she bled.

"Davey…'tis bad?"

"Aye. I'd not lie to you. The bleeding does not stop. And I'm no skilled healer. I've a warrior's ways to deal with it," he whispered, setting the cup aside. He brushed the damp hair from her forehead. "If you've some magic potion in your pack, best tell me of it now. Wait… If the dagger is under a spell, was it poisoned, too?"

"'Twas meant for you."

"I ken that."

"Do not make light of Owain. He will come again."

Davey glanced at the cloth. Blood had spread to all but the edges. He had to hurry, if he was going to do it. Aye, he told himself, hurry, before you lose your courage.

"The boy?"

"He still breathes. Why you want him is beyond my ken."

"Owain will slay him for failing." Just as her ring had failed to protect her from another druid's sorcery.

Davey tensed, hearing how faint her voice was. He truly could not delay any longer. "Lass, let me close the wound. 'Tis bled long enough to clean it."

As he spoke he eased her down and moved to the fire. He took his dirk from his belt and set the blade into the flames. He removed his sword belt and brought the leather end to her lips.

"Bite down on this. I canna have your scream carry when I do not know how safe we are. Can you do that, lass? Or will it be better if I tie a cloth across your mouth?"

Her gray eyes stared up at him, and he knew he had not shielded the anguish of the act he had yet to perform from her.

"The leather," she murmured, closing her eyes.

He used the torn shirt, folded several times, to remove his dirk from the fire. His hand trembled. He felt weak and angry and cowardly, after all. Her sweet lips were closed upon the thick leather, awaiting him to do what was needed.

"Do not move, Meredith." Bile rose in his throat. He had seen enough blood, enough wounds, but not on such fair skin, on a shoulder too small to bear it. But bear it she must.

Dinna think. Dinna feel. Just do it.

He lowered his head, silently begging forgiveness. He kissed the skin above the wound where the strange blue curlicue marked her. A deeply held breath to steady himself, one quick press with the blade and the sear was made. Her eyes flew open. He saw the scream there, but only a thready sound escaped her lips. She shook, and he forced himself to ignore it as he smeared her salve on the wound and gently placed a folded cloth over it.

He kissed the lone tear from her cheek. "Bonnie lass. Cry if you need to. 'Tis a brave way you have about you, but there's no shame in shedding tears."

He lifted the leather free and saw where her teeth had made deep marks. At the sound of a moan he jerked his head up, dragging his attention away from her. The boy stirred and moaned again.

Davey rose with his sword in hand. He would not let the lad's tender years or angelic looks fool him again. He went swiftly to stand over his prisoner and saw that his eyes were open but unfocused. There was a strange glaze in them.

"Can you hear me?" Davey nudged the thin leg with his foot. Getting no response, he began to turn way, but the boy cried out for saving.

"Saving is it?" Davey growled. "You should be

crawling on your knees to yon lady for saving your miserable hide.'' The blank look in the boy's eyes brought Davey's muttered curse. He became aware that he was tied. Davey saw naught of the struggle he expected, only a rigid stillness that ended with a long, expelled breath.

A riddler's puzzle for sure, Davey thought, as he turned back to Meredith. He made her as comfortable as he could, once more filling the kettle, and putting together a few of their supplies for a broth. He gathered wood to keep the fire going and tended to the horses. When he saw that she rested, he took his sword and walked through the woods, making a slow circle around the camp.

Above them, the crags spread out like an incomplete web, with Ben Dearg in the center. Davey moved on, wanting to ensure they were indeed alone there. He sliced and bundled thick grasses as he found them on his walk, until his arms were full and he had to return to camp.

Meredith slept with a thin sheen of sweat on her brow. Davey laid out a thick layer of grass for her bed, then lifted her onto it, with blankets above and below. The massive fallen oak protected her on one side, and he built up the fire on the other. The broth gently bubbled in the pot and he scooped out a cupful to cool a little before he woke her and made her drink.

But he still had the problem of the lad to deal with.

He could not leave him tied as he was, yet the thought of freeing him and allowing another attempt on their lives was out of the question. Davey thought long and hard over what to do, and finally reached an answer.

The boy weighed little as he lifted him and laid him close to the fire. Davey scooped out a cup of broth and added a few oakcakes for his meal. The boy still stared at him with those strange glazed eyes when he untied the rope and just as swiftly retied it, leaving one arm free.

"There's food if you've a mind to eat," Davey said. "But I'll no' be serving you." He saw that pain etched the angelic features as the boy struggled with the numbness of his hand and arm. He tried pounding it upon the earth, but was either too weak or the ties had bound him too long and too tightly. Pity moved Davey, though he cursed himself for it. He knelt beside the prone body. His strong hands quickly massaged the thin limb as, all the while, the lad whimpered with pain.

"Dinna be blaming me for your state, you cur. You set out to kill me an' I'm no' forgetting that. Eat. I'll let you loose to relieve yourself, but you'll spend the night bound like the prisoner you are."

He was not sure the lad even heard him, for the boy was too busy stuffing his mouth as if it had been a long time since food had passed his lips. One look at Meredith's still form and anger replaced pity. Davey should have killed the boy and been done with it. At least he would have made it a swift, clean death. Keeping the boy as Meredith wished might bring Owain after them that much faster. But how was Owain to know if the boy had succeeded?

Davey went back to kneeling beside him, for without his help, the boy could not drink the broth. He allowed him to empty the cup, even asked if he wished more before he began questioning him.

"Where were you to go when you finished with me? Owain was waiting to learn of your success, was he not?" Davey waited, but all he got for his effort was that same blank-eyed stare. "How close is Owain?"

"Davey," Meredith whispered, roused by the barely leashed anger in his voice. "The boy would not know. He would not be told."

"Lady, I must know how to protect us. He has information I need. Seek your rest and leave this to me."

Davey rose and dragged the boy up, tossing him over his shoulder like a sack. He walked to the far end of the fallen oak, far enough away that Meredith could not hear him, but he could still watch that she was safe. He sensed no one near, not as he had last eve, but he no longer trusted his new gift to tell him if danger was close.

Again and again he put the same questions to the boy.

"'Tis the *Tylwyth Teg* that caught me."

"No Welsh words," Davey muttered, concealing his relief that the boy spoke at last.

"The Dark Ones, Davey."

He spun around, neatly balanced on the ball of his foot. Meredith had dragged herself up to lean back against the massive trunk of the oak. She met his gaze without flinching.

"You stubborn witch. 'Tis it your intent to swoon or open the wound again?"

"Bring him to me," she ordered in a stronger voice.

"Will you coddle him now?"

"Davey, have mercy. I know what was done to him. Owain tried to do the same to me."

"The same to you?" he repeated in a stunned voice. "He tried to get you to kill someone?"

"Nay. To steal what he wanted."

It was foolish beyond reason to feel jealous over a man he did not know, but already considered an enemy. All he could think about was Meredith being turned into a mindless minion obeying one man— Owain ap Madog. And what more had he demanded from her? Davey had to force such thoughts aside as once more she asked him to bring her the boy.

He laid the boy at her feet. "I am going to have another walk around. Call out if he makes one wrong move."

"Wait. Bring my pack. Is there water on the boil?"

"Aye. I kept it hot." Resentment lay thick and hot in his voice as he retrieved her pack. Once more he wondered why she needed him. He could barely contain his amazement that she could speak and sit up after the wound she had taken. But then he recalled that she claimed to be a healer. Still, that she used him for little more than to fetch and carry set ill with him.

Davey stalked off without another word. She unsettled him to where he thought things and felt things about himself that he did not like. But once he began his half-circle walk he dismissed her from his mind and concentrated instead on listening to the forest at night. The faint rustlings of creatures seeking forage soothed him, for they would be silent if anyone lurked nearby. Unless, he realized, Owain had the power to make all seem normal when it was not.

Davey no longer heard the soft murmur of Meredith's voice or the boy's replies to her questions. Even the sound of the water tumbling over the stones had lessened. He watched where he stepped, and a few times took care to stop and listen. The third time he did so, he could not stifle the yawn that caught him unaware. He could not spend another full night without sleep.

Davey completed his walk, believing them safe enough as he returned to the fire.

"All appears safe," he said, seeing for himself that the boy slept just where he had placed him. Even with the wavering firelight he saw that Meredith's face was pinched with pain.

"I will make more of the tea. Will you sleep?"

"Davey, I need to tell you about Owain. He used the boy. He will use others. There is naught left in him of the teachings we learned."

His gaze returned to her time and again until he took his place beside her. She drew him like a lodestar. The firelight toyed with her features, showing him the fringe of her lashes, the sweet curve of her cheek, the tilt of her chin. He was becoming accomplished at tamping down the desire her nearness stirred in him. He helped steady her hand while she drank most of the tea.

"You're troubled," he said.

"Aye. I have been thinking back to the days I spent with Owain learning what the old priests had to teach us. He pushed them to teach him more than they deemed wise. It was then that he began to work his wiles on me. There was within the priests' possession a book, and it was forbidden to us. Owain wanted it and tried to spell me into stealing it for him. There was evil in him even then, though he claimed only sixteen winters. I was not much older than this boy, and in the end I failed him, for I was caught. There were no lies to be spoken. All knew Owain wanted the book. For all the care the priests took to guard it, in the end he had that, too."

Her voice had grown so faint at the last that Davey almost had his ear to her lips. Sweet was her breath with the scent of the herb tea, but this close he saw the pallor of her flesh. He backed away and urged her to lie down again.

With her good hand she grabbed hold of his arm. "You must be on guard against him. I have placed a *snaidm druad* around us. But go not into the wood until I awaken. And sleep this night, Davey. Sleep."

"This thing you speak of? 'Twas what you did last eve?"

"Aye," she whispered, closing her eyes. "A druid's knot of protection."

It was later, as Davey restlessly tried to find the sleep he needed, that Meredith's words came back to him. *In the end he had that, too....* So Owain had stolen the book from the priests. But what had he stolen from Meredith?

Chapter Ten

By late afternoon Meredith's salve and teas worked their healing powers on her. She could sit easily and converse in a stronger voice. Davey fought a restless impatience to be away from this place, but kept it hidden from her. She needed another day of rest before they moved on.

He learned that the boy's name was Dai, that his mother was Welsh and that he knew naught of his father. His eyes had lost most of the glazed look, and Davey accredited that to whatever Meredith brewed and made him drink. What he did not learn was what Dai had been ordered to do once he had slain Davey. No matter how Davey worded his questions, he could not trip the boy into telling a different tale. He claimed that he would be found and rewarded.

"Aye," Meredith whispered for Davey alone. "With a spellbound dagger in his heart. 'Tis Owain's way not to leave any to tell tales."

The opening was there for Davey to question her about what else Owain had stolen, but he found he could not give voice to his suspicions. He sought a distraction and quickly found one.

"Meredith, on the morrow we will again journey forth. I will not have the boy, Dai, with us. I cannot trust him. Nay," he said, holding up his hand. "You will not argue with me over this. You claim to need me to protect you. Then allow me to do so."

"Owain will kill Dai if he seeks him out."

"I will leave the boy with the chance to free himself. What he does after that is up to him."

As he said the last he stalked away from her, refusing to hear any more arguments, refusing, too, to be swayed by her compassion for the boy. Davey had not lied to her. He did not trust Dai. The boy, whose glazed eyes were quite clear now, watched Meredith with a look of adoration. Davey knew it was not jealousy that prompted his decision. He could not even blame his gift of perception. But he trusted his warrior's instincts, and they screamed at him not to trust the boy. To explain his decision would waste time and breath. He resented the ember that burned inside to explain to her, resented it and stamped it out. She had charged him with protecting her and he would, even against her will.

Meredith watched him go. She summoned a spell to make him change his mind about Dai, but also knew that Davey had taken a stance and would not waver in his implacable will. Even if she pointed out that the boy would cause them no trouble, Davey would not relent. He stayed away deliberately, caring for the horses, honing his sword on a stone he removed from his pack. She watched him as the sun dipped down behind the massive and forbidding crags.

She had not told him enough about Owain. Yet to do so would violate her oath. Torn, she agonized, while Davey put together a meal from the last of their supplies. She ate without tasting, trying to snare his gaze, but he avoided her.

He had conceded to her wish to loosen Dai's bonds, but this night he did not want the boy sleeping so close to them. She knew that the boy watched her with shining adoration and that it seemed to annoy— nay, anger—Davey.

When the fire had died to coals, Meredith struggled to rise and went to where Davey sat on a rock overlooking the pond.

"You should be sleeping," he said before she spoke a word.

"There is something I must tell you. It cannot wait. I confess a desire not to tell you at all, but your decision about the boy forces me to."

He turned to see her silvered in moonlight, appearing dark and mysterious as her voice. Once more she wore her cloak with the hood up, and that hid her lovely features from him.

"Davey, have you truly known anyone so evil they would kill and commit acts of depravity to preserve their own life?"

"I have seen evil done in many names."

"None like Owain. He refuses to accept mortality. He practices the blackest of arts to ensure that his life will never be forfeit."

"Say plainly what you are circling, Meredith. If

you want me to fear the man, I gladly admit that I do. It is one thing to fight a man of greater physical strength and skill, another to battle one who can call up spells and magic.''

"Then you are wiser than I could wish. Never lower your guard, Davey. But I have come—''

"If you are renewing your plea to take Dai with us, the answer is no. I will not be swayed by any words.''

"But you will listen." She placed her hand on his shoulder when he made to rise. "There are many who would accuse us of making human sacrifice. The priests I follow do not. But Owain, ah, I break oaths to tell you that he believes and practices as much. He has slain innocents in his belief that such deaths make him immortal. But they are not clean deaths, Davey.''

Her hand rose to cup his cheek. "By my faith, I swear this is true. The book he stole—''

Something in her voice caught at him. "'Tis more than that. You know what he does. You have seen him.''

She felt shame enough to turn away, but Davey deserved better. She faced him, but could not admit or deny what he said. She trembled under a welter of emotions she was too exhausted to sort out, and she found herself held gently against him, absorbing his strength and his warmth.

"Lass, I've no wish for you to remember what brings you pain. If I could, I would take it all from you.''

Meredith rested her head on his shoulder and gazed down into the water. Her breath caught, for the water shimmered, then cleared, and what she saw there made her cry out.

Davey spun to put himself in front of her, his body blocking hers from whatever danger there was. But all was serene.

"What did you see?"

"Sightless men slain behind us. Those riders I sensed earlier," she answered in a deadened voice. "Hold me, Davey, please. He knew where we went. He knew."

"Aye. 'Tis not a thing I was going to tell you, but he had to know, else how could Dai be waiting? So Owain is somewhere ahead of us."

Davey took her again in his arms. Her hood fell back, revealing a mute appeal he could not help but see. Desire rose like a sea tide with a storm lashing it to a frenzy. He barely controlled it. His mouth sought the lips offered to him. He gentled his mouth at the last moment to a mere brush against hers, cherishing the fact that she offered the kiss.

She was still weak from her wound, but somehow found the strength to wrap her good arm over his shoulder and draw him closer. Her lashes drifted down, hiding her eyes from his penetrating gaze. He held her without restraint, but close enough to feel the heat of his body.

Their lips met again, hers sweet and fragrant with herbs and innocently closed. Davey wished he was as pure of heart as she needed him to be. The warmth, the softness of her mouth usurped his control. He traced the curve of her lips with his tongue, tucking little kisses in each corner. He was greatly rewarded by her sigh.

She rose on tiptoe with unconscious grace and need, pressing closer to him. Her deep perception of his desire for her heightened her own. Their breaths mingled, became one, flowing like a moment of life from one second to the next. She could not absorb the sensations that swept over and through her, spreading from wherever she pressed against Davey. From her lips, from the places where his strong hands held her and stroked her body, passion heated, then burned, hot and urgent.

When Meredith rose yet again against him, pushing up as well as forward in an attempt to assuage the fierce need rising, Davey nearly gave in, so great was his own desire to mate with her.

Her kiss was more potent than his memory served. Her innocent abandon wreaked havoc with his conscience. But those little pleasure sounds she made ran through him, arousing a wildness he thought he had broken to his strong will. His blood raced as his hand slipped down to the curve of her buttocks to press her body against his. The barrier of their clothing added to his frustration. He had to drag his lips away from hers.

He had experience enough to know her cry was one of protest. Honor fought with the urge to satisfy her need and his own. He scattered kisses across her forehead, her eyes and her cheeks in an effort to quell the heat of his racing blood.

His name came in a whisper from her lips, and then her mouth found his and he was as lost as she to the passion blazing between them. With both hands on her hips he pulled her closer, guiding her in a twisting, abrading dance so he could part her legs and thrust his thigh between them. For a few moments he held her still, waiting for her to pull away, to make one sound of denial, but she moved against him with soft, drawn-out moans. His hands tightened on her hips. She twisted and shifted in his grasp, and with each movement of her body rubbed his swollen shaft.

He thought her to be innocent, believed it, and yet her moves, sighs and kisses spoke of knowledge. As if she sensed his thought, the tip of her tongue skimmed his lower lip and he gave way to the hunger incited.

Meredith no longer thought of right or wrong. A surge of feminine power and need swept her body and mind. Davey caressed her back, took her mouth and aroused her senses with the practiced ease of a man who gave as much pleasure as he took. She was so lost in the passion that rose between them that she attempted to raise her wounded arm, and cried out when a wrenching pain lanced her shoulder. And the pain was no less when Davey broke the kiss. She missed it immediately, that deep, slow penetration that imitated the mating of male to female.

She sobbed against his chest while he held her, gently rocking her to and fro. He whispered meaningless words, his crooning voice a comfort to her. What had possessed her? All her protestations that they could never be lovers were for naught the moment she'd lifted her lips to his. His body was still taut and heated, but he shielded his thoughts from her and said naught, just held her until their hearts stopped racing and their breathing was once more even.

Fear had driven her into his arms. She knew that, and would not lie to herself. *Owain.* Just thinking his name was enough to set her trembling again. For too long she had held fear of him at bay. Did Davey understand what she'd told him? Dared she repeat it?

Davey was silent now. He still held her, with a light touch so she could free herself. But Meredith did not want to leave the haven of his arms. She was falling into a trap. She could call this desire between them naught else. Yet to deny being drawn to Davey like a flower to the sun was to deny herself life. Why now? she questioned. She needed all her thoughts and life force, all her power, to prevent Owain from obtaining the gifts. The failure with Dai would not stop him. Naught short of death would stop him.

And what of Davey? What must he think of her now?

Davey was not aware that he shielded his thoughts from her. It was just as well that he did. Anger would not be the emotion she expected after what had happened between them. Yet anger consumed him. He needed to be away from her. He never thought clearly with her near. Why now? She had been firm in telling him that desire could not be, that passion had no room in her plans or her life. Yet she showed no sign of leaving him, and he, cursed to hell, could not send her from his side.

Had she tempted him in order to get him to do her bidding and take Dai with them? Every instinct warned him against such an act. But how to deny her when she was all that he wanted?

Again he wondered, why now? The suspicions rose and he beat them back. She could not be in league with Owain. She feared the man. Could fear be more powerful than her given oath that she would take no lover until her goal was reached? These questions plagued him, and made him desperate to be away from her.

She took the decision from him by stepping back, then turning toward the fire. "I will weave a stronger knot so you can sleep this night," she intoned in a voice of feigned calm, as if the past minutes had not happened, or had meant naught to her.

"Aye," he whispered to himself, "weave another knot like the one you have woven in me."

She stopped, but did not turn to look at him. "You are wrong, Davey. Your heart and mind are bound by naught but your own will. Seek there if conflict exists within you. Lay it not at my feet."

He flinched from the reprimand implied in her words and her voice. Every time he thought himself safe from her probing, she proved him wrong. He saw her falter in her steps, and hurried forward to her side.

"Let me tend your wound. And waste not breath in arguing."

"As you wish, Davey," she said, after he led her to her bed, "think, too, on what I told you about Owain and what will happen to Dai. I do not wish the boy's death—"

"You never cease to gain your way," he interrupted, but the words were said without heat.

Meredith did not answer him. She lay still as he changed the binding over her wound, and when he was done, he remained kneeling beside her.

"Owain," she began.

"I'll not hear his name again this night."

With more strength than she realized she grasped his wrist. "You will hear what he did to me. You will listen and understand why and how he seeks control of those who try to deny him."

"Ease yourself, Meredith. You undo these days of rest with this fury. I will bide here and listen, if for no other reason than to rid you of this poison that festers for this man."

"Animal," she corrected, her eyes filled with loathing.

"Aye, I will not dispute that with you."

She eased her grip on his wrist. "Owain is my elder by six winters. When I passed my thirteenth summer he told me that we would be mates, but first I had to prove myself worthy of him. He demanded I steal the priest's book. My refusal was for naught. He brought to the door of my hut the gutted carcass of a hare. He warned me that each day I delayed I would find a slain animal, each larger than the one before. I did not believe him."

"Did you go to the priests who watched over you with this tale?"

"Not then, not until a week later. There were no animals larger than the buck he left. He pointed that out to me. If I still refused to steal what he wanted, he warned me he would kill a man next.

"No one believed me. Not until my screams

brought the encampment running the next night. None knew the man dead before my hut, nor was there anything to tell us who he was. I accused Owain of his death, but it was pointed out by the elders that I did not see Owain kill him. Owain was being trained, for with his powers and those they had yet to teach him, he would be the one chosen to instruct our yet unborn prince. There were no others to equal him, and many were silent when I asked for justice against him.

"But I believed Owain, and I feared him. He laughed when I said he would be damned for slaying an innocent man. He simply did not care. I understood then that Owain had some part of him missing. He felt no remorse, no guilt, naught of normal feelings. There were times in the days that followed when I wondered what it was I fought against. And yet I refused to do his bidding.

"Chance brought Owain the opportunity to steal the book. Rather than fleeing with it, he remained within the camp. Once again he made demands of me. He needed to make a very special sacrifice. One that would grant him greater powers than those who taught us. 'Twas the reason he needed to have the book."

Davey stilled her fingers which plucked at her cloak. He noticed the habit whenever she was distressed. She looked at him, but he had the feeling that she was not seeing him before her.

"Meredith, you need not continue. I believe when you tell me he is evil. There is no need to these painful memories."

"Mayhap I do this more for me than for

hap I am the one who needs to remind myself how truly depraved Owain is. Please," she whispered, focusing on his stern features. "Will you listen?"

"Never beg me. No woman should ever beg a man. Not for this, the hearing of a tale."

"I would wish," she said, lifting her good hand to his cheek, "that this was a made-up tale. Mayhap the pain would be less."

"If I could spare you this—"

Her gentle fingers laid across his lips silenced him. "Listen. 'Tis all I ask of you now."

"Then have done, for in truth, the sound of his name on your lips sickens me." He felt rather than saw her withdraw. "Curse my unruly tongue. Finish, Meredith, and purge yourself. If you can speak of it, I can be strong enough to listen. So he had the book he desired so greatly," he finished in an encouraging tone.

"Aye, he had it and he denied it. I did not know his purpose for stealing the book was beyond what he claimed. He longed to try the full range of his powers, and the old ones held him back. The priests knew he had stolen the book, for none other professed interest in it. When he refused to answer their charges, he said it was to protect another. Me. He then accused me of stealing the book. And once more Owain warned me that I would accede to his wishes or pay a terrible ʼce. But I could not do as he bid, much to my sor-"

eyes held such anguish that Davey could find to describe it. He wanted to hold her, to beg e, and yet understood that she needed to share this with him. He held her hand within his own, the clasp light, but he hoped it lent her strength to hurry and finish this.

"Into my care had come two orphan girls. Branwen and Olwen were sweetly innocent and a great joy to me. Although Owain was confined to his hut, with a guard set before it, there were a few others who believed as he did. They wanted all the powers that were once ours to be practiced once more.

"They took my little ones. None other could have. And this time I was believed when I brought the accusation against Owain. No matter how I begged, no matter how the priests threatened, he refused to return book or children. He paid for it with a terrible maiming, and with banishment."

Her eyes brimmed with tears that spiked her lashes. She made no sound, nor did Davey. He could not know the depth of her grief, nor would he deny her the chance to cry for those innocents lost. He came beside her, leaning against the massive downed oak, and drew her to him. Thus they slept at last.

Meredith's tale accomplished one thing. Dai rode out with them in the morning.

Chapter Eleven

There was unspoken haste in the pace they set as the three of them rode hard for the next two days through thick forests of oak and alder and stands of fir. Davey did not know this land of the western coast, and ofttimes they had to return the way they had come to cross ravines, or found their path blocked by huge tumbled stones. Over the moors the riding was easier, through the tall summer grass and heather that stretched to barren summits. And always the familiar scent of the sea rode with them.

They avoided all habitation. Davey set snares, and Meredith found edible plants growing wild on the sides of burns where they watered the horses. Dai remained with them, serving where and how he could. Davey still did not trust the boy. It annoyed him that Dai and Meredith conversed in their lan- which he could not understand. He knew it that he bound the boy to a tree each night, and the horses. He was not unduly but each time he dressed Meredith's wound, he recalled those deadly moments when the blackened dagger had flown from those boyish hands.

Meredith wisely held her tongue. Time and actions would prove her right about Dai. The guilt she felt in failing her two innocent charges never left her. If she could, she would use her gifts to put an end to Owain. Killing him would destroy her, and her people needed her.

Waterfowl flew off from Loch Maree. Another few hours would see them at Torridon's gates. She turned in the saddle to tell Davey they were close, but saw his attention focused behind them. In the distance along the track she could barely make out a robed figure on a donkey. One of the friars from St. Dutho's she thought, but said naught of it when Davey once more looked ahead. He appeared deep in thought, and she was unwilling to shatter the fragile peace between them.

Dai half dozed in his saddle. His horse's reins were tied to the packhorse, and those to Davey's stallion. The boy had been very quiet since they broke their afternoon fast, and Meredith wondered if he were taking ill. She first smiled, then laughed as a seagull swooped down, nearly touching her shoulder. She wished she had a bit of bread to toss it. The gull squawked loudly as if to scold her for the lack of tribute, then glided away. Her eyes were sparkling with pleasure when she shared a look with Davey

"'Tis a look that I will treasure, Meredith, fo▪ shines from your face.'' He saw that his ▪ brought a delicate rose tint to her cheeks.

"Aye, 'tis a long time between laughter. But look, Davey. Down below is the place we seek."

"Will you keep me in the dark about what we do here?"

"I mean to have the cup, Davey. By barter or for coin. The vessel is plain. With a simple knot, much like my ring. I do not know if it belongs to the lord here, or some other, but before the night is done it will be mine."

With the change in her voice, Davey noted the quick shift in her very presence. Here again was the woman he'd first met. He even felt the strange tingling power radiating from her as he rode by her side. Mayhap what he had said to her was true—that her telling him of her past with Owain had rid her of the poison. She appeared calm, but firm of purpose, and his admiration, as well as his ever-present desire, grew.

She reacted with surprise when he reached for her horse's bridle and drew them to a walk. "You must discuss your plan with me, Meredith. I cannot go all unknowing into the keep. What role will you have me play?"

She realized with a start that he was serious. He held no anger at the thought of taking orders from her. She had deliberately not told him, thinking to avoid argument, for Davey was male enough in his ways and thoughts to want to have everything done way.

"Will you be my husband, Davey?"

"Aye, if that is what you need. And what of Dai?"

"brother. 'Twould allow us to stay together,

and would ease your mind about where Dai was and what he did.''

She made to ride on, but still Davey held the bridle.

''If you be my lady wife, then remember meekness would serve you best. We shall say I return with you to celebrate your sister's marriage.'' He paused, frowning as he sought to picture the map of the western lands that Micheil had recently acquired. ''Somewhere far enough away…'' he mused to himself. ''The Island of Mull,'' he stated. ''Does that suit?''

''We will need to travel by sea once I have the cup. We go to England.''

''And do you think a ship awaits us? I need time to arrange passage….'' He stopped, seeing her shake her head. ''What's amiss?''

''Naught. 'Tis all arranged. You need do—''

''There are times, my lady, when you make me feel as useless as tits on a boar!''

He released her horse's bridle and walked Ciotach forward to view the keep below. A small fishing village nestled on the shore of the loch. The boats were already back with the morning's catch, for he could see nets set out to dry. The thatched huts were closely packed, like the heads on a sheaf of wheat. On a rise stood the keep, surrounded by a tall wall of wooden stakes. The gates were closed, which did not bode well, to his mind. He saw naught of men practi? their arms on the moor, nor were there signs of There was an air of abandonment about the truth, Davey would have believed the k? but for the curl of smoke rising in the

He beckoned Meredith forward but did not look at her. "I assume you have been here, much as you first came to our stronghold at Halberry. Was Torridon keep as you see it now?"

She ignored his curt tone, just as she had ignored his angry remark about being useless. She did not understand it. She had been truthful about why she needed him. In all else she was perfectly capable. What was there for him to be so angry about?

Meredith directed her gaze to the keep and village below. She realized the rightness of his question to her. Slowly, she shook her head. "'Tis not at all as I saw it. If the lord is gone will they still allow us to enter? Surely they would offer shelter to weary travelers?"

"I know naught of who holds Torridon. If, as you say, the lord is gone, 'tis a gambler's chance if they will allow us inside. No sense in waiting to find out."

Davey led the way down a rugged path. He scanned the thick woods where all manner of brigands could hide and prey upon unwary travelers. It spoke ill of the lord that the brush was not cleared. He held his reins in one hand, and the other he rested on the hilt of his sword. But they passed unscathed to the moor and were soon before the gates of the keep.

Meredith had said nothing about his precautions, though they were unnecessary. She knew the woods clear of all human predators. Davey appeared strong and bold to her eyes. The inkling that he be needed in this manner wormed its way thoughts. She chided herself for not having sooner. Of course he would want to lead.

He had been trained for such things. Would he ever be able to reconcile himself to the full ability of her powers?

Her musings were interrupted by Davey's arrogant demand for entry. She listened as he repeated himself several times, his voice growing louder and more demanding. Finally a wizened face topped by sparse gray hair peered over the top of the wooden wall. She had a feeling that the old man was standing on his toes to see them.

His voice was cranky with sleep, his words incomprehensible to her. But Davey answered him in kind, with a thick guttural sound to his voice. She sat quietly as they parried back and forth, with neither apparently giving in.

At the last words of the old man, Davey sat in thought, and when he turned to look at her, she was taken aback by the fierce intensity of his gaze. She felt pinned in place, and her breath caught.

"How long ago were you within the keep?"

"Before summer," she said quickly. "What is wrong? Why is the gate not yet opened to us? Davey, why do you stare at me as if I am a sudden stranger to you?"

"You said you would have the cup by barter, coin or whatever means necessary, did you not?"

"Aye, I said that." Growing alarmed, she found words tumbling forth. "And I told you I was forbidden to use my gifts to maim or kill. Tell me what has happened here!"

"They are dead. The lord, his wife, servants, me at-arms, even some of the crofters were struck by sudden death. A bloody flux, the old man said, and none had a potion to stop it.''

''Davey,'' she pleaded, holding out her hand to him. ''You cannot think that I had anything to do with this?''

He would need be blind and deaf not to see and hear the hurt he had innocently inflicted. He shook his head, then voiced his denial. ''Nay, 'tis not what I meant. I would know if you noticed anyone or anything amiss while you were here?''

''Oh,'' she whispered, understanding that she had been too quick to misjudge him. ''I took no note of anything untoward. I ate here within their hall, I drank their water and slept beneath their roof. The lord...Duncan was his name, a most kindly man given to much laughter, as was his lady wife. There were no strangers here. But Davey, that was months ago.''

''Aye. But the old man refuses—''

''You know I must get inside.''

''Well, then, my lady, I suggest you weave a spell and fly. The old man will not allow any into the keep. He said he was ordered to hold it closed until the men from the Earl of Ross arrive.''

''When?''

''He does not know.'' Davey stroked Ciotach's neck.

''Davey, if all died within, who gave the orders to him?'' Meredith asked with a frown. She nibbled her ower lip with the edge of her teeth.

Seeing her concern, Davey admitted that he did not v. ''Nor can it matter.''

"But it does, Davey. How else did the old man survive?"

"That I can answer." He stroked his horse's neck again to still his restless prancing in place. "He claimed he was visiting his daughter in the fishing village the night most were taken ill."

"A sudden onset, this bloody flux." Meredith, as a healer, knew both the good and ill of most plants. Both yew and mayapple could effectively kill. Both were easy to come by. She suddenly twisted in her saddle to look at Dai. "Look at me," she demanded. "Look, I say!"

Dai was slow to respond to her order, but once he met her gray-eyed stare he could not look away.

"Were you here with Owain?"

Davey, too, had turned at the sound of her voice. He stared at Dai, his hands tense on the reins. Ciotach reacted with a head toss and a snort, sidling away until Davey firmed his hands to still the animal.

"We await your answer, Dai."

Meredith offered no sign that she heard the sharpness of Davey's voice. She held Dai's gaze with her own as if she would force the words forth. In seconds, Dai looked away.

"Boy, I will not ask again. Answer the lady, or I will cut you loose to fend for yourself." The boy bowed his head until his chin touched his thin chest. "It appears that you have your answer, even if he is too much the coward to admit to you what was done here."

"Dai, 'tis true? You helped Owain do this?"

"I do not want to die!" the boy cried out, flinging himself from the saddle and running.

He attempted to flee, but Davey was on him in moments, grabbing hold of the back of his tunic and lifting him up in the air. He ignored the boy's struggles as he returned to Meredith's side and dropped the boy at her horse's feet.

"My lady, I beg your mercy," Dai whispered, kneeling there with his head bowed once more.

"Dai, I could not hold you to blame for any sinful act Owain committed. I asked if you were here. I need to know if he killed these good people. You beg my mercy, and I ask you for the same."

He looked up at her.

Meredith shared a glance with Davey, for Dai's angelic features were set in a mutinous expression. She ordered him to answer, she demanded it, and finally, near exhaustion, she tried coaxing an admission from him. He said naught. Not a sound or sigh escaped his lips.

"Accept it as fact that Owain got here first," Davey said. He rubbed the back of his neck in an attempt to relieve the tension that seemed to form a knot there. "We waste time. He will not answer. Better to think of where we will camp this night."

"Here," she replied.

"Here? Are you mad?"

"I pray not, Davey. I told you I must get inside. The moon is on the wane. And I—"

"And next you will tell me that you *will* fly over the wooden stakes!" He flung himself from the saddle, muttering to himself, even if it did naught to ease the turmoil churning inside him. He was uneasy remaining so close to the wall. Uneasy, too, wondering what wild scheme Meredith would hatch to get them all inside. He busied himself stripping Ciotach's saddle. He listened to Meredith's voice whispering as she walked in a circle around them. 'Twas likely, he thought, that she wove another of her druid knots to protect them.

But even after she sat quiet and sorted through the food pack to put together a scanty meal, he could not rid himself of the feeling that he had missed something in his speech with the old man. And the damn boy who refused to talk!

He believed that Owain had slain an entire keep to get the cup. And would he slay them at the end to have it all?

"Davey?" Meredith drew his attention. She hoped to distract him from whatever thoughts brought such a black scowl to his face. When he stood over her, she pointed to their meager fare. "'Tis little enough to share. The heel of bread is rock hard, and the oakcakes dried. We need water, as do the horses." From where she knelt, she glanced up at him. With an absent motion she pushed aside the loose tendrils that escaped her braid.

"Davey, are you aware of what I said?"

"Aye," he replied curtly. *Aware?* Was she daft? How could he not be aware of her every breath, her every move?

"Could you ask the old man—"

"Would you drink or eat anything that he could provide?"

"You have no reason to snap at me, Davey. But I see that you are right. The loch is not far. We could replenish our water there. I wish there would be time to bathe."

"Not there. 'Tis not safe. As for the food, split my share between you and Dai. My desire for food has fled." *Would that may desire for you went as swiftly!* But even as he thought it, he found himself dismissing the words. He did not want his desire to end, he merely wished to satisfy it.

He turned away from her, not wishing those penetrating gray eyes to read what was in his own. "Tell me how you intend to get inside with the gates barred?"

He snapped at her like a summer storm, all thunder and quick lightning strikes. Meredith knew not what angered him, but he would learn to speak in a civil tongue to her.

"I intend to spell myself into a bird and fly over the walls, as you suggest," she stated with serious regard, glaring at his back. He stood so straight and tall, with such a bold and commanding air about him. Meredith found her heartbeat quickening as she remembered what had passed between them last eve.

"Under these conditions, my lady, your wit astounds me."

"I marvel at it myself, oh great warrior."

"As well you might." He shot her an angry glance over his shoulder, quickly looking away. She knelt on the blanket with her head tilted to the side, and he wanted naught more than to take her up before him and ride away from here.

"'Tis sorry I am, Davey, for answering you so."

"Well you might be. Do you not feel the unease? I cannot even think of words to describe it. I do not like this place. In truth, I cannot say if the deaths here bring it about or 'tis something more. You, with your greater gifts, must sense something of what I speak?"

Meredith gazed uneasily about them. Dai sat away from her, tossing a stone from hand to hand. He seemed to pay no attention to them, as if he were alone.

"Meredith?" Davey prompted.

"Truth, Davey. All I sense is the cup within the keep. If Owain attempted to shield this place, I would be able to tell you." But could she? The book held powerful spells. Ones she had never been privy to. Spells that wove evil, and perhaps brought death. But if she put her thoughts into words, Davey would forbid her to gain entry to the keep. At all costs that must not happen. She knew if her life was at risk he would do what he could to stop her.

"That is all? You have naught more to say to me?"

"What more can I say? I feel as you do. There is a lingering sense of the dead here," she stated firmly. "As soon as 'tis dark I will go inside."

"Stubborn wench! But pray tell me, oh great admirer of marvels, what would thou have me do? Shall I mount guard over our paltry possessions? Or the horses? Or Dai there, who appears lost in his own game? Shall I sleep while you risk danger? Or will you whisper another spell and silence me?"

"What ails you, Davey?" she asked, coming to her

feet. What he felt she could not define or name, but it was very strong.

"I want us away from here now. If you insist on getting the cup this night, then do so now. Do not ask me questions I cannot answer. If we delay, we risk our lives."

She was not about to argue with him, not when he turned to face her and she saw his eyes. They were dark, nearly black, with a fierce intensity that drew to mind a hunting hawk. It bewildered her. She felt no sense of alarm, but 'twas obvious that Davey did.

"It shall be as you wish. I go now."

Chapter Twelve

"Hold, Meredith. We go together."

"And Dai? What will you do with him?"

But he was already moving to grab hold of the boy, and despite Dai's struggles, within minutes Davey had him bound.

"At least I will not have to watch our backs." He eyed the wall, more than double his height. "I still do not see how you will enter." He glanced at where she had been, but caught a glimpse her cloak as she rounded the wall.

He drew his sword as he ran after her. She had not gone far. A postern gate? Even as he questioned the possibility, he saw the faint pathway that twisted its way downward.

He watched as she stopped to draw her long knife, then used the blade against the wooden joining. She glanced over at him, and in the twilight her eyes were soft, a haunting dove-gray. She turned back to her work, loosening the chinking between the stakes. She refused his offer of help as she pried the blade upward, then began to work the other side.

She turned to him when the don was almost free. "Do you carry the true sword?"

"Nay. You said naught of using it."

"Fetch it then," she ordered.

He eyed her in the deepening dusk. "You must wait right here for me to return, Meredith. Do not enter without me." He could not see if she nodded. She certainly did not answer with words. He spun around and ran for the sword.

Meredith worked frantically to loosen the next slat. There would be just enough room for her to slip through in another moment or two. Davey would be furious with her, but she could not wait. She pushed the bottom slat to the side and crawled through the opening. To all appearances the postern gate would seem to be barred against entry.

She stood up, and listened to the absolute silence. She sensed naught amiss, but something of Davey's unease had communicated itself to her. With great caution she walked across the yard, remembering from her visit the placement of sheds against the wall. This area was clear, she recalled. The hard-packed ground beneath her feet sloped gently upward toward the wooden stair that led into the keep itself.

She twirled at a sound behind her. Davey had discovered her gone. She could not imagine him trying to squeeze through the small opening she had made. It was enough that he stood guard over the means of her escape.

The one thing she could not plan for was the door to the keep itself being barred from within. If the old man slept in the hall... Nay, she would not put barriers before her. She would have the cup in her hands and leave this place of death.

She found the stair and made her way up, realizing as she placed a hand upon the door that she still held her long knife. Her hand stayed as she thought to replace the weapon within the sheath at her linked belt. Again she blamed Davey's unease for the shiver that whispered over her.

A gentle push and the door opened. A black maw waited. She smelled the rot of the rushes, and a faint scent of smoke, but not from the great hearth set against the north wall.

Meredith whispered an incantation of protection for herself as she hesitated at the portal. Her keen sense of hearing told her no living thing breathed within the hall. And yet…she squashed a sudden misgiving and boldly stepped inside.

The cup's presence called to her, just as the sword had. It was considered of little worth, for it was not gold or silver, and was not locked within the great storage chests in the lords' storeroom. Silent as a wraith, Meredith hurried across the hall, ignoring whatever foulness her feet touched.

She realized, too, that when death struck here, it had taken more than human lives. Nary a rat roamed the rushes. Again she felt a chilling shiver shake her body. Although she strained to use all her gifts and senses, she could not find a cause for it.

After a few steps more, a deep need to hurry pierced her. At nearly the same moment she became aware that Davey stood behind her. Like the sword he carried, he was living, breathing steel. He made no move to speak or to touch her.

She gave herself a mental shake, vowing to banish any thoughts that evil was afoot this night. What evil could there be? She would *know* if Owain was near.

Far better to marvel that Davey had come to her without a sound. She strained to hear him breathe, holding her own breath for a moment. The touch of his hand on her upper arm almost made her cry out.

She soon understood. She knew the way and he needed her to guide him. Without faltering she led him to the end of the hall, silently counting the steps until she reached the lord's chamber. No door barred her way, merely a thick woolen cloth to be swept aside.

Meredith closed her eyes for a moment. It was impossible that this small chamber would be darker than the hall, yet as she looked once more, she found it to be true.

''Why do you hesitate?'' Davey murmured against her ear.

She did not answer him, but went forward with one hand extended before her as she counted her steps. Her foot hit the first of the chests, and she bent to feel her way. The fourth one held the cup.

The very air she breathed seemed charged as she neared her goal. She was thankful that no one had locked the chest. Quickly, her nimble fingers slid between layers of cloth stored within, the aroma of rosemary rising as each movement crumbled the dried herb. Down near the bottom she found bulky objects wrapped in oiled leather. Her fingertips tingled, and she could swear that her blood raced with heat just moments before her hand closed upon the cup.

It was a good thing she had a strong grasp upon the bundle, for Davey suddenly grabbed hold of her and swung her behind him. She shook her head as if coming out of a daze. There was someone else in the chamber.

Meredith found him by the rasp of his breathing. She said nothing, and did nothing to distract Davey. Keeping well behind him, she tried to discern who stood at the entry. All her senses and gifts failed her. But still, she knew it was not Owain.

Of a sudden, Davey lunged with the sword, and the clang of steel rang loudly in the small chamber.

She pressed against the chests that lined the wall, and marveled that Davey could see the blade raised against him. It took seconds to realize it was blackened, just like the dagger Dai had tried to kill Davey with. She clutched the cup to her breast and kept her grip firm on the hilt of her long knife. She despaired that she could not see who Davey fought. The small stone chamber rang with the deadly force of blows as blade met blade. Davey would prevail. But she found to her horror that her knowledge was based more on Davey's skill than any belief in the power of the sword.

It frightened her that she was unable to help him.

Dread rose within her. She murmured several incantations to protect Davey. Sparks flew from the constant thrust and parry of blades clashing together. Harsh grunts and labored breathing seemed to come from every direction. She conjured up fire to light any wood or candles within the chamber, but the blackness remained.

Meredith edged away from Davey. Owain had indeed spelled this place, with spells from the stolen book more powerful and deadly than those she knew. Magic and powers would not win them free; only Davey's wielding the Sword of Justice could do that.

Shock and hatred chased away her fear. A cry had her once more pressing against the wall. Was it Davey? Had he been wounded? How could she help him?

She saw that the two combatants' swords must have locked together. There was the faintest hint of gleaming steel. Unable to cry out, she breathed deeply in an effort to control the renewed fear she felt for Davey. And she smelled smoke.

A strange taste filled her mouth. She knew she had to warn Davey. But how? To call out would distract him and possibly bring about his injury or death. Meredith tried to calm herself. There was no choice. She had to lower her shields. The grunts were louder, but farther away from her, and while the steel blades still clashed, the clanging noises did not come as fast or as furiously as at first.

What she was about to do could prove to be as dangerous to Davey as warning him aloud.

Davey? Heed me. There is smoke. You must end this quickly.

Only Davey's training saved him. He heard Meredith in his mind. Heard her and felt the stroking caress of her voice as she warned him. He nearly dropped the sword and his guard as she repeated her warning about the smoke. But it was the danger to her that spurred his attack with renewed fury.

He forgot that this special sword would fly true at another's blade each time he thrust and parried. The man who fought him seemed tireless, and no matter how Davey feinted, the man refused to be drawn away from the opening to the chamber.

Davey no longer needed to hear Meredith's plea about the smoke. He could smell the stench for himself. He slipped and faltered as he suddenly felt what Meredith did—a chill of fear that began at the nape of her neck and snaked its way along her spine. Those few moments when he was unguarded, as he struggled to block Meredith from his mind, allowed his silent, ferocious opponent to beat him back against the chests lining the back wall.

Davey, despite the disability of darkness, had taken the measure of the man he battled. By his sword thrust, Davey judged him taller, heavier and with a longer reach to the blade he wielded.

But Davey's rage lent him strength. Meredith was his to protect. He heard and felt her rasping cough as thick smoke poured into the chamber. Sweat soaked his body, dripping into his eyes to sting and blind him. He had to finish this quickly. Scorching heat burned his lungs, and once more his distress was doubled, for he felt Meredith's as well his own.

"You slow, quivering pile of jellied bones," Davey taunted. "I'll see you bleed your life out on the rushes."

Davey expected no reply and received none. He used both hands to slash the sword from side to side, driving a wedge for himself. He ducked and rolled, drawing his boot knife, and his aim hit true when the blade flew from his hand. He heard sound then, a choked gurgle and a whispering sigh as breath rushed out and the body fell.

"Go!" he shouted to Meredith.

Instead of obeying him, she clasped her hand to his arm as he freed his knife. "Davey, you are wounded. Let me help you."

The heat of battle still mantled him, and he felt nothing from the cuts he had taken. Rising, he freed his arm from her grasp, only to slide it around her waist and pull her against him.

The cloth covering the chamber's opening was smoldering. They could hear the crackle of flames and see the reddish glow that filled the hall beyond.

Davey snatched up the hem of her cloak and tossed it over her face. "Do not let go of me," he ordered. "Take a deep breath and hold it. I swear to you I will get us out of here."

Whatever Meredith had done, he felt it all. Holding her close stilled the agony that gripped him when he thought of the rash promise he had just made to her. But he had no time to dwell on the jumble of his emotions. He stumbled forward, slicing the cloth barrier with his sword.

Like jagged monstrous teeth, flames rose from the floor of the hall, licking the walls and wooden supports.

"We run," Davey shouted, knowing the chance of their escaping without injury was small. He sheathed his sword and swept Meredith into his arms.

He had run halfway down the hall when a roaring crash sounded behind him. Davey glimpsed a sheet of flame that licked and climbed the wall. Sheer panic gripped him for an icy moment or two. He was no coward, but trying to outrun the fire seemed the dream of a bletherin' fool. He did not want Meredith burned to death, nor did he ever envision such an ending for himself.

He dodged and ran through the thick smoke, tears blinding him as he headed for where he thought the hall's doors burned.

Davey! Put me down! I am too much a burden for you.

He ignored Meredith's invasion of his mind. The heat from the wall of flame where the doors had stood nearly brought him to a halt. Agony came with an attempt to breathe. Smoke, thick and black, closed his throat. He plunged through, stumbling and nearly dropping his precious burden. Dire need lent strength and agility, and he righted himself.

Flames from the timbered palisade lit the bailey. Davey knew he had mere minutes before he gave way and they both would perish. Disoriented, he spun slowly, trying to find where the smaller postern gate was located. He could batter that down and get them free. It was only then that his eyes cleared a little and he saw the barrels of pitch against the walls.

Deliberate! They had been meant to burn alive within the keep! He had not known he had any fury left, but it burst from him. He would kill that whoreson Owain ap Madog!

Meredith renewed her struggles. She silently

pleaded with Davey to release her and save himself. She could barely draw breath through the folds of the cloak he had wrapped around her, and when she did, it was heat-filled, smoke-fouled air that seared her throat. She knew he suffered far more than she did. Fear for Davey lent her strength, but Davey started running again, and she ceased her efforts lest he fall.

Davey heard her gasp and felt her surrendering stillness in his arms. She depended upon him. And he knew it to be an act of faith that had no foundation. He, no more than she, knew where they could go to get free of the flames surrounding them. He ran toward the back of the keep, beyond praying for divine intervention to find a way out.

Solid sheets of flame met him there, too.

Another pitch barrel exploded with a roar, sending a cloud of thick smoke toward them. Fiery debris rained down on them. Davey kept moving, seeking something, anything to help him. The sheds and animal pens built against the far timbered wall were engulfed in flames. But the air was clearer here. Davey realized this was where the fire had begun.

He stood, breathing shallowly, as his teary eyes made out the burned timbers of the palisade.

"Hold tight." His voice was a rough rasp as he gathered himself for one last effort. He chose a route, ducked his face against the hood of Meredith's cloak and hurtled toward the flames. At the last moment, he turned and used his back and shoulder to batter a path for them, and then rolled free.

Chapter Thirteen

Davey could not have known that the spot he picked had been cleared in early spring of all brush. Rains had eroded the earth, and the incline dropped sharply. The force of his thrust to roll them free of the flames was more than enough to tear Meredith from his arms, and they tumbled with increasing speed down the rock-strewn slope.

Meredith cried out several times, tearing the cloak away from her eyes. It was Davey's name she called. She could not see him in the drifting smoke. Frightened, she gulped air, then again cried out for Davey.

He heard her calling from somewhere above him, but he had not the strength to answer her. He had come to a stop against a jagged boulder and, coughing and gasping, was stunned by pain. It slowly came to him that he could breathe, and while the air was still smoky, a wind drove most of it away.

He wanted to close his eyes and rest, but the danger had not passed. He and Meredith were out in the open and their enemy had to be near. Davey tried wetting his lips and found no moisture. With a groan he could not stifle, he used the boulder for support to help him stand. Seeing Meredith staggering toward him, he struggled to call out to her.

He shook his head as if that would clear his vision. "Are you hurt?" he asked when long moments went by and he heard no sound from her. In the dark it was nearly impossible to see her face, though it was mere inches from his own. "Lass, answer," he rasped, listening beyond his own rough breath for the sound of hers.

"Hold me."

Davey reached for her, pain spearing every inch of his body. He managed to draw her close, and for long minutes they stood entwined, while above them flames still lit the night.

"We are not safe here," Meredith whispered, taking hold of his hand. She needed rest and water before she could use her healing powers on Davey. He was still dazed, for he did not know the extent of his injuries. There were many cuts, and his skin was reddened and blistered from the fire. Her own throat felt as parched as his. He had been strong for her when she needed it most, and now she would be strong for him.

"Horses," he muttered, pushing himself away from the boulder he had used to support himself. He knew he should draw his sword. He could not believe that Owain did not wait close by to attack them. "Do you sense him near?"

She did not look at him as she shook her head. She still had to work out for herself what had happened within the chamber. Her mind felt as if a thick blanket had smothered her senses. There was no reason to worry Davey, but her fear was bone deep and quite chilling when she thought of how much power Owain had gained. Power he was unafraid to use against her.

It was that fear that prompted her to stop. "The horses will be gone." Speaking caused a spasm of coughing that brought tears to her eyes.

Davey staggered to a halt beside her, breathing heavily of the windswept air. She was right Owain would not leave them a chance to escape. What they needed, he thought as both his vision and his mind cleared, was a safe, quiet place to rest and make plans.

He did an abrupt about-face. "The village."

Two steps more and he staggered. She wrapped his arm over her shoulders, bracing him with her body. It would be dangerous to expose themselves to villagers neither of them knew. But a gentle probe revealed Davey's determination to find some respite. Meredith sighed. He would prove stubborn if she argued with him. Arguing with Davey required strength, and she had none left.

Owain finished his search of the packs that Cei and Pwyll had brought to him, along with the horses that belonged to the pair he hunted.

When he first discovered the sword sheathed on the saddle he felt an instantaneous uplifting of his spirits. Finally his gods had smiled upon him and blessed his endeavors on their behalf to restore the ancient beliefs, so that they would once more be worshipped in the old ways, as written in the precious book he had coveted, then stolen.

A cold rage encompassed him after he had an opportunity to examine the sword, and discovered that while it was an exceptionally fine blade, it was not the Sword of Justice. Feeding his rage was the knowledge that he did not have the Cup of Truth or the maid in his possession. What turned cold rage into malignant enmity was the news that the man Meredith had found to protect her still lived.

Owain knew where the cup had been hidden. Not its exact location, only that it was within the keep. He had not the maid's power to be drawn to those sacred objects he sought to possess. Thus his need of her continued.

The death of his man David meant little more than annoyance to Owain. He would offer David's death as another sacrifice. The four men who had followed Meredith and her warrior from Halberry were sacrifices, too; Owain had easily vanquished them days before, in the woods. But it was not enough. Not nearly enough, for he had failed.

He stood and turned. His gaze swept over Cei and Pwyll and came to rest upon Dai. The boy was still tied, as he had been when Owain discovered him. Dai had failed him, too. Owain refused to accept failure.

The water was so sweet and cold it made Davey's throat ache. He drank deeply, then sipped from the roughly carved wooden cup, his eyes closed and soft sighs on his lips.

Meredith was no better. Her thirst slaked, she sat on a flat rock on the shore of the loch, splashing water on her face. The villagers had offered what little they had when she and Davey had stumbled into the fishing village. The coarse bread and fish offered to them, along with rough, mismatched garments, were all they had to spare.

No one questioned their story of having lost their way, and approaching the keep to ask for shelter, only to have the fire break out and their horses bolt.

Flames could still be seen, but the fire was dying. She turned away. Davey looked a little better after she applied goose grease to his face and hands. She knew before he looked at her that he wanted to know what had happened within the chamber. She was also sure that he would bring up the matter of her disobeying his order to wait for him.

She was not to be disappointed.

He sat below her, corking the leather water bottle, his gaze fixed straight ahead. "I still cannot understand why Owain tried to burn us alive, Meredith. I know he is after the sword and the cup, and you, but why would he risk your death?" The last was said in a voice still husky from all the smoke he had inhaled, and in a musing way, as if he was still unclear what it was he wanted to know.

"I believe the fire was meant only to draw me out."

"Only? I beg to differ with you. My life was to be forfeit."

"Davey, please, I did not mean to make little of that. I..." She stopped and considered how she could explain to him that every sense had been blocked somehow. A chill shivered down her back and she saw the way he looked at her.

"You are cold?"

"Nay, the shawl is warm enough and my cloak will dry by morning. All our clothes will."

"Meredith, this is no time for you to pretend you do not know what I am asking you. What happened?"

She shrugged. "I am not sure. Owain has grown more powerful. I could not sense him near."

"But when I asked you, you said that he was not—"

"I lied to you!" She rose from the rock, walking away from him.

"Why?" he asked softly.

"I am frightened by what he did. I could not protect you as I should have, and I could not protect myself. You cannot understand what this means, Davey."

He heard despair in her voice and wished his exhaustion would flee as swiftly and as easily as his thirst had. It was an effort to stand, when all he wanted was to lie back and sleep, but Meredith needed him.

He stood behind her, and before she could move away, he wrapped his arms around her. She was shaking. "As long as we are together he will never, ever harm you."

She twisted around to face him. "Davey, you do not—"

"Hush, lass. Neither one of us should be doing anything more than resting. We need to find our horses, too."

"I told you, Owain has them. He has Dai, too. And he will—"

"Most likely kill the boy for failing." Davey ignored the way she stiffened and pushed against him to free herself.

"Are they close?" he whispered. "Could I stop him?"

She almost smiled, as she was sure he meant for her to do. Not over the coming death of the boy, but his asking her what he knew was impossible. Davey could not battle an ant for a crumb now.

"Come, I will show you."

She drew him back to the water's edge, and there she whispered her incantations. The wind ceased abruptly.

"Look at the water, Davey," she ordered, and saw that he did so, but reluctantly. The water churned and glowed, then swirled in a circle that stopped suddenly. With a faint shimmer the vision formed in the still water, showing a man with a faint black aura surrounding him.

"Owain," Meredith murmured in a voice devoid of all emotion.

Davey stared at the man Meredith's power revealed in the water. No, he thought, that was not right. He knew the water was there, but it was smooth as the glass in a church window. And just as clear, he realized after a few moments.

His admiration for Meredith grew anew. He could not help the envy he felt that she had such power and commanded it. He stole a glance at her. She stood beside him in apparent calm, but he sensed the agitation beneath. Her eyes were fixed on the vision of Owain.

Davey directed his attention there, too. Fair hair, slender build, dressed in a friar's robe... But Davey concentrated on the man's eyes and saw the evil within them. The handsome face was spoiled by the greed that shone there. As Davey watched, fire flared, the flames turning from golden-red to blue mixed with green, and then at their heart a white core appeared. But he could not see what Owain did. He only looked up in time to see the twisted rage that marred the handsome face, the silent scream of rage that opened his mouth.

In the vision, Owain raised his arm and pointed with a hand that resembled a claw.

Transfixed, Davey watched as if he were standing across from the man himself. The fire before Owain leaped higher, fed not by wood, but the man's incantations. Colors twisted through the flames, making the fire appear a thing alive and totally controlled by Owain.

The glow beneath the water strengthened as if fed by the fire within its heart. Davey glanced at Meredith, but she stood frozen, unable to move.

When he looked down again, he saw the boy, Dai. A shadow moved behind the boy, cutting his bonds and dragging him forward. The boy's legs collapsed. Whoever held his arms forced him finally to stand.

Davey knew what was coming. The fear he had experienced earlier in the burning keep rushed back to him. He grabbed hold of Meredith, sheltering her against his chest. He was unwilling to watch, unwilling to be a party to the evil of Owain ap Madog.

Meredith sent forth a keening wail. She fought

down the sickness that brought bile to her throat. She knew she had to stop the scrying, but Davey held her so tightly that she could not free herself.

"Davey, let me go. I will not let him win. He meant for me to see this. To punish and to warn. Owain has twisted all our teachings. His power comes from the Dark Ones. But I swear to you," she sobbed against Davey's chest, "I swear that he will pay for the taking of innocent lives. The old man, all those in the keep, the boy and those men he slayed for following us."

Davey heard the last whisper and recalled she had mentioned something about others slain, but had not told him that any men followed them. He knew then that Micheil and Jamie had sent men after him. It could be no others, and guilt for their deaths weighed heavily on him.

"Meredith, you say he knows that we watch. Does that mean that as you used this water, Owain can use fire?"

"Aye. 'Tis the way of the gifts. Each will have a force of nature to use."

"Could you spell protection around us?" he whispered into her ear, his lips hidden by the folds of her shawl.

"Davey, I told you that his power has grown."

"Can you do naught to stop him from seeing where we go?"

She felt Owain's anger, but did not allow touch her. "I will try."

Without moving, she dispelled the scry water, and then, turning slowly within t

Davey's arms, she murmured her incantation for protection. The moment she stopped speaking, Davey urged her away from the shore of the loch.

"Do you think you can get past the village without being seen?" he asked.

"Davey, I will not leave you. Owain is too close, and that makes it most dangerous for us to be apart."

"I am counting on his being near."

"Your thoughts are muddled from all that has happened. You must be as tired as I. What sense does it make to seek revenge now?"

"Can you do as I ask?" Davey's voice was rife with impatience.

"I will, if you grant me good reason for it," she snapped.

"We need our horses. There is reason enough. Give me your answer, Meredith, for every moment of delay will help me to fail."

She reached up and touched his bearded cheek. "I would not have you face him, Davey. I would not lose you."

He snatched her hand from his cheek and brought her palm to his lips. "You will not lose me. Now, my lady, will you go and give me peace of mind?"

She shivered from the warmth of his lips and breath ᵒon her palm. He used it as distraction, she knew, how well it turned her thoughts....

ʳeredith?"

, I can go."

briefly touched her fingertips. He took a
ᵉn turned back. She was in his arms be-

fore he said a word, offering her mouth. The kiss was harsh, and over too quickly.

"I will not fail you again."

"Davey..."

He was running from her, and then the darkness swallowed him. "Aye, my warrior, I could wait in safety, but I will not." She did not care that her cloak was still damp as she exchanged it for the shawl, which she then wrapped their own clothing in. Taking up the leather water flask, she hurried after Davey, but in following him, made sure she was not so close that he would sense or see her.

She almost smiled when she thought that there was no way he could lose her, for he carried the sword and she the cup, and the gifts called to each other as strongly as Davey called to her.

Chapter Fourteen

The sky had lightened to the faint predawn gray by the time Davey reached the woods above the still-smoldering fires of the keep. He had no path to follow; only his senses guided him. He thought of Meredith and knew he should not. As always, the woman proved a distraction from what he needed to do.

Owain had made a grave mistake in taking his horse. He could know naught of the training the war-horses received at the hands of his clan. And Davey was counting upon this as he moved cautiously through the forest. It was Meredith who told him where Owain was. Not directly. She had said that each had a gift for using a force of nature. But Meredith needed water to scry, and Owain, no matter how powerful she believed him, needed real wood to build his fire.

Surely, Davey thought, all gods would favor him in avenging the death of so many innocents, and lead him to where Owain was camped.

Davey staggered and almost fell. He caught a sap-ing to stop his fall. There were only so many hours when rage alone gave strength, and he was nearing the end of that time. He forced himself to remain where he was, breathing slowly and deeply, and listening. The overhead canopy was too thick for him to see the sky. No night creatures rustled around him. Quiet as he had been, he knew it was the reek of his clothes that kept the small animals away. Or he could be very close to the camp he sought.

Davey freed the sword and his belt knife. The ground below gave off the scent of rotting leaves as he once more moved forward. His foot was lifted for another step when he heard the snap of a dry twig. Within seconds he had ducked behind the shelter of several close-growing oaks. He waited, sweat beading his brow, his heart pounding, and thought of the trap to ensnare him and capture Meredith.

No matter how he strained he heard no other sound. It had to be close to dawn, for he could make out the faint shapes of bushes and trees. From far off he heard the cries of curlews, but naught sounded closer to where he hid.

He had not become a warrior to hide from his enemy. He thought of each attack, each twist to his plans that Owain had brought about. He remembered the wound Meredith had taken and the deaths Owain had caused. Davey needed to rake these moments over and use the fury they generated to give him strength.

Owain would not escape him this time. Meredith would never have to fear her enemy again. And it was more than past time for Davey to move on.

But he found himself not moving. What was h

doing? He had made a vow to protect Meredith until she reclaimed and returned four special gifts to her people. What right had he to endanger that, simply for revenge against the man who thwarted him? What right, indeed?

Davey closed his eyes briefly. He had the sword and she the cup, and most of all, Meredith was free of Owain. The loss of the horses was not truly important. He still had a sporran full of gold to buy more. And was he not playing into Owain's hands by trying to attack him?

What true hope did he have of succeeding? None. He knew himself, knew his strengths, had honed his fighting skills for more than half his life, and now had to concede that he had chosen the wrong path.

Cowardice had naught to do with his decision. Keeping Meredith alive and unharmed and free of Owain was all-important. If he kept going, he would risk that.

Davey looked longingly toward the forest where he had been headed. Fear for himself never entered his mind.

Davey?

He started, his eyes darting from tree to tree, and then grew calm when he realized how Meredith communicated with him.

I am returning to you.

Meredith lowered her head and sagged against the thick trunk of a fir. He would be angry that she had followed him. But she was so thankful her prayers had been answered that she considered it a small price to pay for his safety.

* * *

Owain waited for the warrior to come to him. He had not killed Dai. He had found a use for the boy, who now wore the robe of a friar, although he was still bound where he slept near the fire. Cei was hidden a little beyond their camp, and almost directly opposite him Pwyll waited. Like the snapping jaws of a beast, they would have the warrior between them, and there would be no escape for him. Then, alone and unprotected, Meredith would have to concede that Owain had won, and she would in the end join forces with him.

He licked his lips, his excitement growing. A small voice urged patience and caution, but he found it very hard to obey. Soon...soon...

The moments slipped into minutes. Owain stared at the spot where he was sure the warrior would approach their camp. He would have the sword. Without thought, his hand made a caressing motion over the hilt of the blade sheathed at his side. He smiled, thinking of how unwisely Meredith had chosen a warrior— one whose youth would be more an enemy than Owain himself. Youth and pride. He counted upon those to gain him what he wanted, what he needed, what he must have.

And so he waited.

Davey found that Meredith watched him approach with a new respect in her eyes. There was no need to speak, for both shared the thought that they needed to put distance between themselves and Owain as quickly as possible. They headed south and a little to the west, keeping to the edge of the forest track until the agony of taking another step overcame them both.

Davey ordered Meredith to sleep first, in a small grassy space where a flattened outline showed that a deer had found it safe. He prowled the area, not daring to stop moving in case he, too, should yield to the demands of his body to rest.

There were two paths of thought that were able to keep him awake: his desire for Meredith, and his desire to confront and then kill Owain ap Madog.

The first brought a rueful smile, for there was little he could do in their present state to further that cause. Still, he paused in his patrolling to look at where she slept. The light was dim, rich with green shadows. She slept with one hand beneath her cheek and the other clutching the cup to her breast. He studied her face, the curve of her brow, the thick fan of black lashes, the line of her nose, the sweet curve of her mouth. Desire rose in him like a hot tide. He knew it was a reaction to the danger that had passed. He knew how deeply this one woman drew him. He had put her at risk when he'd forgotten his duty to her.

He could never again forget that.

Lovely, passionate, desirable and courageous. He did not know another woman whom he wanted or needed more in his life.

He eyed the woods, judging the time to be late afternoon. A faint growling reminded him he was hungry. His gaze returned to Meredith, and he saw that she was awake and staring at him.

"Come, you need rest, and I have had enough to be able to heal you."

He accepted the invitation to be close to her, and ignored the rest of what she said.

"Lie down beside me. I promise I will not hurt you," she murmured.

The half smile on her lips stung his pride. "I have no fear of that. And the burns no longer hurt."

"Hush," she whispered, scooting over to allow him to lay his head on the bundled clothing. "Just close your eyes, Davey." Her fingertips barely touched his brow. The extent of his exhaustion nearly overwhelmed her, and she knew herself to be a strong healer.

Meredith discovered another difficulty. Leaning over Davey, studying his face, touching him, caused a warmth and a strange fluttering within her. She had shielded her mind from him, but there was no way to shield her heart. Here was the man who had turned aside from his inbred need to have revenge on those who brought harm to him or those he protected. She knew he had done this for her.

She trailed the tips of her fingers across his closed eyes and caressed his cheeks with a gentle touch. The skin was reddened and blistered. She saw how her healing skill brought sweat to his brow. She touched the bruises on his shoulder, even through the cloth, and eased the pain there. She closed her eyes and touched his body, healing cuts and burns wherever she found them.

Her warrior. He had nearly been killed. Tears fell down her cheek, unnoticed as she murmured in the old tongue and sought the earth's power to make Davey strong again.

As Davey lay still beneath her gentle touching, an incredible heat built in his body, to an almost painful intensity. He did not open his eyes. It seemed too much effort to do so. Each place he was burned, bruised or cut received her attention—first the shiver of her touching him, then the heat, growing until he wanted to move, needed to move, but could not. When she transferred her attention to another injury on his body, the warmth lingered but the pain was gone.

Davey was floating, someplace where there were no shadows, no true light. He heard naught, and breathing very deeply brought only a faint scent that he could not name. Thought became impossible and he stopped struggling. He rested in a place that was not a real place at all.

Meredith sighed deeply as she rolled to her back. She trembled with exhaustion, but there was more to be done. She sat up and uncorked the leather water flask to drink a little. It was nearly empty. Setting it aside, she rose and removed her cloak, then quickly divested herself of her clothes. She freed her hair of its braid and slipped the leather sandals from her feet.

Turning back to Davey, she drew the sword from his side. The brush and trees grew thickly around their small space, so she could not walk far. It was not the earth that she wanted clear, but the thick leaves overhead, so she could see the sky.

A massive lightning-struck fir gave her the space she wanted, for the new growth had not yet had a chance to block out the sky. She could see the first stars.

For a few minutes, she experienced doubts about what she intended to do. She had not the right. On the other hand, she had not been forbidden, simply because no one believed that saving the life of her chosen warrior would mean so much to her.

She glanced back at where Davey slept, and her resolve firmed. She knew, more than most, that the gods would either heed her plea or refuse her. She never lost sight of the fact that once the gifts were returned to the priests, her life and Davey's would mean little. But buying a bit of time was worth whatever price was demanded.

She nicked her finger on the blade of the sword and gently squeezed a few drops of blood on the blade, then on the moonstone in the center of the hilt. She used none of the formal words she had been taught; her plea for aid came from her heart.

Tiny flashes of fire shot from the stone. The hilt she held grew warm, then heated until it was uncomfortable for her to hold. She did not release it. The gods demanded ceremony, and tested those who asked for their aid.

Raising the blade to the sky, she begged each of her gods to hear her. White spears of light joined the flashes of blood-red fire coming from the moonstone.

The sword shook with the power she demanded to be set free. Up and down the blade ran tiny flames, and they soon covered the hilt and guard, and ran over her hands. There was no heat to this fire, only a warmth.

A gentle breeze stirred the trees and blew her straight, black, thigh-length hair out behind her.

Within moments the wind increased, chilling her naked body. She stared up at the night sky, and at the
brilliant stars strewn on its carpet.

Meredith fell to her knees, still holding the sword
blade upright, and she pressed her forehead against
the warmth of the hilt. In the ancient tongue of her
people she begged, as the most humble supplicant,
that the light and power and knowledge that the gods
had once been wise to invest be returned to the sword.
The night turned cool, but a thin sheen of sweat covered her bare skin. She did not move as the wind
abated, and still she knelt, slowly raising her eyes to
the heavens.

Above her one star appeared brighter than its closest neighbor. And still she waited, silent now, until
the second star appeared.

"Look down upon me. I come to you with a pure
heart," she murmured. "I am here to serve our prophecy. I have reclaimed the Cup of Truth. I hold the
Sword of Justice. I give unto your keeping the warrior
chosen for me. I trust you with my life and his. Grant
to me this plea for your aid. You are all-knowing, and
aware of the power the Dark One commanded to
stand against us. I beseech you to give me what is
yours alone to bestow. Hear me," she cried out, "preserve your Cymry. Aid your faithful servant, Meredith."

Meredith saw the third star shine with a hard brilliance, and it hurt her eyes to look upon the trinity.
She felt a faint, slow churning in her belly, and fully
recognized her own fear, but fought to control it.

She offered no bargain to her gods. She had naught

to offer them that they did not already possess. Her arms trembled with the strain of holding up the offered sword. Within moments she shook and saw that the blade itself was running with white flames. She could do naught to hinder the descending arc of the sword, for it moved not by her will. And when the point of the blade touched the ground, it did not stop, but plunged into the earth itself until it was buried to the hilt.

She bowed her head. She waited now. She was a vessel, no longer a woman with thoughts and feelings. This was what it meant to serve with a pure heart. She believed. She had dedicated herself and lived only at the gods' direction for what she was chosen to do.

She felt the tremor of the earth beneath where she knelt. She stared at the face on the sword hilt, at the curved rays surrounding the visage that held all the sorrows and all the wisdom in the world. Her mouth and throat were parched. As she watched, there appeared a gathering of light in three white-hot spears that pierced the heart of the moonstone.

She lifted one hand to touch it. But that was not enough. She wrapped her fingers around the hilt, and more drops of blood slipped into the carvings.

And from the carvings into the earth itself.

Who are you?

"I am yours. I am servant. I am vessel. All that I am is yours to keep or to kill."

Are you truly worthy of the task set before you?

"I was judged worthy by those who serve you. Only you know if their judgment is true."

Will you surrender your life?

"It is yours."

And the life of your warrior?

"It is yours." A tiny curl of terror shook her where she knelt. They would see and know. But she could not bargain. She would not.

The same warm, white fire that had encompassed the sword cloaked her now. She feared that she would shame herself when the sky grew brighter, but then, in a blink of an eye, the stars were gone.

Meredith sagged, her hands still grasping the sword. The earth tremors had stopped. The white fire was gone. She had thought herself weary when she began, but that was no longer true. She rose, and as she did so, pulled the sword free. No earth clung to the blade. It was clean and shining. The hilt and guard appeared the same. The stone revealed no sign of the brilliant light or fire that had touched there. But she knew. Knew she had been accepted and answered. As had Davey. And she would never tell him the price to be paid.

Chapter Fifteen

Davey stirred awake with reluctance. He kept his eyes closed, using his ears and other senses to reassure him that there was no immediate danger. The scent of crushed grass rose as he stretched, then sat up, quickly searching for Meredith.

She sat across the way from him, her back cradled by the massive, protruding roots of a half-dead tree. She was sorting greenery in her lap, but looked up and smiled at him as he raked a hand through his hair. They both ignored the loud rumbling from his belly.

Davey looked around the clearing as his memory returned in a rush. He looked at his hands and saw no signs of battle or fire. He realized he felt as if he had slept the night in his own bed at Halberry. Rested and whole was the best way he could describe how he felt. He looked everywhere but at Meredith, and could find no reason for this awkwardness. A few minutes later he knew he acted foolishly.

He studied her. She appeared pale and drawn, almost too weary. Disturbed, he saw her gaze skitter from his. He waited a few minutes more, but she would not even glance at him.

"Your healing skill is truly a gift of your gods, for I feel a new man this morn."

Meredith did not look up, but nodded as she finished sorting the wild thyme and mint she had found.

"What is wrong, Meredith?"

"Naught that we can fix now."

"Aye, I see your point. No horses or food. Owain still searches for us, and here we sit like bletherin' fools waiting for him to find us."

"I see you are truly healed in body and spirit."

His eyes narrowed. Mockery? From Meredith? "What has happened while I slept this healing sleep of yours?"

"Naught."

"You lie. You healed me. I see for myself the cost to you and am humbled. But I wonder if the price you paid was more than—"

"You speak in riddles, Davey. Do not mock or make light of your well-being by thinking of costs. What the gods give they often take as easily."

She had forgotten how quickly and quietly he could move as he came to his feet in a controlled rush, then crossed the short distance that separated them. One glimpse of his dark, intense eyes and she saw again the very dangerous man he could be. Wisely, Meredith did not offer him any resistance when he took hold of her upper arms to stand her in front of him. She said naught of the herbs that fell to the earth. Nor did she attempt to turn away when he held her chin with one hand so she was forced to look up at his face.

Her skin was warm where he touched it with his thumb and fingers, and soft, so very soft. Desire hit him with a fist of hunger. He longed to press his mouth against her own, to taste and feel her. He watched the subtle darkening of her eyes as she became aware of his thoughts. And when he reminded himself of the bargain they had struck, it did no good. She had healed him, and in the giving, she had opened herself to him.

"Play me no simple, innocent maid this morn, my lady. Your healing gave a piece of you into my keeping. I would know what bargain you struck with your gods to do so." He did not attempt to curb the huskiness in his voice. He wanted her to know what she did to him.

And she did know. Her breath caught. Her gaze could not hold his. She felt heat mantle her cheeks. She longed to close her eyes, but darted them from side to side as if she sought a way out.

"Davey?"

His name was a whispered plea he refused to acknowledge or answer. He leaned closer, ignoring the voice of reason that warned him he was wrong to do this. Desire had a stronger and more passionate voice, for it gave him what he wanted. A gentle nudge lifted her chin and angled her mouth for the slow descent of his own.

It was not with the strong desire that heated his blood that he kissed her, but with a sweet coaxing that yielded rich plunder. He tasted wild mint as, lightly, softly, he let his mouth drift to her cheek and then back to her lips. In seducing her, he seduced himself, using his slightly opened mouth to steal her breath, and give his own. His lips teased hers, dipped into corners, then slid across the full bottom one. His fingers curved up, brushed aside her thick braid and found the delicate curve of her ear.

He caught her lobe between his thumb and index finger, rubbing gently, squeezing lightly. He was rewarded with a small cry. His other hand slid from her arm to the tree trunk behind her. He wanted to touch and feel the soft weight of her breast. He forced from his mind the urge to press her down into the already crushed grass and lie upon her. He forced from his mind the image of the two of them entwined, but he could not keep the feel of what it would be like from his loins. Claiming Meredith as his had to be the nearest thing to heaven.

Davey made no effort to shield his thoughts or the images that flashed in his mind's eye. A most delicate probing showed him that Meredith had warded herself tightly against him.

Anger that she denied them both the beauty and feeling of completeness, with no barrier between them, skimmed along his nerves and hardened his kiss for long moments. Then he eased his mouth away and contented himself with the trembling of her body leaning into his, with her quickening breaths and the tiny, soft sounds that she made. They almost, almost broke his control.

Beware. The word chanted like a litany through her mind. Strength, and the need she had to resist Davey, floated through her thoughts. She wanted to touch him. She wanted to run her hands through his hair, to hold him tight and then allow the full wash of pleasure to drench her senses. Wicked. Dangerous. Seductive. Her warrior was all three. And she wanted more.

Her body ached with need. She had to be strong, had to fight the insidious lure Davey held out. She must listen to the voice of caution that warned her again and yet again not to give in to the magic he created between them. *Beware. Be wary. Remember the promise made freely only hours ago.*

But skillful seduction led, and did not force her, down a path where passion brought every sense alive.

She tasted the wild mint she had eaten earlier, and now it tasted heated, pungent and of Davey. The scent, too, was sharper, and she moved closer to him, crushing the thyme and mint that she had dropped so the scented oils were released and rose with heady fragrance around them. She curled her fingers tight into her palms to stop herself from touching him with more than her mouth, but she could do naught to cease the trembling that came from inside herself. Where he still rubbed her earlobe, heat came in shivery bursts. The sensations were all new to her, new and overwhelming. She wanted to stop time and revel in each one, but he distracted her when he caught her lower lip between his teeth. There was no pain, but the laving of his tongue drew a long, low moan from her.

Her heart beat hard in her chest. She could not seem to draw enough air. Her legs were unsteady, and so she once more pressed against him, knowing full well his hardness and strength. And when it appeared she would give in and touch him, going so far as to raise one arm, fingers open to clasp his head and bring his mouth fully to hers again, he lifted his lips from hers. The move severed the charged heat that passed between them. She listened to his harsh breathing, saw the nearly black blaze of his eyes and the flush of passion across his cheeks. He no longer held her at all.

She saw his attention fix on her uplifted hand. A corner of his mouth curled. She lowered her gaze to the cleft in his chin. She wanted to place a kiss there. His words chased away that notion.

"Were you truly going to stop me?"

"Aye. I thought it best to do so."

"You lie, sweet innocent. You offer a man a banquet of delights that he would share with none. And your gods, my lady," he commented caustically, "could never give you the same in return."

Gray eyes flashing, she raised her hand to strike him, but he gripped her wrist.

"Have I struck too close to the truth?"

"What I do with my gods is between them and me, Davey. You are not one of us. You are not and never will be of the Cymry. You can never understand how I serve them."

She stared at his fingers enclosing her slender wrist, stared until he released her, and then she stepped to the side to go around him, but Davey would not allow that.

He studied her features until he could no longer

avoid her eyes. He tried to penetrate the shield she placed between them. He thought there was something more she wanted to tell him. He waited, blocking her from leaving him, and soon realized that she had said all that she would to him.

He brushed the hair back from her brow, sliding his hand down to lift her long braid. "'Tis a poor return for the healing you gave to me. I...I canna seem to help myself," he said, sinking into the thick Scots burr of his childhood. "Come, lass, say you forgive me."

The wary look she adopted made him stop stroking her hair.

"'Tis no' easy for me to admit a wrong, lass. Nor to admit that I am jealous of the power your gods hold over you."

She needed to hear no more. She *knew* he spoke the truth. He was jealous. Since she barely had her rioting senses under control and his nearness threatened that, she nodded.

"Aye, I will forgive you. But you must promise me never to broach this again, Davey."

The green shadows gave her eyes a silvery cast. He brushed the back of his hand across her cheek.

"Promise me, Davey."

"Would you have me lie to you after all we have been through together? Do not ask for such a promise from me. I feel something has changed within you. Something that is causing you pain. This new closeness is strange to me, Meredith. I keep expecting to hear your sweet voice in my mind as I did when I lay in a fevered dream, and later in the keep. I canna see the reason for you to hold yourself from what we could share. You know there is more than passion between us. I want…och, lass, you know very well what I want.'' He let out a heavy sigh and stood aside. ''I will not badger you. I—''

But whatever he intended to say was not spoken, for panic filled both their eyes at the sound of men's voices and horses coming toward them.

Chapter Sixteen

"Up!" Davey ordered, dragging her across the clearing to the thickly growing firs.

Meredith wasted no time. She reached down to grab hold of the back hem of her cloak and gown, bringing the cloth forward and up, where she tucked the ends into her linked belt forming baggy breeks that would not impede her. Davey lifted her high and she caught the limb above her. The branches were stout and strong, and she easily climbed midway up the tree, where the greenery hid her. But to her dismay, Davey did not follow her up. He ran his foot across the crushed grass that held the imprint of his body, then looked to see where she hid. Nodding, he ran to the opposite side of the clearing and disappeared.

Meredith wanted to scream at him. She could not, for mounted men-at-arms streamed by below her, mailed and armed. She could only count them as they rode past: sixteen men and four packhorses.

Far more important to her was Davey. Where was he?

Once Davey realized that the men came from the south, he recalled the old man telling him of men-at-arms being sent to the keep that had burned. He kept pace with them, from deep enough in the woods that he could not be seen. Those packhorses were his target. Not all of them; he reminded himself not to be greedy and bring about a search for the thief.

He thought the men-at-arms foolish to be strung out as they were, riding single file. He was busy sticking small branches and leaves wherever he could on his clothes. Most of the men were out of sight, all but the last four and those packhorses.

The last man in line made no effort to keep the pack animals close to the horse he rode. Davey rolled to where the final horse would pass, whispering in so soft a voice that someone would need be on top of him to hear that special croon he used for horses. It was an inborn talent the three brothers shared, and the animal rewarded him by not shying when he used his knife to cut a few sacks free.

He gathered his booty and disappeared before the horses were out of his sight. He had no idea what he had stolen, but he was sure that he and Meredith could make some use of it.

Davey, humming as he entered the clearing, went directly to the tree where Meredith was hidden. He tossed the sacks on the ground, then stood close to the tree trunk.

"Your thief is returned, so come and feast with me, my lady." He peered up, but the thick leaves and branches did not allow him to see her. "Meredith, 'tis safe. Now come down." A few moments more and he understood what the sudden dread crawling up his back meant.

"Meredith!"

He knew it was a waste of time to climb the tree. He did it anyway. He had gone past midway and was looking down when he spotted a small, cloth-wrapped bundle wedged in a notch between a stout limb and the trunk. He was sure he knew what she had left for him. The cup.

Some distance north, one of the men-at-arms heard a cry, and asked what the noise was. "Sounds like a hound from hell."

"Wolf," several replied.

Others looked around them, and some were seen crossing themselves to ward off evil, for the howling continued.

Meredith drifted in and out of a drugged haze from whatever vile potion Owain had forced her to drink. She knew she rode before him and was tied and gagged. She struggled to remember what had happened, but the effort proved too great. She thought they were riding fast, for the wind was strong against her face. Davey would be furious, like her gods, for surely they had handed her over to Owain by allowing him to find her.

Then the blackness washed over her and she felt herself falling forward, only to be jerked back by Owain's grip.

"You will never escape me again, Meredith," he gloated. "I have studied this warrior of yours and know he will come after you. When he does, I will kill him. The Sword of Justice and the Cup of Truth will be mine. And you, most of all.''

Davey had come down from the tree holding the cup as his last link to Meredith. His breath grew short as he slumped against the trunk. His heart beat too quickly in his chest. He opened his mouth to howl out his rage, but no sound emerged. He had lost her. He had belittled her service to her gods, and they had punished him by giving her to that evil beast.

Meredith! It was a silent scream from his mind to hers. Naught came back to him. He needed to find her.

But where and how?

He had nothing but himself to depend on. No magic spells, no incantations, no way to see into the future.

He scanned the clearing, keeping fear for Meredith at bay by forcing himself to first discover what had happened there.

Something had lured her into climbing down from the tree. He recounted how the noises of the men-at-arms had made them run, then separate. That party had headed north as Davey trailed them. He made an ever-widening circle in his search for hoofprints or broken brush—something, anything to tell him which direction Owain had taken her.

He was skilled, but Owain used the black magic of a sorcerer to cover his trail. There was no sign to follow.

Davey returned to the clearing. He eliminated

north, for he would have seen them head in that direction. Where had Meredith said they needed to go?

He was staring at the woods, his hand on his sword hilt when the hairs on his neck raised. Someone watched him. He opened his mind and used his greater sense of perception while he considered the brush, grass and trees as possible hiding places. He heard the snap of dry wood and drew the sword. Whoever Owain had left behind was clumsy. The man made more noise than a herd of deer, which Davey reminded himself, was not all that much noise, but still enough for him to be ready for an attack.

He took a few steps into the center of the clearing, then stood his ground. He was sure now where his attacker was going to come forth. Battle ready, Davey knew he was more than willing to spill blood, but not kill the man. He still needed to know which direction Owain had taken Meredith.

What appeared from the woods left Davey choking on his rage.

Ciotach whinnied and limped into the clearing.

Davey slammed the sword into his sheath. He swallowed his rage when he saw the whip marks on his horse. The stallion extended his neck, teeth bared until he caught Davey's voice and scent at the same time.

Davey refused to allow the despair that rose within him to take a firm hold. His horse needed care and he needed the horse. But as he worked with the little he had, he kept silently talking to Meredith, hoping against hope that she would somehow hear him and know that he was coming after her.

* * *

Groggy as she slowly opened her eyes, Meredith glanced around. The night was as black as a bottomless pit. A small red glow indicated a fire burned to embers. She had to close her eyes. A dull headache pounded slowly at the base of her skull. Her mouth, throat and lips were dry. She was still bound, her wrist bindings too tight, her ankles the same. She did not know where she was. Her chest hurt when she took several deep breaths. She was in some kind of a stable. Someone across from her snored. The restless stamping of the horses was very close. No voices, not even the one she dreaded to hear... She had some vague memory of Owain talking to her, asking her questions, telling her things.

Owain, so terrifyingly beautiful with his fair hair, and his eyes holding the glint of madness behind his anger.

Meredith wanted to squeeze her lids tight and block any view. She longed to sink again into the black void holding sway over her. She fought not to drift away again. She was not sure how much time had passed. Was it one day or two or even more since Owain had captured her?

The pounding increased until a band formed across her forehead. Every effort to think brought pain like shards of glass piercing her skull. She froze when she heard someone restlessly turning, crushing the straw that formed their beds. She did not want anyone to find out that she was awake. She had to put the pieces together. She had to find a way to escape.

The one thing she was thankful for was the knowledge that Owain would not kill her. She mentally shrank from a memory of his hands, and a cruel twist to his mouth after he had whispered something to her. What had he said?

Trying to remember was a struggle she could not win. The blinding pain slicing across her forehead and eyes made thought nearly impossible. This time when the black void beckoned, Meredith eagerly welcomed it

Davey stumbled on the twisted path that led him toward the coast. His lame horse followed him. He lost count of the times he had almost fallen. Meredith needed him, and that alone gave him the strength to go on.

Hunger no longer bothered him. He quickly stifled the near mad laugh that escaped. The sacks he had stolen carried grain for the men-at-arms' horses. He had lost Meredith for naught but his own reckless behavior.

Behind him the horse snorted and Davey stopped. He heard the faint tumble of water over rocks and turned to the right. Minutes later he unwrapped the binding he'd made of his torn sleeve, and bathed the stallion's shank and fetlock joint. While the horse drank, he washed the dried blood from the whip marks, cursing Owain for lashing out at an animal. Davey remembered what Meredith had told him about Owain's kills and was thankful that Ciotach had been spared. But it did not remove his guilt. Better the death of the horse than Meredith in Owain's clutches.

Bitter bile rose in Davey's throat. He stood up and

moved down the burn, then knelt where the water was not muddied. He repeatedly tossed water on his face, needing the cold sting to keep him awake. He fumbled at his belt for the precious cloth-wrapped cup that Meredith had last touched. He felt closer to her when he held it. The moon showed the dull gleam of the metal with its endless entwined knot design. At a glance it was not an object to be coveted, but Owain wanted it. He wanted this cup and the sword. And Davey knew that Owain counted on his coming after Meredith to trade them both for her. Not that Owain would. Davey's life would be part of the bargain, and Meredith would never be freed.

He scooped water into the cup and held it high.

"Meredith said 'tis a cup of truth. If her gods are listening and watching, then see that I drink from this cup." He drank without stopping until the cup was empty, and once again held it high.

"She told me this was a special gift to her people, like the sword. Surely you cannot see her fail to return them. She cannot free herself from Owain's clutches. He has learned a black power that she cannot overcome. I serve her, and through her, I serve you. But in my jealousy and need to be first in her thoughts and heart I…I failed her," he cried out hoarsely.

"Hear me! Help me! I will offer you my life once she has reclaimed and returned all the gifts to her people."

His head bowed in despair. The words were simple and heartfelt because his life did not matter without her. He had had the responsibility to protect her. He alone had been the one to fail. And he would continue to fail unless she was protected from harm until Davey found her. *Och, sweet maid, what have I done to you?*

He raised his head to look at the night sky. The stars appeared sprinkled like gems on a merchant's dark cloth, and the moon glowed with a pearlized sheen that seemed to target the cup he held.

"I drank from your cup. You know I speak the truth. Meredith is within your keeping. Guide me to her. Let me help her as I promised."

He saw the image of Meredith in his mind. Beguiling, lovely Meredith. Her long black hair gleaming, those gray eyes staring directly into his. The tint of passion on her cheeks, the promise in her smile. He closed his eyes and remembered the taste of her, wild mint, and the desire she could not hide. Slender against him, trembling but always strong... Courageous Meredith, defying him, bearing the pain of her wound, soothing and yielding one moment, cautioning and ordering him the next. Meredith. The one woman he knew was meant for him. 'Twas true of his brothers, and of himself. One woman found and wanted as no other. Only that one special woman would do for a life's mate.

He stared at the moon and the lacy dark clouds that rimmed one side. Was Meredith looking up, too, and wondering where he was? Did she know that he was alive and coming for her? Did she fear Owain? Did her heart and mind tell her that Davey would do anything and everything a lone man could possibly do to be with her again?

Had she heard him calling her?

An anguished groan rose from deep inside him. He gave it to the night.

Davey knew what he was going to do. Blasphemy! And he did not hesitate over the complete irreverence toward the sacred teachings of his youth. He was not denying the existence of God. But asking for help of other deities, even acknowledging their being, was enough to condemn him to hell. He almost laughed. He was already in a hell of his own making. Naught could be worse.

He slammed the cup into the water, scooping up enough for him to drink once more.

"Hear me! My life for hers!"

What he meant to be humble came out as defiant. He was overcome by such a smothering darkness that he fell to one side. His hand holding the cup dipped into the shallow water, but his grip remained firm. He tried to see, but his eyes would not open. He attempted to move and his limbs refused to obey his bidding. He managed to get his free hand on the sword hilt. The sword quivered at his touch.

Mad! He had gone truly mad to think that the sword had moved against his hand and body as if eager to drink the blood he had promised it.

"Please, hear me," he mouthed. "Please…"

Chapter Seventeen

Meredith tossed restlessly, almost resisting the dream. It lured her with a gentle assault, offering comfort and holding out the promise of her heart's secret desire. She was afraid. Not of where the dream would take her, but of what it would reveal. Secrets were best kept secret.

But the dream was insistent. And she found herself stepping into a glade she knew was not a place she had ever seen. Within this place fear was absent. She stared down at herself. A gown made of cloth of gold, thin and finely embroidered with a rainbow of flowers and birds, draped her body as if it had been made for her. The sleeves were long and flowing from her wrists, the neckline bejeweled around its square cut. Her hair was loose, and she touched the narrow golden circlet she wore. Who was she to be dressed as royally as a queen?

Sunlight filtered down in lacy patterns through the leaves of the trees surrounding the glade, and played over the flower-strewn grass with delicate shafts of golden-green light. The pond, with its banks lined with rocks draped with little carpets of moss, from palest yellow to deepest green, had a flawless surface. The water was as clear as a precious divining crystal.

Meredith stepped closer, drawn as always to water, and saw the pale sand bottom. Not one leaf marred the smooth spread of sand. No birdsong intruded, no buzzing of insects disturbed the peace of the glade. She could feel the magic of this place and sense an unseen presence watching her. But she had no fear that any harm would come to her there.

She realized that she was free of worry, free of the blinding pain in her head. From the earth through the soles of her thin leather slippers and up into her body came the healing force that she had mastered as her own. A great sense of well-being filled her.

She raised her arms with joy and spun in place. She crushed tiny plants of wild thyme, wild mint and rosemary so that their heady fragrance filled the air. A smile curved her lips, laughter bubbled up and she felt herself blessed by her gods for this gift.

Too quickly she sobered and stared around her. All such gifts came with a price.

Davey dreamed. He thought he was strangely dressed, in boots, breeks and a tunic of black. Silver glinted from the mail shirt he wore when he lifted his arm to push aside a branch barring his path. The Sword of Justice shot sparks of gold and silver wherever the sunlight lit the forest path he followed, and he carried the Cup of Truth in his hand.

The harp song drew him forward. Where it led him, he did no know, but its will had become his own. He soon realized the sense of well-being that filled him. Nay, 'twas more than that, he amended. He felt stronger, near invincible as he strode along.

The song had grown faint, and panic rose, for he knew to lose the song was death to him. He ran forward, gasping, then stopping when he heard again the delicate melody that lured and beguiled him to whatever waited ahead.

The fragile air coming from the strings reminded him of Meredith's voice. The song sounded like a woman calling her lover, her heart's mate, her soul's only joining for all time. There was promise there and he allowed the song's special brand of magic to touch his soul, heart and mind.

It was a warrior's instinct that brought his hand to the hilt of the sword, but Davey truly felt no fear. He sensed no evil awaiting him as once more he allowed the lovely song to lead him forward on the forest path.

Like Meredith's voice, the harp song was eloquent and passionate, too. Desire to be with his chosen lady rose within him. He hurried now, sensing and hoping that he would find her soon.

Then the glade was open to him and the music and its magic felt silent. His breath caught to see his heart's desire standing in a shaft of sunlight. She glowed in a cloth-of-gold gown, with a golden link belt, and wore a golden circlet on her brow.

"I knew you would come," she said in a voice sweet and silken as a melody.

"You're a witch, to draw me to you with magic."

She laughed. "Some men would call me thus. Let them. You know better, Davey. You know me."

"Aye, I know you." He stepped closer and noted her thoughtful glance at the cup he held. "I have come to return this to you for safekeeping."

She stood close enough to reach out and touch the cup. She looked into his eyes. "You drank from this."

"Aye." It was not only the act of drinking from the cup that precluded him from lying to her, it was Davey's choice as well. In her eyes he caught a glint of some unknown emotion that unsettled him. He glanced around the glade and allowed its peaceful aura to soothe his spirit.

"Was that you playing the harp?"

"Did you hear music, Davey?"

"Aye. 'Tis what drew me to follow the path that led here. You will laugh, but I thought it sounded like your voice calling me to join you in this dream."

"I would never laugh at you, Davey." She gestured to indicate the glade. "Aye, 'tis but a dream we share. But I did not summon you. I could not."

Owain.

The name and the man stood between them.

Davey refused to allow that evil into this place. He thought instead of what she said about not summoning him to her because she could not. "Do you know why I was sent here?"

"All things come. All things pass. All will be known when 'tis time."

"You have said those words to me before. Strange that now I remember Peigi saying the very same thing to me. She gave me something of my mother's, something I forgot. She also said I was not to open the cloth until I had need.''

"And do you have need?"

"I have need of you," he said softly, taking hold of her hand. "You said this dream is a gift."

Meredith felt her body tense into coiled knot. She'd never said those words to him. They were her thoughts and she had thought them long before Davey suddenly appeared. She stared at their entwined hands, and then at the cup he still held.

"Davey, what have you done?"

"Done? Naught but come to you." He thought he understood when he saw her stare directed to the cup. "Look at me, Meredith." It annoyed him that she was slow to obey. "Look into me. Do you see guile or subterfuge within my eyes, my mind or my heart? You can read me as easily as I read a warrior's battle moves. You know by my own admission that I have drunk from your cup." He raised that very cup between them. "The Cup of Truth, you have said. None can lie no matter what liquid is tasted from this vessel. And am I not loyal to you alone, my lady?"

She looked into his dark brown eyes and found no guile nor subterfuge there. She also used her power to look into his mind. He made no effort to shield himself from her. She *knew* he did not lie to her, knew he *could not* lie to her. But then, there were lies of omission, and there she judged him guilty.

She wanted to escape his intense scrutiny. Very softly she said, "You said this dream is a gift and all gifts from my gods must be paid for. You asked them for this and they have granted you your wish. I hope the price you will pay is worth—''

''Cease! 'Tis my gift and yours. Will you waste this dream time with recriminations? I will not. Meredith, och, lass, I ache with missing you. I needed to be with you as I need air to breathe and water to drink. Will you flay me for this?''

Who moved first, she could not in all truth say, but soon she was in his arms, held tightly while she listened to the steady beat of his heart. Here then was her protective shield. In this man she had her warrior and her soul's mate. But she could never tell him. Never share with him what was in her heart.

He rocked her against him, and the tiny moves of their feet crushed more of the wild herbs until the two of them were enveloped in the heady scents. Everywhere he looked was glazed in a golden-green light.

He stroked the long length of her silky black hair, then closed his eyes, the better to absorb the sensations of her soft, slender body gently abrading his with the rocking motion he had begun. He thought it was like a dance, but surely one he had never enjoyed. What was to be between them was as yet unknown, but he fully indulged himself in the prelude.

Just holding Meredith thus brought him to heaven. He sensed her smile before she lifted her head and peered up at him.

He read no coyness, only joy, from her expression. He did not want to talk. Words, he thought, would fail him. He measured the shallow unevenness of her breaths and realized his own were none too steady. Heat rose from her skin and he filled himself with the scent of her. Fire curled to life in his groin. She quivered within his embrace.

He memorized each feature of her face, letting the heat rise, until the scent was ripe with sensual awareness known to every rutting stallion. She closed her eyes then, and he savored that small act of surrender.

Meredith opened her mind to his. She slipped her hand behind his neck and stroked the soft, dark brown hair that lay at his nape, feeling the strong, corded muscles beneath her fingers as she urged his head lower and raised her lips to meet his.

"Kiss me, Davey. Kiss me until there are no yesterdays, no tomorrows, only now."

He sealed his lips to hers. He was Davey, his firm mouth taking the softness of hers, his beard rubbing her tender flesh, but he was Meredith, too, with her yielding mouth, feeling her flesh abraded by his. The need for each other seemed to explode through their bodies so that the ground tilted and they were enveloped in a golden-green dome where sensations ruled.

Davey felt the same wonder as Meredith as they kissed in a dreamy incandescence that was more powerful than either of them had ever known. He had a man's carnal needs balanced on a blade's edge with the tender seduction she required of him. What he felt for the woman in his arms was simply indescribable. He wanted her with a passion that excluded all else. Meredith was his heart and mind. She ruled his body and heated his blood. His emotions, thoughts and physical response were open to her through the strength of this complete link.

Meredith knew when Davey dropped the cup. She

clung to him with both of her hands now. Her body molded to the hard, muscular shape of his. Davey's intense pleasure was her own, but doubled as the link prevented her from hiding the first bloom of desire that shimmered to life inside her. She felt the catch of his breath as her lips parted and he claimed the new territory granted him. Scents mingled with heat. The fragrance of her own arousal was distinctly female. Davey's carried a darker, stronger male scent. Mingled together, they made a heady aroma that made her press tighter against him.

She trembled when he traced every curve of her delicate ear, his breath touching her overly sensitive skin to add another layer to the intoxication of being loved by him. The warmth of his gentle lips skimmed and kissed her cheeks, her eyelids, her temples. She reveled in the fact that he saw her as someone lovely and sensual and so desirable he would give his life to possess her.

His lips traced her jaw with a string of kisses. He opened his mouth on her neck, tasting, and she tasted herself as sweetly salty on his tongue. There grew a new intensity to his pleasure that increased hers.

Deft fingers, made impatient with need and the fear that this stolen time might be too brief, saw sword belt and circlet cast aside. Those same deft fingers, hers untying his tunic and his unlacing the sides of her gown, worked hurriedly in concert to rid themselves of the clothing keeping them apart.

Flesh on flesh. She had never seen herself as soft, so silky soft and fragile that he had to force himself to be gentle with his caresses. She knew the hard muscular length of his body, knew it from the wounds that had led to fevered nights when she had washed his body with cool water, through her scrying, had aided in his healing. But she had only seen him then, not touched. She was utterly still beneath his exploring hands.

She tried to tell him what he made her feel, but her whispers were unable to penetrate the lustful passion that held him in thrall. She was tantalized by the swell of her breasts and hardened nipples nestled against the crisp, dark, curling hair of his chest. She burned as he held her hips, his aroused flesh finding the damp nest of curls.

A coiled knot of tension began to unravel. She ached. Davey's head lowered to nuzzle and lick her breasts.

His lips heated against her skin as he fell to his knees. He teased the aching fullness of her breasts with feathery touches of his tongue, nipping at the firm, silky globes with small love bites. She grabbed hold of his shoulders, her only anchor now.

"No man ever knew a hunger such as I," he whispered. He laid his head against her belly while his lips explored that sweet curve. 'Twas a wicked madness that seized hold of her. His lips were now hot against her skin and she had a moment's panic in thinking he would leave her naught that belonged to herself. But excitement built as, more urgent now, his kisses traveled to the black mound of curls between her thighs.

The tremors within her body grew and grew until she shook like a leaf caught in a storm. She gasped at his gentle exploration and felt herself tense, but Davey shared with her how precious the gift of her trust and herself was to him. Her moan turned into a groan of pleasure.

He held her firmly when she shied against his fingers combing the soft curls, stroking her, slipping ever lower until they found the petal-soft flesh that hid her maidenhood.

Beneath the soles of her feet she felt the awakening power of the earth that had been hers to command. Light glowed around them when she opened her eyes, and she heard the harp song trilling a sweet, sensual melody. Magic. That was what they made together. Strange new sensations called up a restlessness within her. She wanted something more, but knew not its name. Her flesh yearned for his. She wanted to join with him, to complete what they had begun in their first cycle of life. Spreading like heated honey through her limbs was a pleasure so intense she thought she would die of it. But rather than die of the radiance exploding through her, she tasted the first bite of ecstasy.

He nipped her thigh, and she brought her hand to her lips, stifling her cry as his mouth found her. She knew this was his gift to her, given to no other woman. He stole her hidden flesh with a cleverly plied tongue that had her twisting and arching against him.

The searing intimacy left her limp. She sank to her knees and he took her into his arms, his lips feeding dreamily upon her own.

"Join with me now, Davey," she begged in a hoarse voice. "Please, the time flees."

He followed her down, covering her body with his own. She no longer wanted or needed a slow arousing of desire. The same wild abandon that held him gripped hold of her. Her nipples stabbed his chest and heat filled him. His hands slipped beneath her, lifting her as he eased himself to claim her maidenhead.

She wrapped her arms around him, kissing his cheek and jaw, tasting salt, sweat and man. The pain was sharp but somehow sweet as she yielded the delicate skin that protected her virginity.

Mine. Now and then. Here and forever.

His words, hers, it mattered not. Her hair was a black, silken tangle caught beneath her; his fell over his shoulders, drifting back and forth to tease and caress her breasts with his movements.

Beautiful.

Their smiles were lost in a kiss.

He was beautiful to her. Watching him, she felt his muscles flex and strain, felt his strength and power as he strove to bring them to the release they both craved.

She lay like a vision of pale cream against the black silk of her hair, soft, yet strong, and giving, so very giving. Her breath quickened, and she shifted to take him deeper. She held him tight when his thrusts came faster, harder, and she closed her eyes, knowing when the moment approached. She shared with him the spilling of his seed, the welcome rapture it brought to her.

She had become the earth mother, and he the water

of life. One could not exist without the other. And here, joined as one, was the sanctuary made from their magic.

But this was a stolen dream, and warnings came that their time was done. He resisted. She coaxed. 'Twas a gift, a gift to cherish no matter where their paths took them. He needed one last kiss before he yielded to her wisdom. Had she known how deep his surrender was to her?

They dressed hurriedly now, for the harp song had gone, and long shadows filled the glade. A light wind sprang up and even the dance of the leaves overhead seem to whisper to them...*hurry, hurry.*

But there was one last thing that Davey would not be denied. He fetched the cup and dipped it into the still pond water, setting off ripples that covered its once flawless surface. Meredith watched him as she set the circlet back in place on her head. He came forward and knelt before her.

"Drink with me, my lady, and make a vow," he said, holding up the cup to her. "Vow with me that there will be a day when we will join and never be set asunder, if not in this life, then the next."

She touched the rim of the cup with snaking fingers. If she drank from the cup and made the vow, her gods would be denied. Death in this life was only the smallest of prices to pay. She thought to tell him, but there was within his eyes the knowledge of what he asked her. How could she deny him? He was her soul's mate. Had been. Would be forever.

Meredith took hold of the cup.

Chapter Eighteen

Something pulled him from his dream and Davey fought against it. He would not leave her! But the image of the well-defined glade had already disappeared. Gone was the harp song and the forest path. Meredith still stood, but she faded while he watched. He tried reaching her, crying out her name lest he lose her. His plea went unanswered. His curses were spilled to dark shadows.

He finally opened his eyes and found himself drenched in sweat. His hand gripped the sword, and above him the moon was covered with dark clouds. He was empty. The pain sliced through him, worse than any wound he had taken. He cried out his loss, but there was none to hear him or to care.

Ciotach snorted and Davey turned to see the stallion grazing his way toward him. Davey sat up, running his hands through his hair. He had to find some way to regain control of his rioting emotions.

Repeatedly telling himself that it had been a dream and naught was real did little good. Meredith *had* been with him. He *had* kissed her, and held her slender body against his own. He *had* loved her.

But when he glanced around he saw that he was still in the same thicket where he had finally bedded down when he could not walk another step.

Ciotach reached him, and he pushed aside the stallion's snuffling nose with all the irritation he felt.

He was going mad! Had anything been real? The cup! He fumbled at his side until his hand closed over the cloth-wrapped bundle. He tore open the leather tie, and cast aside the cloth. He held the cup with both hands, just as he had in the glade to Meredith.

"Sweet saints! Where are you?" he cried out.

He did not know why he held the cup with one hand and turned it over, with his other palm cupped below.

"What are you doing, you bletherin' fool?"

He had no answer for himself. But he waited what seemed like an eternity and was rewarded for his patience and his faith. A tiny drop of water hovered on the rim, clinging there as if reluctant to fall. But fall it did, into his waiting palm.

Such a tiny drop, no bigger, really, than a grain of sand. But Davey felt this incredible soothing presence flow through him, calming his fear for Meredith, bringing him a strange sense of peace that all would be as it was meant to be. A flow of warmth spread from his lap and he was distracted to look down at his sporran.

"All will be known when it is time," he whispered. He opened the hide and drew forth the little cloth that Peigi had given him. He did not remember when he had tucked it in his sporran but he welcomed having it. Here was the source of the warmth, he thought, as his hand closed tightly around it. Peigi had said that his mother gave this to her for safekeeping for him.

He had not thought of his lady mother in a long time. He remembered her bright, rich chestnut hair gleaming with light, and her eyes so serene. They said he had her eyes, and her coloring. He knew hers had not been a love match, but years together, and the bairns she had borne, had strengthened her bond with his father. Davey's gift of sight had come from her family. 'Twas said her mother could read the ancient runes and follow the stars.

One of the three little maids that his brother Jamie claimed as his now carried her name…Onora.

Davey whispered her name as he opened the cloth. It was too dark to see, but by feel he guessed he held a stone. He lifted it between his thumb and index finger, holding it up.

In moments he held cold fire in his hand as all the starlight accumulated within the small stone. He closed his eyes against both the glare and the sudden pounding in his head. He was helpless to stop it, had always been helpless, although this time, for the first time, he rejoiced at the coming of his gift. He barely stifled his impatience as the image took time to form.

In that waiting time, before he understood what he was seeing, Davey realized why the stone was special. None of the sickening or weakening that usually accompanied his glimpses into the future was present. And the pounding in his head lessened.

"Bless you, Mother," he whispered. "And you, Peigi, for remembering."

When he saw the stable in the clear glow of moonlight, he knew Meredith was there. He could see solid shadows of what appeared to be bodies lying in a half circle around her. His heartbeat quickened and his breath caught for a second.

Meredith was there, the other half of his self. All that he needed to make him whole.

Davey had never attempted to focus his gift of second sight. It used him at its own will, at times revealing a vision that made no sense until an event came to pass.

But that was not true on this night.

He was in one place, Meredith in another, and he was able to watch her. It was not enough. Naught would be until he could hold her in his arms again. He had to know where she was, and where Owain intended to take her.

Davey blocked everything from his mind. With his eyes closed he called to her. He thought and hoped and needed to believe that in their shared dream and joining, an unbreakable bond of communion had formed.

Naught that he silently whispered roused her from sleep. He could and did watch every breath she drew. He ached with a need to touch her, but either Owain had used his black arts to shield her or Davey's own gift was merely a tool of the gods to torment him.

He lost track of the time he stared at the stone, his mind scurrying like a hare before the hounds to find a way to make this work.

When his eyes burned from the concentrated light, he enclosed the stone in his fist. Useless. And it left him as helpless as a bairn.

When Davey looked around him, gray and rosy streaks were already lighting the sky. Morning would soon be upon him. He could not afford to sit there.

He was ready to toss the stone back into his sporran when he looked one last time at Meredith. Only he did not see her. He had a feeling the man standing with his back to him was not Owain. That did not matter. Davey was far more interested in what the man looked upon. Dawn's light revealed a shimmer of water—a large body of water—and small ships anchored there.

Another man joined him, and once again, Davey was most sure this was not Owain. Their heads were close together as they whispered, but they never turned so that he could view their faces.

He truly felt like a bairn for not having realized the power of what he held in his hands. This was naught like his gift to see a glimpse of the future. The precious stone would allow him to keep track of Meredith and where Owain took her.

But he knew he had no time to waste. Stone or no, he wanted to be very close to them. There was still the ring and the harp to recover. Only the gods knew what Owain would do to Meredith to make her tell him where they were.

When Davey went to tend his horse, he discovered the gods had given him another gift, for the stallion's lameness was gone. Riding without benefit of saddle proved no obstacle; Davey had raised and trained their warhorses along with his brothers and often rode bareback. With the stone and the cup secure, he rode for the western coast. And he rode toward his lady.

What Davey had not taken into account was his own desperate need to see Meredith as often as he could. He still feared that the images in the stone would soon disappear. So he looked, and spurred Ciotach to a fast, ground-eating pace. He kept the stone in his hand, glancing whenever chance allowed him.

He did not know what to do with the consuming rage that overtook him when he saw Owain ap Madog put his hands on Meredith.

Meredith came awake thinking Davey called her. She was soon disabused of that. 'Twas Owain who leaned over her prone body, his hand on her shoulder, shaking her to get up. She lifted drug-dazed eyes to his face, blinking, then recoiling at what she saw there.

Her stomach heaved and she gagged, then spewed out the contents of the vile potion he had given her. It gave her small satisfaction when Owain jumped back, but not in time. She had soiled his robe. When he raised his fist, she braced herself and put all the hate and defiance she could into a glare directed at him.

He muttered curses but lowered his hand. Still she was not fooled. He would beat her if he thought it would give him what he wanted. But first he would try to coax and reason, even use inducements and seduction to find the other gifts and Davey. And she already knew that she would seek escape or death before giving in to him.

"*Cariad*, you fight me needlessly. We both want the same things—to see our gifts returned to our people as they were always meant to be."

The Cymry endearment sat ill upon Owain's tongue. She offered no response, not even to continue looking at him. But that was part of Meredith's allure for him, the way she had of withdrawing herself and remaining untouched by all that went on around her. He would break her of this. Break her until she served him as a willing vessel.

Inwardly, Meredith shivered with a cold that would not abate. She could feel Owain's intent to destroy her if he could not bend her to do his bidding. She cringed, feeling his hand stroke her hair.

"As lovely as I knew you would be. Your warrior cannot help you now. If he is not dead he will soon be. And then what will you do against me?"

"The gods will see to you." She knew as soon as she responded that she had been wrong to answer his goad. This was what he needed from her now. He wanted her to know his power, and his soft laughter turned her insides to ice.

"Remember, *cariad*, I serve my gods as you serve yours. I believe it will amuse them as you struggle against what is already ordained. I know the outcome of any contest between us, Meredith. You should have the wisdom to bow to my greater powers and concede defeat now. You will waste yourself in a hopeless struggle fighting me."

At a snap of his fingers the fire sprang to life. Pywll

of the sunken eyes quickly fed fresh wood to the small flame. It caught in seconds, roaring high.

"Look within. See how foolish to depend upon your warrior to save you. Look, I say!" Owain fisted his hand within the tangled length of her hair, dragging her to the fire.

Meredith's wild laughter brought madness to light in Owain's eyes.

"Look within the fire yourself," she goaded. "I see a bright flame and naught else."

Owain looked into the white-hot heart of his fire, but there was naught to see. He murmured incantations in an ever rising voice of rage. He swore and he cursed, but the fire burned and its white heart, which served him so well, refused to deliver up the image of where Davey was.

Her mouth and throat went dry. She looked into the face of madness, and fear unlike any she had known gripped her. The man touched her and his grip was cold, like flesh long dead. A low cry tore from her throat. He had caught her arms behind her back and twisted them. His fingers tightened and sent excruciating pain up into her shoulders. She bowed her head and attempted to move to relieve the strain, but she could not.

Owain twisted her hair around and around his hand. "You will tell me what I want to know. I will make you beg for death before I am done."

She could not utter a sound. She wanted to spit with defiance into his face, but she suddenly realized that any moment of delay she could bring would give

Davey a chance to find her. And she needed him to come quickly.

"Hurting me will not give you what you want. You may know where the other gifts are, but you will never bring them to life."

It was agonizing minutes later that some sanity returned to Owain's eyes.

"If you continue to enrage me, *cariad*, you will pay the price. You gave him the sword and the cup. He will try to come after you. And I know you would love to be bait, thinking he will overcome me. It will not be. Cei," he ordered, "you will wait here for the Highlander. Kill him. Bring me the sword and the cup. I will reward you far beyond your dreams."

Cei clasped his hands together and bowed before Owain. "It shall be as you order."

"You could learn from him, *cariad*." He turned aside, motioning Cei closer but making no effort to hide what he said from Meredith. "Bring me your arrows. I want to prepare them properly."

His smile was an evil thing to see. Meredith bit her lower lip until she tasted blood. She knew what he meant to do. He would spread poison on the arrowheads. Even if Cei did not immediately kill him, the slightest nick would end Davey's life.

"I expected tears and pleading from you."

She looked up at Owain. "You are mistaken about my feelings for him. His life—"

"Spare me your lies. I *saw* you with him. You would defile yourself with a man of so little worth."

"Never! I used him, Owain. Just as you use these men and you used Dai to lure me into the forest."

"I thought that last bit clever. You always had a fancy to use your strength and powers for those weaker beings that were meant to be used."

"Damn you to perdition for killing him."

"He failed me. The punishment for failure is death. But you will not fail me, will you? I will kill you if I must, but I believe your death is one I would truly regret.

"Cei, make sure of your aim. And when he is dead, bring me a trophy. I want the hand that dared touch my sword, and the woman I chose. Yes, bring me his hand."

Meredith screamed, and she kept screaming until Owain placed both his hands on her mouth to silence her.

Chapter Ninteen

Owain waited impatiently for Cei to join them. He had taken a room in a small dockside inn in Apple-cross, after he forced another dose of his vile potion down Meredith's throat.

Dressed once more in his friar's robe, Owain had no trouble in obtaining either the room or passage for himself, his newly widowed sister and their servants. But as he paced the confines of the room, he wondered if he should have left Pwyll to help Cei. The Highlander had proved resourceful. And he had the sword.

Owain avoided thinking about what had happened to his attempt to scry in the fire. He glanced at where Meredith was curled on the narrow bed. Had her strength to prevent him from scrying grown?

He walked toward the small window that over-looked the harbor. He ignored the overpowering stench of fish. With his hands hidden within the wide sleeves of his brown robe he pondered again Mere-dith's refusal to aid him.

Why did she believe as she did? He'd offered to

share a power greater than any man or woman had known in centuries. And she'd refused him. What hold could those mealymouthed ancients have over her? What promises could they have made to her, that she would give her life to them?

Those old priests had waited and watched, schemed and planned for a child to be born to unite their people. But he, too, knew the Cymry. He knew their jealousies, their love of war and their hatred of any man's rule, unless he proved to be more powerful than they.

And Owain would be the most powerful man to live among them. Mayhap more than Cambria would be his to rule.

Let the old ones cast their runes, read the stars and perform their rituals.

He raised his maimed hand in front of him. Aye, he would have his revenge. And he would laugh while they burned.

Owain went back to his pacing. Then he suddenly stopped short. Why was he so sure that the Highlander would track them to the stable? The man was without powers. How could he find Cei? What terrible mistake had Owain made?

"Pwyll! Find me a horse. And guard her. It means your life if you fail me."

Davey had the sword to thank for his life far more than his skill in using it. He had found the stable and the man left behind to kill him. He would never doubt Meredith's word again. She had told about the sword's ability to enhance a warrior's skill. He had not known the blade would deflect an arrow aimed for his heart.

He looked around the rubble of a burned inn that stood on the road leading down to Applecross. He could see the ships' masts just as he had when he looked into the stone. But was he in time to stop Owain from sailing away with Meredith?

Regret for having killed the man before he could question him lasted but a moment. It was more important for Davey to stay alive. He snatched up his own cloak.

He hurried back to where he had left Ciotach. From what he had seen, Applecross was not a thriving port, but more than a fishing village. Mayhap he would find news of Owain's passing. Before he mounted he lifted the stone, smooth and almost round, and held it up to the strong afternoon sun. Its pale yellow color revealed naught of what he wanted to see. His fury was fully under his control, so he did not toss it away but tucked it back into his sporran. He slid the sword home in his belt and slipped the cloak on. It would serve to hide his shabby appearance.

The village was built on a flat below the high mountains of mist-shrouded Torridon. Davey saw ample evidence of men-at-arms with their Ross badges displayed. He also noted several friars walking from the priory. That triggered the memory of Owain dressed in a friar's dark brown robe. Now Davey had a place to start his search. Someone must have seen Owain and Meredith.

Two small merchant ships were being loaded with casks and crates. Davey looked beyond them to see if any ship had sailed and not yet cleared the fiord. There were small fishing vessels but not the mast he searched for. Either his quarry were still here or long gone. But Owain had left behind a man to kill Davey. Owain would not be leaving until he had the sword and cup in his greedy hands.

Davey dismounted. It would take him longer to walk the village streets, but he could do so slowly and thereby search undetected. He hoped.

Schooling himself to have patience, he tried again to call Meredith with his mind. He dodged women with their baskets of fish, extolling their freshness. Off the main rutted road, smaller alleys spread like a spider's webbing. Davey chose to keep his search nearer the docks. If that failed, then he would look elsewhere.

He kept sharp eyes on every friar. His warrior's instinct told him that Owain would use such a disguise again. It was a good choice. There were few if any who would not come to a brother's aid. What Davey especially looked for were any whose cowl was raised. The soft draping of a friar's hood left little more than a profile visible.

A few raggedly clad boys came forth and tried to get him to hand over his horse for stabling. Davey stopped and asked each one if he had seen a friar arrive with a young woman within the last few hours. He described Meredith and Owain. None of the boys claimed to have seen them.

But the knot of boys had drawn the attention of three Ross men-at-arms. As the armed men approached, the boys melted away into the alleys. Davey stood alone.

The three were of an age with him. Davey seized the advantage of hurrying toward them. "Och, lads, I be needing your help. My lass's family spirited her off. Giving her to the church, you see, an' mc having got my da to offer a bit more for a bride. I ken she is here. Traveling with her uncle. He is the one that wants her for the church. If you have ever been in love, lads, take pity on me and lend a hand to find her."

Davey watched as they looked at each other, then back at him. His story was an oft-told tale when families had too many daughters and not enough dowries. And the priests were always encouraging their flocks to send sons and daughters to serve the abbeys and priories. Those without dower performed the hardest and most menial of tasks.

"I have little coin, but I would be willing to offer my stallion to the man who helps me find her."

"What's your intention, lad?"

"Buy passage on the first ship that will have us. Och, listen, we are in love, I tell you. Would you be standing in the way?"

Davey sweetened the offer with one of his gold coins. If they did not hinder his search, but kept the other Ross men away, it would serve him just as well.

He'd started to give Meredith's description when he heard her call his name. He answered her silently, ignoring the concerned faces that swam before his eyes. She was here. Close enough to reach him. His hand slipped through the opening in his cloak to rest on his sword hilt. He would kill anyone who stood in his way.

He pushed the Ross men aside, running toward the docks, begging her to tell him where she was. He never saw Owain ride out, for he no longer wore the friar's robe. Nor did Owain take note of the cloaked and hooded man running toward the docks with three Ross men-at-arms in pursuit.

Davey needed to know if she was alone. She told him Owain had given her something to drink that left her weak and dazed. She explained that Owain had left suddenly, but set his man to watch her.

All Davey wanted to know was where she was. *Near the docks.* But there were three inns near the docks. Afraid he would run out of time before he found her, Davey turned to the men following behind him. He handed over another gold coin, and asked them to search two of the inns. He did not stand around and wonder why they decided to help him; he made for the third. And he talked to Meredith the whole time, telling her he needed her to distract her guard, because he sensed how close she was.

Distract him? Meredith could barely move. She eyed Pwyll where he sat at the small, roughly made table, sipping a tankard of ale. His shrunken eyes never left her. That vile potion Owain forced her to drink had not lasted as long as the first time. She could think, and reach Davey. The one thing Owain did not want was for her to attract attention.

She drew in a deep breath and screamed.

Pwyll jumped from his bench, knocking both it and his tankard over in his hurry to silence her. His bulky body moved fast. He was across the room with hands reaching for her when Davey pounded on the door.

Davey put his shoulder to the wooden door and shoved. It was barred from the inside. By this time he was joined by the three Ross men-at-arms, the inn-keeper and assorted patrons. Davey was elbowed aside.

"Open in the name of the Earl of Ross!"

If Meredith had not been terrified of being crushed by Pwyll's massive hands, she would have found a small bit of pity for the sudden confusion in the man's eyes. These were lands belonging to the earl. It was no light matter to refuse his men entry.

With Pwyll's hand covering her mouth and nose she could not breathe. Black spots danced in front of her eyes. She struggled to pull his hand aside, all the while listening to the arguing and pounding coming from the hall. Now it was the innkeeper, then Davey again, and once more three or more voices demanding entry in the name of the earl.

Pwyll released her. Meredith drew heaving breaths into her air-starved lungs. She watched as he lifted the bar to the door, then opened it. At first she could not see Davey in the crowd of men that forced their way inside the small chamber. Then her hand was grabbed, and she found herself in his arms.

Davey pushed a path through the room, carrying her. He refused to answer any questions, glared at any who stood in his way and finally reached the short hall. There were no back stairs.

"Can you walk?" he asked.

"I think so. Where is Owain? Did you see him?"

Davey's answer was to draw his sword. "We are leaving and woe to anyone who tries to stop me."

But no one did. Outside, he lifted her onto Ciotach's back and swung up behind her. Instead of taking the road down which he had ridden, he headed toward the beach. His only thought was to get well away from Owain.

"Where is the harp and the ring, Meredith?"

"England. We need to go to the manor house on the River Ribble outside of Whalley. The harp is there."

"We will need a ship. Do you know the nearest port?"

She thought a few moments. "There is a village below the castle at Lancaster, and to the south, Liverpool."

Davey set his heels to the stallion's sides. He held her tight against his chest, murmuring thanks to all the gods that he had her safe again.

Chapter Twenty

Days of hard riding, little sleep and worrying about Meredith took their toll on Davey before he found a ship that would sail down the coast to England.

The first few days, Meredith could barely keep any food down, until she had gathered enough herbs to make an infusion that rid her of the vile potion Owain had forced upon her. Davey hated having to push her to go on when she so desperately needed rest. Her slow recovery kept him from asking questions, or talking to her about the dream.

He finally found a stout merchant ship, with a master who forced Davey to bargain hard to take Ciotach with them. Davey blessed the time he had spent involved in his clan's shipping interests, for his knowledge of and admiration for the ship stood well with the master.

Davey covered the stallion's head with cloth before leading him up the plank, for he knew the danger of being crushed between the ship and the dock if he fell.

Davey had not known that Meredith had never sailed before.

"Meredith, I swear to you, 'tis a sturdily built ship," he insisted. "The sea is calm. The ship's master knows what he is doing."

"I heard that one can die of the sickness."

Davey had to turn away. "Not die of it." *Only wish you could.* He remembered the first time he had sailed in rough seas and almost cast himself overboard.

"Davey?"

"You may not be taken with any sickness, only a slight discomfort. Come," he coaxed, slipping his arm around her waist. "We will go aboard now or they will sail without us."

What Davey never mentioned to her when he had to push her along was that every minute of delay allowed Owain to get closer to them. Davey had no doubt of that fact, and he thought that Meredith knew it, too, although she never mentioned her captor's name.

Davey glanced up to see that the loading had been finished. There was no time to be lost, and the passage had cost them dear with their remaining coins.

She offered no resistance when he led her up the wood plank, and he was not above enjoying the way she clung to him. He stood near the rail as the plank was pulled up, the ropes were cast off and the seamen settled to their oars. He led her along the narrow walkway between the stacked barrels and crates as the ship rose and fell in the easy swells. He wanted them both out of the way as the seamen raised the sails. He found them a place to sit against the high-sided planking.

Davey drew Meredith to sit beside him, and wrapped his cloak around her. The ship moved steadily and the wind caught the newly raised sails. For a few minutes he was content to hold her, but Davey was troubled. Since she had escaped from Owain, Meredith had said very little to him. She never mentioned the dream, nor asked how he'd found her.

So he told her of the dream, and as he talked, he wished her head was not resting on his shoulder. He could not see her face as he whispered all that had happened. His voice grew husky when he described making love to her, and then sorrow tinged his tone when he explained how short a time their gift had lasted, and he had been alone again.

The silence stretched between them. Meredith lay very still against the warmth of his body. She could not accuse him of lying. To share the dream as Davey described could only come from his bargain with her gods. And she knew her gods to be unpredictable in their granting of favors as well as the payment demanded. A cold knot of fear formed inside her. What price had Davey paid for his gift?

She did not ask. She had to deny to him that the dream had happened. If she dared to admit the truth, that his desire for her was so powerful that he could, with her gods' aid, reach across the miles separating them to draw her into his dream, she would be lost. She felt the depth of Davey's deep, abiding passion for her, and she returned it full measure. But she had warded herself so he would not know how much she wanted him. It was knowledge best kept hidden or Davey would do all in his power to turn dream into reality.

She fought the sting of tears that came suddenly to her, and was glad he could not see them. There might never be time to join with him in that perfect blending of heart, mind, body and soul. For a moment she allowed her inner shield to lower and imagined the conflagration to rival the heavens if she and Davey were one.

But not now. She had to concentrate on completing her quest. And she had to wonder if Owain or Davey's longing would destroy her first.

"Davey, your dream was just that. The exhausted imagining of a man pushed beyond his limit," she told him, using anger as a weapon against him.

The expected anger from Davey did not come. He sighed and held her tighter.

"Mayhap," Davey said, "whatever Owain forced you to drink has affected your memory."

"Davey, what do you want from me? I did not share this dream with you. That you believe otherwise I cannot help. I told you what it would mean for me to grant this desire more importance than what I need to do. I will not betray my people."

He kissed her temple. "I want your love. I have had it in the past, and now I want you to say that you love me."

"Nay, 'tis more that you want, Davey. You want me to rely on you alone for all that gives meaning to my life. You want to control me, too. In that you are no different than Owain."

She started to pull away, but Davey held her close. She resisted for a few minutes, but she had not regained her full strength, so remained as she was.

"Why do you deny what you know to be truth? Meredith, we were together in the past, lovers then and now. Do you believe I do not know the danger of giving your love to another? It is to risk one's heart. Like my brothers, I know when I have found the one woman, the only woman who can be my life's mate. You reject me. No matter what I say, I cannot make you see that you are wrong. There is strength to be had from our joining. There is nowhere you can go that I will not follow—and not," he said as he strove to leash his anger over her stubbornness, "as you believe, to control you. Lest you forget, my lady, I did not seek you out. I knew naught of these gifts. After what we have been through together, do you so revile me as to compare me to Owain?"

"Davey! I hurt you. Curse my unruly tongue. 'Tis sorry I am. Forgive me, please?"

"I forgive all but your blindness to see what could be between us." He raked his hand through his hair, damp and sticky from the salt spray. But the smell of the sea soothed him. "Sometimes I have this feeling that I hurt you in some way in the past that you cannot forgive."

He cast the words as a lure, much like a fisherman cast his net, but he caught naught for his admission. Her deep sigh as she snuggled against him told him without words that she was done talking. Once more he let her be. He would do as he had sworn and protect her, but once she was free of her obligations to her priests and people, he would accept naught but her surrender.

They sailed the Irish Sea with tailwinds sent by the gods, for naught marred their way. Whenever they put into port, Davey took Meredith with him, afraid to let her out of his sight as he replenished all that had been lost.

They docked near the small town of Ravenglass. Seeing that it was market day, Davey told the ship's master that he and his wife—which was how he'd booked their passage—would browse the stalls while the cargo was being unloaded.

He decided to take Ciotach with them, not unusual in and of itself, for he tried to exercise the stallion as much as he could. Meredith wanted to walk among the stalls. There were sacks of spices, and bolts of cloth, plus all manner of farm animals and horses. Enticing aromas came from baked breads and those stalls selling sweets. It was at one of these, where Davey stopped to buy small pasties drizzled with honey, that he sensed someone watching them.

He glanced at Meredith, needing no words as she communicated her own unease. Davey thought the crowds made it easier for them to hide, but it also made it difficult to discover who found them so interesting.

They walked along, eating the sweets, leading Ciotach.

"You know, it may be no more than some young gallant wanting to know you." As Davey said this, he looked at her and smiled. There was a slight flush to her cheeks and a tint of gold on her skin from the sun. She had put their time on the ship to good use, sewing him a new tunic in forest-green, and for herself a soft wool tunic of white, high-necked and long-sleeved, over which she wore a bliaut of gray. They were not richly dressed, so as not to draw attention to themselves, but Meredith's loveliness could never be disguised.

Meredith scanned the crowd and her unease grew. She bit her lower lip, knowing she had to broach the silence she had imposed on herself about Owain. "Do you feel 'tis Owain close by?"

Davey hid his surprise that she was first to mention his name. "I cannot be sure," he replied. "Getting a ship that did not make as many stops as ours would prove no great difficulty. That would not explain how he knew we would come ashore here."

"Owain would know. Trouble yourself with discovering who watches us."

"Buy things," he ordered. "Buy enough so we need to return to the ship."

"Better to go now."

"I have no intention of remaining with it, Meredith. We could be trapped far too easily." He led the way around a group of women clustered before a spice stall with its rich aromas. The feeling of being watched seemed to increase in intensity.

"You think to continue our journey by land?"

"Aye. There is no place to run or hide on a ship. And that bastard Owain would not care who died with us if he chose to set fire to the sails or cargo."

"Say no more." She clutched his hand holding Ciotach's reins, since the other already rested on his sword. She knew his fear of fire since nearly being burned alive in the keep at Torridon, and said naught, for she also knew how deep that fear went.

So Meredith bought a basket, cheese and bread, and a small length of linen to cover the opening of the basket. With the covered basket held before her, they stopped at each and every stall as they worked their way back to the ship. Although she had made no other purchases, the covered basket hid that fact. She pretended the weight of the basket was too much to carry and gave it to Davey when they reached the docks.

Hoping to confuse whoever watched them, Davey swung her into his arms and kissed her before he lifted her up on Ciotach's back. He tied the basket onto the saddle.

"I will fetch our packs. If anyone approaches, yell *tairbh* to Ciotach. He will fight for you."

"*Tairbh?*"

"In the way of the bull." He smiled at her, but his eyes roamed the crowd on the docks. "All the Gunn warhorses are trained with a few words of command. Do as I say."

He hurried up the plank, afraid to have her out of his sight. He wished there had been time to find a horse for Meredith at the market. To do so now would only alert their watchers. Davey showed no surprise that he believed there were more than one; that was what he sensed. He knew, too, from his talk with the ship's master that they were not that far from Whalley. Off Morecambe Bay was the River Lune, and south of that lay their goal. He gathered their packs from the small space he had found among the stacked barrels, and ran back to Meredith.

Something in her eyes confirmed that Owain was here. Davey tossed her the packs and mounted behind her. Ciotach needed no urging to run.

High above Ravenglass in the Cumbrian Mountains a fire burned before a cave. Laughter rang out. There was a maniacal frenzy to the sound as the white heart of the fire gave Owain ap Madog his greatest wish. He had the druid witch and her warrior running again.

His smile turned sly. He closed his hand around the small circle of silver that he held. Meredith did not yet know that he had found the ring. And he would soon have the spell to awaken its full powers. Then let them come against him.

"Let them come!" he shouted, his fist raised high to the heavens.

Chapter Twenty-One

A fortnight passed before they stood on the hill above the farms belonging to the manor house near Whalley. The late afternoon sun was blocked by a surge of clouds that hinted of rain before the night was done.

Davey had used his well-honed skill as a reiver to steal a fine-boned mare for Meredith to ride. She in turn had surprised him with a talent to not only quiet horses, but to make the mare her own within an hour. If he had not seen it with his own eyes, he would disbelieve any who told the tale. But with the aid of their last two apples and her voice, she had touched the mare, breathed her breath into flaring nostrils and generally made much of her. So much so that Ciotach displayed his jealousy. Davey knew how his stallion felt. He wanted all of Meredith's attentions focused on himself. But she had kept him at an emotional distance, if not a physical one.

He thought she worried, but she would not share what distressed her. She had her shields firmly in place again. All their talk centered on a need to hurry.

His questions of why were turned aside, his concern rebuffed. His probing gained him naught but a growing despair.

He watched her wander off from him as he made another of their rough camps.

Meredith felt his frequent glances touch upon her as she leaned against a tree trunk. The limbs were high enough to provide shade, and privacy came from someone's artful cutting, so that the lower branches drooped toward the ground.

She could not rid herself of troubling thoughts. When her focus should be on Owain and what he was doing to stop them, she could not stop thinking about Davey. If he ever knew what she had done, she did not believe he would forgive her. She had lied to him. She *had* shared his dream. And the memory of those moments when two became one haunted her. *A gift from the gods.* But it went against everything she had been taught and told and truly believed. She knew how much she hurt him by withdrawing from his every attempt to discover what was wrong. But how could she tell him the truth?

That she wanted him. Not in a dream out of time, and not just once.

He called her his life's mate, but she knew him to be the other half of her soul.

"So deep in thoughts, my lady? I wish you would share."

Meredith started. Davey had come close enough to whisper in her ear, and she had not sensed him near. She glanced at him over her shoulder, then turned around. The hunted look in his eyes alarmed her.

"What—"

He silenced her with a kiss, his lips sweetly cherishing and warming on hers for too brief a time. He eased his lips from hers, hungry for more, but kept his promise that he would wait, no matter how bedeviled he was.

"Are you certain the harp is still down below?"

"Nay." 'Twas the truth. She had not been thinking about the harp at all.

"Then ascertain the harp's whereabouts and quickly, for a party of riders just left there, and I swear one is wearing the robes of a friar."

Meredith spun around, edging out from under the tree. She saw the dust on the road and thought there were four, no, five riders heading south.

"'Tis him, I tell you," Davey insisted as he joined her.

"What makes you say thus?"

Davey held out his stone. "Look as I just did and see for yourself."

She stared at the pale yellow stone. She made no move to take it from his cupped palm.

"Go on. The stone belonged to my mother. I assure you that touching it will bring you no harm."

"The stone is yours, Davey. No other may use it."

Davey held the stone between his thumb and index finger, gently turning it over and over, then held it steady.

"I can barely see Owain within it, Meredith. I cannot make sense of where he is. Near? Far? There is naught to see but his face."

Meredith battled fear. She looked toward the thin,

silvery-blue ribbon of the River Ribble. If she could slip away and get down there, she could scry and answer Davey's question. But deep inside she already knew the answer. And the risk of scrying when Owain was close was too great. She had to keep Davey apart from him. She no longer sensed the harp.

At her sides, her hands curled and clutched the cloth. If Owain had the harp…gods help them! All the protection that had been hers from the start of her journey seemed to be slipping away. Or had been taken from her by Owain's black arts. The thought added another layer to her fear.

Could her gods have turned from her? Was the love and desire she had for the very warrior they had chosen for her to be her downfall? If she failed, so failed the dreams of her people.

She brought her hands together and started to rub her ring. She knew that delaying to speak of all this with Davey endangered them both. But his life was the one she worried about. Owain could never kill her. But he could take Davey from her.

Gods, help me! she cried in her mind. Let it not be Owain who has gained the harp. I will journey the rest of my life to find the gifts if you spare Davey now.

She rubbed harder with her thumb over the endless silver knotwork. She could only try a spell of protection to include Davey if he wore the ring. The feeling grew that it would be useless against Owain's growing powers.

"Meredith, what is wrong?" Davey cupped her shoulders and drew her tense body against his. "Tell me what you want me to do. Should I ride after them to see if 'tis indeed Owain? It would give me great pleasure to cleave him in two.''

She shook her head and felt the bite of his fingers as he turned her to face him.

"You are trembling. What is wrong?"

"Davey, do you trust me?"

"With your life," he answered without hesitation.

"My life?"

"Aye, sweet lady. I keep telling you that I love you, that you are my life's mate. Your life to me is far more precious than my own. Hence," he said with a smile, hoping to bring one to her lips, "I trust you to do all in your power to protect what means more than my own life to me."

But Meredith was not smiling. She closed her eyes, effectively shutting him out. This time he had no patience to wait her out.

"Stop your infernal hiding from me! Your precious harp may be gone. You will not even answer me when I ask what you want done. Mayhap, my lady, I should follow my own inclination about Owain."

His hands fell away, and then he stepped back.

"Nay, do not go near him!" Meredith opened her eyes and saw Davey's anger. She threw herself against him, her arms entwined around his neck, her thumb once again rubbing over the knot on her ring while her lips sought and found his. Her heart was in that kiss. There was no holding back. All the passion of many lifetimes, all the desire and love that had bound them through the ages poured from her. She no longer cared what happened to her as long as she kept Davey safe from Owain. She knew what he would do with the harp.

The shields were down. Davey was caught up in his dream again. This was the woman he knew and yearned to have again—the sweetly heated gift of herself, with naught held back. He caught her thick braid with one hand, as if he needed something more to hold on to. He had no thoughts to spare for Owain. Meredith consumed him

When he kissed her and held her like this Meredith felt the world spinning away. All that remained was this reckless desire, this insatiable passion. She whimpered softly under the hungry demand of his lips. He tasted her and her tongue played with his, teasing, then dancing away. His hands slid down to the small of her back, pressing her closer, molding her lower body to his. She caught his lower lip with the edge of her teeth, remembering how he had done this to her and what it made her feel. She rubbed the captive flesh with the tip of her tongue.

He held her tighter until his aroused manhood was like a living force between them. Heat spread from the tide of desire that raced through her.

She touched his hair, her fingers sliding through the dark brown sleekness. She felt his breath-catching shudder as she stroked the bare skin of his nape, pressing against him as if she wanted to become a part of him.

The racking conflict that tore her apart was drowned by the love she felt for this one man, only this man. She wanted to drown in passionate forgetfulness and cast aside all forbidding strictures, every impediment that kept her from him.

With every deepening kiss, with every moment that passed, she was suffused with the magic that made them halves of a whole.

She knew what brought him to the height of pleasure and thereby enhanced her own. The caress of his hand curving over thigh, hip and the fullness of her breast made her follow the same path on his body— only where she was soft, her hand molded hardened muscles that no cloth could hide.

Need raced like flame through her mind and body. Heat spread from every tingling place of contact. She trembled in his arms, overcome by this urgent desire to possess and be possessed. This was a heady power to drink and dine upon—to know that a touch, a kiss, a sweetly uttered moan could make him want her with scorching passion.

She felt his arousal move against her. Potency added to power unfurled. If she was captor, she was held captive by the same enchantment that chained him.

"I want you," she whispered, scattering kisses over his strong jaw, lingering at the cleft in his chin. "More than life, I want you."

A driving fury of need brought fierce hunger to mate his lips with hers. And she answered him beyond any dream. But a tiny insistent voice grew louder and louder, telling him something was very wrong. Davey fought against it, for here in his arms was the woman he desired more than life.

More than life...the words re-echoed, and with

them came the voice of reason, even though his body was on fire, and soaring passion tried to rule his mind.

No matter the hot, searing power that made her most tantalizing and passionate, he knew she acted against the very tenets that she swore by. *We can never be lovers...death to me...betray all...death to a dream of my people.* The words rose from memory, and he heard the ruling passion that came with them. A passion that had naught to do with gratifying the desire of the body and all to do with the fires of the heart.

Never lovers...never.

This would destroy her. Destroy the prophecy. And Owain yet remained the most dangerous threat of all to their very lives.

Drenched in cold, Davey pulled her arms from around his neck and tore his mouth free of hers.

"Davey?"

He held her away from him, barely able to drag air into his lungs as he struggled to bank his hunger for her. Better to bury himself, and far easier to do so. She looked at him with pleasure-darkened eyes. Her cheeks wore a passion's flush and her lips, slightly swollen and reddened from his kisses, were parted as if she would speak.

He shook his head; that was all he was capable of at this moment. He had to force himself to step back from her. His chest heaved with the effort, for he was afraid that if he spoke now, he would hurt her. But a sense of betrayal became rooted where desire ruled, and lay claim to him.

For long moments, Meredith stood, cold and empty

as he withdrew from her. She tried to shield herself before he understood why she had cast aside duty, honor and loyalty to her beliefs and to her people.

It was too late—she saw that in his dark brown eyes and in the tense set of his jaw. She felt it in her body, in the piercing pain lancing her heart.

She lifted her hand, both to stop him and in plea.

With her head thrown back, she stared up at the dark storm clouds that filled her vision. Far-off thunder rumbled. The wind swept the hilltop and stole her words before Davey heard them.

Lightning flashed. Great bolts struck the earth below with all the power and force of the storm unleashed.

Meredith ran toward Davey. She had to touch him, and give him the ring. She had to protect him.

"Davey, I beg you!" she cried out. She heard the first note, heard it above the rising wind and the sudden slashing downpour of blinding rain. She slipped and then flung herself at Davey. "The harp...Owain!"

Too late!

Chapter Twenty-Two

Her extended fingertips barely brushed Davey's callused ones before he fell to his knees with his head thrown back, and a cry of anguish that rivaled the howl of the storm poured from his lips.

The wind gusted with such force that it threatened to tear her away from him. She could no longer reach his hand. It had fallen to his side, clenched in a white-knuckled fist that revealed he used his formidable strength of will to combat the melody of agony Owain played on the harp.

Through the rain and her tears she saw the mask of pain etched on Davey's beloved features. The arch of his body told her what horrors Owain's melody inflicted. To be told what a thing can do was one thing; to see it for herself left her frozen for long minutes. Minutes better served in preventing Davey's suffering.

She circled him, drawing the strongest of the druid fences, the *airbe druad*. For any to cross but the one who made it meant their death.

Another cry came from Davey's throat. Her instinct

was to give him comfort. She fought that need and moved through the rain and the wind toward their packs under the tree.

She tore through them, scattering all until she found the cloth-wrapped cup. She muttered, then screamed out the malign incantation of the *glám dichenn* to wither Owain's hands and destroy his body. Without her, Owain could not key the harp to play the final and most deadly melody.

Her fingers fumbled when she needed them nimble.

Hurry...hurry! The litany played over and over in her mind. If she did not protect Davey now, she would never untwist the damage Owain wrought.

She must succeed in protecting her love from the evil of Owain's spirit. She would do it or die.

Lashed by the storm, many of the thickly leaved branches were torn loose and struck her on her face, back and shoulders. She used her teeth to free the leather tie around the cup, her eyes wild with fury, a boiling rage lending her strength.

She fought her way into the open, lifting her face to the storm. Her hands formed a funnel for the rain to fill the cup. And her laughter rang out when she brought the water to Davey. She begged her gods to intercede and make this cup of life-giving water into the *deog dermaid,* the drink of forgetfulness.

And if her prayers were answered, she risked losing his every memory of their time together.

It was a risk she was more than willing to take to save his life. If she could not be with him, and love him in this time, she would wait for another. He was her soul mate. Heart's blood. The half needed to make whole.

She held the cup to his lips. "Drink, my love. Listen only to my voice. I will defeat the horror he brings to you. Obey me in this, Davey!" she pleaded, knowing the agony of body and battering of spirit he had to overcome.

"I will not let Owain win. We will not let him win. Please try. Drink this. Let me save you."

She held his head cradled against her breast and brought the rim of the cup to his lips. "Davey, hear only me. I love you!" She felt the icy chill of his body stealing the heat of her own. And she held him tighter as he fought to drink the water.

Meredith cried. His body was so tense with the agony he suffered that his face was taking on a grayish cast. "Oh, hear me! I will not let that foul servant of the Dark Ones take his life. He is mine. Given unto my care. Destroy him and your destruction will encompass me. Gone is your prophecy! I beg your aid to save him! I beg you," she wailed, trying to be heard above the storm. She dropped the cup and never saw it fall between them as she knelt in the rain and mud to hold Davey in her arms.

"He will not win. He cannot." She whispered in sobbing breaths.

The heavens opened in a deluge of such force of wind and rain, thunder and lightning that the earth shook and the trees were torn from their roots.

And still Meredith held Davey against the unleashed fury. Her throat was raw from screaming and begging for cessation of Owain's vile playing of the harp. When she could not make another sound, when there was no breath or strength left in her, she felt a great shudder rack Davey's body. She fell to the side as his weight collapsed on her.

There on the rain-soaked ground she held him, rain passing for tears, for she had none of her own left, but the cries went on in her mind. And so she waited out the storm, waited out the decision of the gods she wanted to renounce for what they allowed to happen to her love.

Owain watched it all. The rain spat and hissed, but did naught to put out the fire he had built. He plucked the strings of the harp he had killed to possess, and saw his enemy writhe upon the earth. Helpless he was, like a newborn babe without recourse, having to depend on another for his very life. Meredith would fail him in this.

Owain glanced at the churning river below, then at the black undersides of the clouds that wept furious rains. Even the stiff wind that bellowed his cloak behind him like a huge wing, pleased him immensely. Had he called the storm he would have rent the earth far more fiercely than what he saw before him.

He rolled his fingertips over the strings, the notes discordant, as they were meant to be. He smiled with a madman's glee to see Meredith try to stem the small trickle of blood from her lover's mouth. Escape him? Never. Choose another over him? Never.

He whispered the words, those precious words that released agony and horror, pain and death upon the unknowing, his clawed hand barely able to brace the harp against his chest while he plucked first one string, then another. This was power! This was what those ancient ones were afraid to use.

But he saw within his fire's heart that the dark, near-black blanket was being stirred. An eerie white mist was shredding the darkness, a mist that slowly crept around the two entwined figures and hid them from his view.

His eyes bulged. Spittle flew from his mouth. He had to swallow the bitterest of bile as he saw his chance to kill his enemy and claim what was his disappear under the covering mist.

"Nay!" The wind caught his scream of rage.

In the heart of his fire the mist lifted and swirled. He saw Meredith turning as if she knew that he watched her, and wanted him to see. A cold smile twisted her lovely mouth as she raised silvery-gray eyes toward the dark, rain-laden clouds scudding across the dismal sky.

Owain looked on in horror as his woman, his near equal, kissed the lips of the man he had sworn to kill. Was now killing with every hard, punishing slash he made to the harp's strings.

He was wild in his frenzy, slamming his good hand on the harp—beyond cursing, beyond belief as he heard her speak to him.

"He is mine, Owain. His life and his love. Pluck away at the strings and see your own death come to pass."

He threw the harp into the fire. "Watch it burn," he shouted. He laughed when he held the ring high.

"You did not know I had this. Like the harp, the ring is mine! I will destroy all if I cannot have them!"

But a thick squall from the blackest of clouds settled above him, and smoke rose from the hissing fire until in moments it was reduced to thick, sodden ash. And there lay the harp and the ring, untouched by flame or rain, a last mournful note rising from its strings.

Despite her exhaustion, Meredith dared not close her eyes through the night and well into the next day. The discomfort of damp earth, sodden clothing, hunger and thirst meant little when she could listen to the deep, even, healing breaths that Davey drew in his sleep.

She had been aware of the storm's abatement, but more puzzled by the mist that shrouded them. She sat within the circle of the *airbe druad* with Davey's head and shoulders resting on her lap. She stroked his sweaty brow with her fingertips. Her eyes burned and her body cried out for rest, but she refused to move, refused to disturb Davey's needed sleep.

Where Owain was now was not something she cared to think about. If the mist that veiled and protected them from his sight was truly god sent, Owain would be dealt with when the time was right.

Her burden to stay awake was great indeed. She caught herself nodding off to sleep and fought the insidious pull. She thought of the first time she had seen Davey in the flesh, not in half-remembered dreams or scryings. She traced the shape of his lips, seeing his smile and hearing his laughter. She brought her fingertips to her own lips, placed a kiss on them and rested them on his mouth. His sigh was more felt than heard, but for now it contented her to touch him.

She shifted a little, attempting to relieve her legs, which were growing numb with his weight resting on them. She ignored it, pushing her discomfort aside, and instead wondering about Davey's memory when he awoke. Would he know her? She closed her eyes against the painful possibility that he wouldn't, even if she knew she had no choice. Better to use her time to think of a place for them to go. And she still had to recover the harp.

Meredith shivered. The night was growing cool. She dared not leave Davey. Temptation rose to have a fire's warmth for them both. Davey stirred in his sleep, turning his face to rest against her belly. She smoothed his hair over his head and down his shoulder.

Her hand fell to the earth. It was moments later that she understood what she was feeling: the vibrations of drumming. But that could not be right. She stared out at the night, black-on-black shadows, for the moon was hidden behind a thick bank of clouds.

A whinny from one of their horses told her that what she felt was riders coming toward them. Fear grabbed her. Could it be Owain? But he would know that he could not cross the line of the *airbe druad* and live. Would that stop him from sending another man to his death?

She knew the answer to that. He would not care. And once the line was crossed, the spell of protection was broken. She had to rouse Davey now. There was no way she could move him on her own.

Meredith fought down the panic. Mayhap it was not Owain. And mayhap she could spirit herself and Davey away.

Chapter Twenty-Three

She shook Davey and in a voice filled with desperation whispered to him that riders were approaching. She had violated so many of her teachings to keep him alive, but as her hand touched his belt knife, she hesitated. *Forbidden to maim or kill.* She snatched her hand back from the hilt.

The sudden jerk of her body did what her whispers had not. Davey opened his eyes and turned over. Night. The same or…? He could not complete the thought, for his head ached. He felt the dampness of his clothes and that of the lap that pillowed his head.

"What ails you, lass?" he asked in a voice groggy with sleep.

"Riders," Meredith answered. A small cry of gladness passed her lips. "You are awake?"

"Aye. I willna say much about it. Sweet saints, what happened?"

"Davey, this is no time to ask questions. There are riders below us near the river. I do not know if Owain is among them. Can you stand?" She tried to lift him, but her strength was spent. Her puny effort merely allowed her to move her legs.

"Give me a minute, lass. My head is feeling like I broached a cask of ale and finished it alone."

"We have no time. You must move. We need to hide." There was naught of gentleness in the way she scrambled free and caught hold of his hands as she tried to make him rise.

"Do you still see or hear the riders? I am thinking they are long gone. Likely looking for a low place to cross and naught more." He lifted his hand and raked back his damp hair. "Come tell me why you have been sitting here shivering. I know you can build a fire."

"Everything is wet, Davey. There was a storm. And then Owain—"

"Speak not that vile name to me. I swear my head is about to crack." He rolled to his side, then managed to get to his knees. He accepted her support to stand. "We will go down to the manor house. They will give us shelter. You are shaking worse than me."

"There is death down there, Davey. Owain has the harp." Meredith was glad of the dark that hid her face from his far too penetrating gaze. She saw that he was steady on his feet now, and she moved away from him. He was right about the riders. They were gone.

"We are too open here, Meredith. We will take the horses and go down by the river. I remember seeing a thick growth of brush and trees near its bank. We can find some dry wood—" His speech was cut off by the way she clung to him. He cradled her face in his hands.

"First warmth. Then talk. Agreed?"

"Agreed." Her head bowed and came to rest against his chest in thanksgiving. She felt him smoothing the damp tangle of her hair. Strength flowed from him into her depleted body. And warmth. Delicious warmth that she absorbed as if he were a fire.

"Meredith, were you hurt?" he asked, wishing he had light to see for himself.

"Nay. He did not touch me."

"Then let us leave this place." Davey said naught to her of his trouble remembering exactly what had happened. It was all vague, but in a way that disturbed him. He felt weak, too, although moving around helping her gather their belongings eased the ache in his head.

Davey sensed Owain out there, or if not him, someone he'd set to watch them. Davey kept silent about that. Meredith needed to get warm.

His weakened state and lack of light made him walk slowly ahead while she led the horses. At first he rested his hand on his sword, but halfway down the hilltop, he drew the blade, sensing danger. Twice he veered off from the direction he had been heading to avoid being trapped.

It was the silence that warned him—the lack of any sounds made by small night creatures on their evening hunt. He could not see dark shadows moving, and no breeze stirred the leaves—yet suddenly there was a rustle. It ended quickly, but he heeded the noise.

The riders burst upon them without any other warning. Light bloomed from rush torches, held by three men on foot. Four riders circled around them, their very silence far more menacing than if they shouted.

"Meredith, free Ciotach." Davey stood his ground, not looking to see if she obeyed, and whispered the Scottish words that brought the stallion to battle readiness. None of the men had come close enough for him to strike a blow.

He sensed the stallion rearing as he trumpeted his challenge to the strangers' mounts. What Davey did not sense was Owain's presence. He had no time to ask Meredith if she saw a sign of him being with these men bent on attack. Two of the riders came at him, one from the right and the other from the front.

Davey held the sword with both hands, swinging it from side to side. There was an unaccustomed weakness in his limbs that he had to compensate for. That the blade would do its work he had no doubt, and moments later tested that belief against a rider's strike. The sword bit through the other's blade, leaving the rider holding a stub in his hand. There were a string of curses then, the voice thick and guttural, giving orders to seize them both.

Ciotach came between the other rider and Davey. Like the trained warhorse he was, he used teeth and hooves and his greater size against the smaller mount and the man who rode him.

A man near his own height came at Davey on foot. He swung his sword like a scythe, with Davey's death the harvest he sought. But Davey's exhaustion fled with the familiar sounds and moves of battle. Rage settled like a cold knot in his belly. He heard the other man's hissing breath, the keening of the sword as it sliced and slashed, but found no target. The man labored mightily, grunting with effort, then crying out when Davey's sword cut his body. The man dropped his sword, doubled over and scampered away into the darkness.

A horseman rode close to taunt him, but not within reach of his sword. Davey did not rise to the lure of separating himself from Meredith. He knew she kept her horse guarding their backs, with Ciotach keeping other riders away.

Davey stood braced to fight, always more aware of the danger to Meredith than to himself. His training had been to attack, but he dared not move to leave her vulnerable. He was concerned, too, with those others who waited in the dark. Their watching eyes crawled over him, judging him and the sword he held.

"Come meet your death, you thieving whore-sons!" Davey taunted. "Come, cowards, this is a thirsty blade."

A man raced by, swinging his sword with a meaty fist, as if he were in a practice yard slicing at a quintain.

Davey easily dodged both blade and horse, his backswing laying the flat of his sword against the horse's rump. It was no playful tap. The animal humped its back and nearly unseated its rider while kicking out with its hind legs, missing Davey. The rider jerked his mount around and tried to ride Davey down. Davey took exception to the attack and dispatched him readily. The riderless animal raced off.

Another horse's squeals of rage came from behind Davey: Ciotach claiming victory on someone's mount. From the sounds of Ciotach's battle frenzy, Davey knew the attacker's horse would not rise again. He could only hope that the rider went down with his mount and stayed down, giving him one less to worry about.

Three long whistles halted the attack. Torches were flung aside, and the men seemed to melt away into the darkness. In mere minutes, as suddenly as it began, the attack was over and he and Meredith were alone.

Davey, still caught in the heat of battle lust, held his sword in a two handed grip, and circled the area. The attackers had not only fled, but had taken their dead with them. He saw Meredith run to grab one of the still-burning torches. With a soft voice and soothing words he calmed Ciotach.

After he spent a few minutes stroking and praising the stallion, he turned to Meredith. ''Was this another of Owain's tests?''

''Owain was not with them.''

''I know that. 'Tis not what I asked. We must not tarry. Who knows if those men will take a notion to attack us again?'' Leading Ciotach, he went to stand before Meredith. ''Did any of them hurt you?''

''None came near me.'' She shivered and the torchlight wavered in her hand. ''You were cut. That wants tending.''

''It can wait,'' he said, searching her face. She hid something from him. It was not the first time he'd sensed it. He set his lips in a tight line and gritted his teeth. He was not about to ask her, only to be denied. With an abrupt motion he snatched the torch from her hand to lead the way.

They found a nest of moss against massive boulders. Davey soon had a small fire going, and its warmth and light were most welcome. He cleaned the sword, but when Meredith made an attempt to tend to the few cuts he had, he shrugged her off.

"We cannot stay here," he said, with a thoughtful look around. He saw the dark shadows beneath her eyes, and realized he must look the same. They had been driven by Owain's pursuit these last weeks without enough food or rest, but this attack made him realize how very vulnerable they were.

"I cannot go, Davey. The *crwth* is not far from here. And somehow Owain recovered the ring. I will not leave until I hold them in my hands and know that Owain is defeated."

"Even if the price paid is your death?"

Across the fire she saw his eyes, as dark and hard as stone, regarding her with some emotion she could not define.

"My death is a risk I have always been aware of, Davey," she said softly, hoping to defuse his anger. She knew very well what caused it.

"Risk? Aye, 'tis a truth you speak. I ken the risks we've taken from the first. But what of my memory, Meredith? Was losing it part of your acceptable risk? Why have you not told me what happened to me?"

She wasted no time asking how he knew. "Davey?"

"Speak me no lies! Just tell me!"

"Stop shouting at me. I am not your enemy." She pushed back from the fire, wanting to hide in the shadows. How to explain to him what had happened? If Davey knew how easily Owain had used the harp to bring him to his knees and render him helpless, she could destroy his belief in himself and the sword. There would be no controlling his rage. Although he did not ask about the ring, she feared that Owain might find the key to loose its protection spell. That admission would shake his trust in her as well.

'Twas a price she was unwilling to pay.

"I can feel you scheming, lass. Is the truth so terrible that you cannot tell me, after all we have been through together?"

He had spoken of risks. Davey was strong. She had only to look at the dearly beloved features, at his face of strength and sensitivity, to know that she could tell him anything, everything. But inside herself she found a small, hard core of resistance that held her back from crossing over to where he sat, leaning against one of the massive rocks.

The decision was taken from her, for Davey rose and came to sit beside her. They sat with their shoulders touching, and then he lifted her hand to touch his lips to her palm. She felt a sweet, insidious warmth flow through her. But it was not desire that had brought him to her side, for his body was tense.

Davey still held her hand, but rested it on his thigh. "Mayhap 'tis best if I begin with what I do remember." He waited for some encouragement, and when none was forthcoming, sighed deeply. "Och, but 'twas a strange feeling that came over me. He did some vile thing with the harp, for I heard this wild clanging of chords, like no music I recall. I was helpless to shut it out. It crawled through me, lass. And I could do naught to stop it. That is the last I remember."

"'Tis enough," she whispered in a small voice. "More than enough," she added, bowing her head to hide what he might read in her expression and feeling like a coward as she did so.

"Do you know where he is?"

"Somewhere close by."

"Could you find him?"

"Davey, you cannot go after him now. This…this thing he did with the harp hurt you in ways I barely healed."

He caught her chin with his fingertips and raised her head. Leaning over, he studied her features as if imprinting them on his memory. "If you are willing to risk your life, will you decide for me if I will risk mine now?"

"Do not ask me that." She had to close her eyes against the blaze of his.

"Coward," he murmured. "Look upon me. Look, I say."

She lifted the thick fringe of her black lashes slowly, and her gray eyes took on a sheen from the fire, but she leveled them upon his.

"When we began this," he whispered against the corner of her mouth, "you were willing enough to risk my life in your quest. And I, bletherin' fool that I was, took that risk willingly. I'd not lose you now. You have waited each time for Owain to move first. Poor war tactics, lass. Far better to attack when your enemy believes you to be weak."

Davey kissed her cheek, then the tip of her nose, and smiled to see her face tilt the tiniest bit upward, offering easier access to her lips. But Davey denied himself. He needed his wits about him, and kissing

Meredith wiped thoughts of duty and war from his mind. But he could not help himself from nuzzling her neck, brushing aside her still-damp hair.

"Tell me where he is, lass. Let me seek him out," he urged in a soft and very seductive voice. "Else I will be forced to think that you protect him."

Those last words penetrated the sensual web he had woven, and she leaned away from him. She would have risen and put more distance between them, but Davey slipped his arm around her waist and held her fast.

"What makes you accuse me of such vile treachery?" she demanded. "If I protect anyone, 'tis you. Do you understand naught? All was clear to me. And then...then you showed me what it meant to desire someone more than loyalty owed or promises given. 'Tis your life I will not risk. Your life he would take, and thereby slay me."

"Then 'twas no dream when I heard you say you loved me?"

He wore such a self-satisfied look that she raised her hand to strike it from his face. His strong fingers caught her wrist in a grip that did not hurt, but one she could not break.

"Do not blame me for learning to be devious. You force me along that path by your secrets. I will not crow with victory won by knowing that you said it. I will not even ask if you meant it. But I will not be denied knowing what else is hidden behind those eyes that ensnared me from the first."

She was bent back as he leaned over her. His breath was hers. He did his own fair share of ensnaring, with dark eyes that probed for the smallest crack in her

shield. She refused to yield to his greater strength.
But she was guilty of hiding things from him. The
fire was behind him, and his face was in shadow. She
longed to kiss him into silence, spell him to sleep
while she hunted Owain and thereby freed Davey
from risking his life. But killing Owain was forbidden
to her. Of all the vows she'd made, 'twas one she
could not break.

"Och, lass, look here. We are at each other's
throats, and that whoreson laughs to know he set us
at odds. Keep your secrets, but let me hear you say
you love me."

"Aye, 'tis true, Davey. But ask me not to say the
words, for naught can come of it. You have known
that, too, from the first. Never did I lie about that."
She felt his pain and seized upon something she *could*
tell him.

"Davey, I did not tell you that Owain has more
than the harp to aid him. Somehow he has recovered
the ring. If he finds the right spell for it, he will un-
leash a power greater than my own. As it stands, he
already knows a spell to block me from sensing him
near to us."

"Aye, he would enjoy being able to approach us
unseen." He moved away and drew her up with him.
"Remember that for all his spells and blacker arts, he
is yet a man." He spoke to her, but his head tilted to
the side, listening with all his senses open. "Och, lass,
we will have a good laugh on Owain, that fumbling,
pitiful excuse for a man."

"Davey! What ails you?"

"Naught. Everything is as right as I could ever
wish." But he answered in a distracted way that she

could not help but notice. He felt her hand on his cheek, attempting to make him look at her. He resisted her urging. Her sudden silence told him that she, too, was aware that they were no longer alone. Davey only hoped that she could not sense his fear of hearing that harp play. He had a vague, terrified memory of falling into a black pit whose sides were so smooth he could not get a handhold. Fear had taken hold of him, more than he had ever known. And he was cold, numb with cold....

With a rough shake of his head, he rid himself of that strange memory and recalled instead the feel of Meredith's arms around him, her lips pressed to his and the sound of her voice calling him back to be with her.

He raised his leg, one hand dropping down to finger the *sgian-dubh* secure in his boot. He had deliberately left the sword across the fire, where he had been sitting. Owain had the arrogance to believe that he would win. Davey would prove him wrong. Unless his every warrior's instinct and all the new senses of perception he had were wrong, Owain was creeping up on their camp.

Davey glanced at Meredith. *Dinna let her see the fear and the dread in my heart and mind.*

But that is exactly what she saw.

Chapter Twenty-Four

Owain made them wait, aware, on edge, anxious and certainly anticipating his strike. The chance attack by those outlaws had allowed him to observe the results of his own attack with the harp's music on the Highlander, as well as his tactics in battle. Owain had watched, and cursed when the man refused to move far from Meredith. He had hoped to snatch her away in the dark. He would have sired a great race with her bloodline. Now she had befouled herself by claiming to love that sword-wielding beast.

Owain had a passing regret for slaying Pwyll out of rage at the harp failing to kill the man who stood between him and all he wanted. Far better to have Pwyll to distract the one while he stole the other.

He smiled to see the Highlander's swift, searching glances that probed riverbank and wood. He would not be found unless he wished it.

With a delicious sense of anticipation, Owain lifted the small harp. He cradled it in his arms much like a man would hold a babe. Despite the failure to kill, he knew it was no fault of the magic he held to do his bidding and rid him of the thorn that had pricked him every step of the way.

He waved his hand over the strings, thinking of the deadly melody he would play. To see his enemy helpless and on his knees before him brought a great sensual pleasure. While he held his enemy in helpless thrall, he would have the maid. And the gifts. All of them together again. And the power... He delighted in the shiver that crept over his body, for when he won the maid would be forced to key the spell on the ring.

Meredith would not be able to deny him then. Or ever. There would be no one to deny him ever again. Whatever he wanted...riches, lands, men on bended knee and women to serve. He would have kings begging for his aid.... He could be king.

He *would* be king.

He blinked his eyes to rid himself of the visions that swam in his mind's eye. Down below him vaporous fog lifted from the river and wafted over its banks. But the tiny fire still glowed like a beacon and drew his gaze.

How close should he be? he asked himself.

As near as he could get to see pain strike, to see Meredith once more unable to defeat him.

Owain hurried to the spot on the hillside where he had brought his enemy to his knees. And once there, he stood with his arms outstretched as if he would gather the heavens and hold them captive.

His eyes glowed as his triumph played out in his mind. With every breath he took, he felt the power surging through him. Each incantation he whispered brought forth the dark forces of the gods he served.

He would win. There was no other outcome.

He, Owain ap Madog, cast out, maimed, his name purged from all memories and all writings, would rule the world, and woe to those who opposed him.

Down at the riverbank, Davey made preparations to meet Owain. He knew he would need his every skill, and every bit of courage to withstand the agony Owain would use against him. Davey knew how much Meredith loved him when she removed the ring from her finger and, using a length of ribbon he had bought for her hair, slipped the ribbon through the ring and tied it around his neck. She had naught now to protect herself but her own spells, though Davey did not intend for Owain to get anywhere near her. He had slipped away from the fire after he found a candle stub in their packs.

He smiled at her when she saw him warming the tallow and pinching off small pieces.

"Truly, I am not daft, lass. What you see is as much a weapon as that sword." He would say no more.

"Stay with me, Davey. Owain cannot cross the *airbe druad*. It would kill him." She did not care if her heart was in her eyes for him to see. One of them—Davey or Owain—would not walk away. And she was too afraid to scry in the river to see which one would live and which one would die. Even the thought was a betrayal to Davey, a lack of faith that smote her with guilt. She knew he needed her belief that he would triumph over Owain and his evil. She forced a smile and blew him a kiss.

"You ken, lass, I need to be free to move as I see fit. I cannot allow him to pin me to one place. That gives him all the advantage. He has had enough of that."

Davey stared hard at her for those last minutes before he slipped away. He impressed on his memory the sight of her black hair tangled like a wild mane, those eyes seeming to whisper every word he longed to hear, and her lips, red where she had bitten them, parted now but silent. He recalled what she'd said about Owain killing him and thereby slaying her. Davey knew the feeling and the belief of those words. Without her, there was no life for him.

He yearned to linger for a last kiss, another word just to hear the sound of her voice. But he was a warrior going to battle for their lives, and for the dreams of her people. He would not, could not fail.

The water was icy as he slipped into the river and let the current carry him downstream. Owain was out there; he could feel him. Davey caught hold of tall reeds, being careful not to pull on them, for their roots were shallow. He parted them and made his way to the bank. He lay there, slicking back his hair to get rid of the water that dripped into his eyes. He could not see Meredith or the horses. He thought, but could not be sure, that the river made a slight bend above where he had come out.

He rose to his feet and, keeping to a crouch and using every bit of natural cover he could find, made

his way up the slope, above where he had left Meredith.

A thick growth of saplings barely allowed him passage. He searched for any sign of movement, but not
a leaf stirred. Even the horses were still and silent.
He could see the small eye of their fire, which they
had allowed to die down. It reminded him that Owain
used fire for his scrying.

Davey crept from the stand of saplings and nearly
fell when a loose stone rolled under his foot. He
twisted his body and regained his balance. As he
moved forward once more he saw what he had been
waiting for; on the hilltop was a spurt of fire.

"Owain ap Madog!" he bellowed, throwing his
voice as he ducked and dodged to circle around behind him.

But as Davey circled Owain, small fires broke out.
At first they dotted the hillside, then brush caught and
burned brightly. The flames all had white hearts and
made no sound. It was a feint and naught more,
Davey thought. And to his disadvantage, for he could
not hide himself.

Owain was not waiting for him on the hilltop.

Davey could not see him, could not hear him. He
had to believe that Meredith was safe from Owain; to
think otherwise was to destroy himself.

But where had the coward hidden?

He had trouble searching for his enemy. The flames
hurt his eyes, while fire was Owain's element to use.
The burning brush also created deep pockets of
shadow, any one of which could be Owain's hiding
place.

He had sworn to himself that Owain would not be
first to attack this time. It put him at a disadvantage
to always be on the defensive.

"Come out and fight me like a man, Owain!" Once
more Davey yelled, then moved, this time heading
down the hill toward their camp. Owain had to be
down there. Meredith would draw him close, she and
the cup. Owain knew he had the sword.

But before Davey got close, he stopped and made
ready against the harp song. And none too soon. He
both saw and faintly heard the first insidious notes
played. He half ran, half stumbled down to where
Owain stood, close to Meredith's protective circle.
She stood within, holding the horses, her eyes wide
as Owain implored her to give in to him.

"I will spare his life, since that is precious to you.
Look to him, Meredith. See how he falls. Just a pluck
of one string, not yet the full melody played. Will
you try to heal him yet again?"

"Owain, forget this vision you have," she answered. "You will die if you use what was not ever
meant to be touched by you. Hear me. Know that I
speak the truth to you. Cease now. Cease and I will
help you find—"

"I need not your help!" he raged, his clawed hand
almost ripping the strings from the harp. He turned to
see Davey brought to his knees, but was disappointed:
the tall warrior still advanced on him without any sign
that the harp's music affected him. Again and again
Owain played. He howled with rage.

"What have you done?" he screamed at Meredith.
His foul curses were aimed first at her, then at Davey.

The more he raged, the greater the fires grew, until the whole hillside was lit with cold flames.

Meredith saw what Davey could not. Owain's face was wild with desire for death. All reason fled from his eyes, and she knew for him there would be no escape from that which he sought to bring to others.

Spittle fell from his lips in his frantic mutterings. When he saw that Davey still came toward him, he threw down the harp and drew forth a sword.

Meredith bit her lip to stop a cry. He was going to use Davey's own sword against him.

Owain held the sword with both his good hand and the clawed one. He raised it over his head, screaming his evil spells as he ran toward Davey.

Just shy of a sword's length, he stopped short. "Tell me how you withstood the harp. Tell me! What magic power has the witch given to you? How could you? I saw you brought to your knees. I saw it!"

Davey's smile was cold and tight. He could see Owain's mouth, and the eyes that carried a madman's fury. But he could not hear what he said, just he had not heard the evil song he had played upon the harp.

He lunged with the sword. Owain retained enough sense of self-preservation to sidestep, and brought his own blade down on Davey's outstretched arm.

Davey pulled back, but the edge of the blade sliced across the back of his hand. As it did, he recognized the sword. This was no outlaw's poorly tempered blade, but his own finely made steel. He swung around to the left, but Owain was no longer there. Davey spun in place. His sword deflected Owain's blow. He put his trust into his own abilities as the better swordsman, and delivered a constant flurry of thrusts designed to keep Owain defending himself, without the chance for attack.

But Davey knew he would not be able to keep this pace up much longer; what Owain had done with the harp the first time, had weakened him. He went after the madman with cold rage guiding his hands and feet. He watched the glitter of hatred grow in Owain's eyes.

Davey went after him again. Steel rang on steel and sparks flew. He had to wonder if Owain had not somehow cast a spell on his sword, for the blow he had delivered should have cracked the blade.

Dragging air into his lungs, Davey stood back, but circled, always moving around Owain, who swung the blade and forced him to keep his distance. Davey feinted again and again, forcing Owain to keep moving in an ever-tightening circle. Davey sliced Owain's arm. He caught the edge of his sword in the folds of Owain's robe, but blood flowed when he yanked the sword free.

Now he reversed his feints to the right, leaving his back exposed, and when his foe took the bait, Davey spun round, using the sword like a staff for battering.

Owain staggered, then fell to his knees. He dropped the sword and lifted his hand, which was covered with blood. His mouth moved, but no sound came forth.

Davey did not trust him to be mortally wounded. He had to make sure.

He delivered the death blow with such force that the sword pierced body and bone, and the earth itself. There it stood, vibrating for long moments until shafts of blinding white light shot from the face on the hilt. Davey shielded his eyes with his upthrust arm and turned away.

He had to struggle to remove the twisted bits of candle tallow that he had used to plug his ears against the sound of the harp. He saw that the fires lit by the madman had nearly gone out. And he had to look again, had to know that Owain was truly dead.

Staring down at the body, he said in a voice lacking all emotion, "Your death will never pay for the lives of the innocents that you took. May all the hellfires burn bright and consume you, Owain ap Madog." As he pronounced the last word, he grasped the sword to free it. Fire ran from the rays, spreading out from the face to run down the blade. Davey could not let go of the sword. Another blinding flash of light and only ashes remained of Owain's body. Davey shook with exhaustion. He forced himself to sift the ashes to reclaim the ring.

He heard Meredith crying his name, and he spun around to see her running toward him. He opened his arms to her and she flung herself against him. Tears flowed down her cheeks.

He crushed her against him, slowly rocking her. "'Tis over, love, and long past time to take you home."

"Aye, Davey," she answered with a sob in her voice. "By all the gods' mercy, I was so afraid for you, but I never once faltered with doubt that you would win."

"There were minutes when I thought I would fail, but no more. There is naught here for us. Come away with me. Come away now, love.'' Davey knew he had one more battle to face. Meredith had reclaimed the gifts, but he had yet to claim his final prize. Would the priests let her go?

Chapter Twenty-Five

Old Roman roads marked the way for Davey and Meredith as they headed toward her homeland. Across the broken stones of the once-standing wall of Offa's Dyke they rode, into a land of wild beauty that called to their hearts.

Meredith warned him that they were being watched and shadowed by the Cymry. He understood why so many forces of England's might had failed to truly conquer these people. The tracks they rode along were little better than the paths animals followed. No man could fight an unseen force that used the natural growth of trees and bushes, rocky defiles and water courses to aid their defense.

The middle of his back itched more than once, feeling an arrow from one of the famous Welsh longbows aimed at it. But he found signs of their welcome to Meredith in the offerings left by the campfire—of food and flowers, a leather jack of wine or stones polished smooth. No matter how many times Davey looked, or swore to stay awake and catch sight of the watching Cymry, he never did.

It was an annoyance and not his first worry. That honor went to Meredith, with her new reserve. Her mood was light and they often shared laughter, but she skillfully avoided any physical contact when she could. If she could not, her manner turned cool. When his blood ran hot, this new demeanor left him sometimes angry, most times confused. He wondered if this was her way of showing him that what he wanted most and what she said she desired no longer held true.

The subject was taboo. Any mention of the future was answered by the first words she had spoken to him so long ago in the courtyard of his clan's stronghold.

"All things come. All things pass. All will be known when it's time."

"And when is the time?" he would ask.

"Soon," she replied. "Soon."

This answer did not content him. It made him most anxious. The deeper they rode into the Cambrian Mountains, fording rivers and streams whose names he could not pronounce, or backtracked along lengthy vales, the greater his fear that he was gong to lose the one woman he loved to the seductive wild beauty of this land.

He rode behind Meredith and listened closely as she told him about this land that she loved. *Hiraeth,* she called it, saying there was no name in Norman or English that truly explained the love of the land. He understood and appreciated this, for he felt the same way about his Highland home.

Birdsong filtered through the thick growths of oak

and larch, the latter of which, she told him, was used to build a smoky fire to drive away evil spirits. She picked vervain flowers whenever she found them, needing them, she said, to purify the gifts. He had glanced at the pack carrying the sword and the harp and the cup. She wore both rings now, since he had reclaimed one and returned the other.

There were times when he rode so deep in thought that he was not aware of his surroundings until she called him several times. She did so now, pointing out that they had a visible escort.

He was startled to see them joined by a group of small-built, dark-haired men with eyes that revealed naught of their thoughts.

"Davey," Meredith said softly, "they come to escort us to Alawn's hall. Be patient a little while longer."

"Patient?" he repeated. "I have been so patient that sainthood enters the realm of possibility for me."

"Your anger serves no purpose. I promise you that all—"

"Aye, I ken it well," he snapped. "All things will be known when 'tis time."

"'Twill not be much longer, Davey." She knew he did not fully understand, and as she urged her horse into a canter, she heard him call to her. It took every bit of will she had not to turn back.

Davey found his way blocked by the men crowding around him. He held the reins tight lest Ciotach take exception and, reading his mind, try to trample everyone who stood between him and Meredith. Davey muttered curses in his own tongue, just as the men guarding him—for he could see no other purpose for them—spoke in their own incomprehensible language.

He may not have understood the words, but the gestures made, with brandished longbows and knives, told him that he was not to attempt to follow her.

Meredith knew he would come to no harm. Just as she knew how much she had wounded him with her reluctance to allow any physical intimacy. Davey never gave thought to how much it hurt her to deny him. But she had many thoughts to ponder and needed distance from him. He so easily stirred desire to life with a mere look from his dark eyes. His touch or kiss would weaken her will.

She needed to prepare herself, and thought she had. It was no easy task to think of facing the priests. She did not require use of her powers to discern that the way she chose would be difficult. And she could not help Davey when his time came.

When Meredith dismounted before the wooden hall where she had grown to womanhood, she found that Alawn waited alone for her. She had no fear of him, although she knew that many did. But for her, his dark blue eyes were always kind.

She kept no secrets from him, for he had the power to read mind, heart and soul of all who came before him. His thick mane of white hair fell below his stooped shoulders. He held his rod of yew, with ancient words carved into the wood. He used the rod for purposes of divination.

His thin lips wore a wide smile of welcome, as wide as the arms he held out to her.

"Well come, my child. You have weathered your trials and become stronger for them." Alawn held her to his chest, accepting that she would tell him what troubled her in good time.

"Come inside. There is food. And others who wait to greet you."

"You know that Owain is dead?"

"Aye. I watched." His eyes reflected his sadness. "There were some who said he was cursed with a *dlui fulla,* but I showed them that none had made a madman's wisp of straw or grass, or pronounced the horrible incantations that led to his malignant thoughts of seizing all power unto himself."

"There was no other choice but his death," Meredith said quickly, in defense of Davey's actions.

"There never was another choice of what was to be done with him. But come, help an old man. You were sorely missed from our hall."

Beneath her hand, his white wool robe felt soft, but of a thicker weight. He had aged while she had been gone.

"Aye, 'tis a truth to that. I feel the cold more no matter the season."

She laughed. When she was a child, he would startle her with some remark or answer to a thought she had. Now she felt she was home.

Alawn paused before the hall's great doors. "My child, no matter what you decide, and it will be a decision based on your free will, this will always be your home. But there is no rush."

"You do not know Davey as well as you think if

you can say that, Alawn. I fear for him being left behind.''

''He is wiser than you believe. He knows there are matters that he is not a part of. You were well pleased with him?'' He studied the lovely features, as dear to him as if she truly was his daughter. ''Aye, I can see that you are. Look deep into this one's heart. Your doubts will fade. But I hear Emrys and Brehon making a fuss, just as they did when you were little. Always thinking I kept you too much to myself. Bah!''

When Davey entered the hall with his escort, he first searched for signs of Meredith. He had been kept apart from her for three days. His hosts—he had come to calling them that, since it was impossible to think of the men who hunted with him, and tried teaching him to shoot a longbow, as his guards any longer— had provided him with fresh clothing and a bath. What he wore was as fine as any clothing he owned.

He had contributed to the feasting by bringing down a large red stag. He tried to argue that his arrow's flight could not have been the killing shot, but it was a task beyond him when he could not communicate with words. And the task was doubly hard when a few cups of mead had passed his lips. He swore he would bring home a cask or two for his brothers to taste. He had thought he had a good head for drink until he tried matching these smaller Cymry men cup for cup.

''Well come to our hall, young warrior.''

Davey turned at the sound of the voice behind him and faced three old men, one of whom bore a striking resemblance to old Duncan, one of the oldest croft holders in Clan Gunn. All Davey wanted to do was ask where Meredith was, but perceived that he would hear that oft-repeated refrain "all in good time." Well, he would wait them out.

"You will be rewarded for your patience," the middle one said. "I am Emrys. On my right is Alawn, and here is Brehon. We give the blessings of *Hu Gadarn* upon you for keeping our lady safe. We raised her here in this hall."

"'Tis not your babble he wishes for, Emrys," Alawn said, his eyes twinkling with some hidden knowledge. "He is impatient to see our maid."

"Do you give some blame to that?" Brehon asked. "I, for one, would rather look upon Meredith than either of you."

Davey stared. He could not help himself. There was no time for light banter when matters of grave import had brought him to this place at this time. Before he could remark on this, Alawn held out his hand.

"Our lady comes to join us. We will not keep you. There is much needed to be said between you two."

They parted before him, and he saw Meredith, but not as he knew her. She was dressed in a white flowing robe much like the three old priests wore, but there the similarity ended.

There were small groups of people in the large hall, and many stopped her to speak a few words of greeting. Davey seemed rooted to where he stood. The woman who made her way toward him had an aura of wild, barbaric splendor.

Her glorious black hair fell to her hips in loose

shining waves. She wore a wreath of greenery and flowers, with ropes of gray pearls entwined. Her linked belt was gold, judging from its gleam, and a small jeweled eating dagger rested within. But it was her face that held him a silent captive. He knew her to be beautiful, but there was a glow and serenity he had never seen before. Her gray eyes were clear, he was glad to note. Gone were all the doubts and shadows he had seen too much of during the last weeks before they arrived here.

She came to stand before him. Davey drew a deep, shuddering breath that brought with it the faint scent of flowers heated by her body. She smiled at him, a tiny bit amused by his speechless stare. He grinned, and still did not know what to say or do. Thoughts of taking her into his arms and declaring before all that he claimed her as his crossed his mind.

"We cannot, Davey," she whispered, taking hold of his hand. "We are required to sit at the high table. This feast is in your honor as much as mine."

"I need no feast. The only hunger I have is to—"

"Hush!" She leaned close to scold. "There are those here who can read such thoughts, not that they would invade a guest's mind, but still others have sharp hearing. We will have time later. I promise you."

"Alone?"

She looked away. "Aye. There are matters of great importance to us both that need to be discussed."

"Then I am content to enjoy your company."

And he was content. He had the three old priests to talk to as well as Meredith. The food was simple fare but plentiful. Wine and ale and mead, which Davey declined to drink this night, flowed from pitchers without end.

He understood without being told that no mention was to be made of Owain or of the reason he was here. He spoke of his home and his clan and brothers. He did not know if any took note of the times he clasped Meredith's hand or gazed upon her with love glowing in his eyes. He truly cared not who saw. He was more than willing to proclaim it aloud, but these were her people and it was her place to make any announcement.

Meredith left him for a little while when she gave in to the clamor for her to sing. The harp she held was naught like the one that Owain had used, and Davey was thankful for it. He sat as enthralled as others in the silent hall as she sang. Not one word did he understand, but the music found a place in his heart.

He noted, too, how others watched her. Their faces held expressions of love and devotion, admiration and respect. Would they ever let her go from them?

Her song changed to a lively tune that brought forth a great deal of laughter. He smiled and stifled the hard need driving him to be alone with her. He would not give her up. He could not.

Chapter Twenty-Six

The night was cool and the breeze scented with smoke and forest as Meredith led him from the hall to a small hill. Moonlight draped her with delicate light, giving her an ethereal air. But her hand in his was real enough as she stood beside him looking over her land.

Her silence shook his confidence that she had brought him here to tell him what he most desired.

Meredith thought back to her avoidance of being with Davey under all the watchful eyes, until tonight. To see him and not touch him, to hear him speak and want his lips on hers was too much torment. So she had waited, and now the time had come.

"These last few days were hard on you," she said at last.

"And I hope as difficult for you."

"Did you doubt that, Davey? I wanted to be with you. Surely," she said, turning to look up at him, "you knew that?"

He had to take her into his arms, unable to last a moment longer without at least holding her. "'Tis sorry I am for saying that. My temper got the best of me. I feared that you no longer wanted me. You will be mine?''

'''Tis not as simple a question as you believe.''

''I willna have another answer but 'yea, yours now and forever.'''

She stroked his cheek. ''If I were anyone but who I am, I could repeat those words to you. But I am not.''

''Do you reject me, then? Was all this some sham—''

She did the only thing she could to silence him. His mouth was still open when she pressed her lips to his. The strength of the feelings between them could not be denied. Not by time, or words, or being apart. While Davey lived there could never be another man for her. She gloried in his strength, and the will he had to temper it with gentleness.

Fire coursed through her veins and warmed every part of her body. A low moan of yearning escaped her as he pressed against her. There was so much to love in this one man. His steadfastness in the face of danger, his courage and strength of character, and the genuine goodness of his heart. And he was hers.

His fingers twisted in the silken sheen of her hair, tilting her head back for the hunger of his lips exploring her every feature, her earlobes, the bare length of her neck. Her hands clasped his head when he brought his hunger back to her lips.

''I love you, you and only you,'' he whispered.

''*Eneit,*'' she called him, shivering with the heat of

passion that erupted between them. *"Eneit,"* she said yet again. "My soul."

"You love me. I know you do. Come away with me now. Tonight. I swear by all that is holy I will do everything in my power to make you happy."

She ached with the need to deny him yet again. She leaned away from his descending lips, knowing their power to make her forget everything but Davey and the love she had for him.

"Please, listen to me. Tomorrow the priests will ask what you wish. You can tell them that you ask their permission to wed me." She narrowed her eyes and stared at him. "You will say yea to them?"

"Nay. I want you for a moment's sport. Goosling! Och, lass, that you should even tease me. Of course I want you to wife. And I will forsake all others to have it so. But why," he asked, nuzzling her chin, "must we wait? We can tell them now."

"Davey, I cannot. Please, they are set in the way of things. There is little they would refuse you after what you have done. To give people back their dreams, to have within their hands what was wrought by the ancient gods for them... Their feelings are powerful."

"And they want just as powerfully to hold on to you," he noted with a touch of bitterness. "I saw that for myself in the hall tonight. I ache with wanting you, not only to make love to you and know that you are mine, but for a thousand days and nights of sharing."

"Then let me go now." She scattered kisses on his lips and chin and neck to soften her request. And it was a request, for she had not the strength to leave his arms.

"Tell me this. Is there some test set for me to prove myself worthy of you?"

"Davey, oh, Davey, how can you think thus? Did I not tell you from the first that you were chosen for me? Oh, my beloved, you have no reason to fear them. They love me and wish to see my happiness. And I…'' She stopped herself from telling him of the doubt she had. One that had grown and would not be rooted out no matter how many times she reminded herself that he did love her. Her, the woman, and naught else.

"Until tomorrow," she whispered as he let her go. "And dream of me."

"I do naught else." He almost stopped her from going, but stilled the impulse. There was something more that she had not told him. He threw his head back and looked up at the night sky. Three brilliant stars fairly close together captured his attention and held it for long moments. Tomorrow was not so far off. He could wait a few hours to see his will done. And Meredith's, he added. She wanted this as much as he.

When dawn's light streaked the sky, Davey was already up and dressed. The dark tunic he slipped over his head appeared almost black in the light of a single candle. The water he splashed on his face held an icy bite, a warning that summer was near done. Leaving his companions asleep in a smaller hall, he went by the cookhouse. A smile won him a bit of cheese and hot bread slathered with butter to break his fast. He sat out in the morning's chill on an up-turned barrel.

He expected the summons to the main hall and kept watch to see who would fetch him. He was surprised to see that the old priest Emrys, wrapped tightly in a heavy cloak, was the one who looked for him.

But instead of returning to the hall, the silent Emrys led him to the forest's edge. He gestured toward a barely defined path.

"Go, my son. What you seek is there waiting."

Davey experienced a vague disquiet and a touch of dizziness. The feelings were very like when his gift of second sight would come. But it ended as quickly as it started. He caught a smile on Emrys's wrinkled lips before he turned away and left.

The thought of this being some sort of trap never entered into Davey's mind. Yet he found it strange that he thought he knew this forest growth. Passing strange, yet he shrugged it off. He had never been to this place.

He had to push aside low-growing limbs as he fol-lowed what he thought was a deer track. The sun was fully up, and on the path ahead the rays gleamed like a beacon, guiding him forward.

A faint sound came to him and he stopped to look around. This could not be the place of his dream, but the music... Nay, not a harp song luring him forth, but the sweet, haunting song of Meredith's voice. His first beguilement with the lovely, mysterious maid had been the sound of her voice.

He started to run then, ducking where needful,

shoving aside the forest growth to make passage for himself. He remembered his dream. Recalled the sound of the harp song and how he had likened it to Meredith calling him, her lover, her heart's mate. He knew the promise that waited ahead for him. A promise well worth the wait. All things would be known when the time was right.

Her passionate song brought to life the belief that there was true magic in this place. He ran harder, anxious to see her. Desire heated his blood as he reached the end of the path and found himself in the place of his dream.

Sunlight filtered down in lacy patterns through the leaves of the trees surrounding the glade, and played over the flower-strewn grass with delicate shafts of golden-green light. The pond, its banks lined with rocks draped with little carpets of moss, from palest yellow to deepest green, had a flawless surface. He could see the clarity of the water, for naught hindered his view clear to the bottom. Not even birdsong dared to compete with her sweeter voice. No bee buzzed to disturb the peace of this glade.

She stood at the edge of the pond, facing away from him, weaving her magic on his soul. He envied the bright shaft of sunlight that held her captive.

Davey was afraid to move or make a sound.

This could not be a dream. He would surely die if the vision in cloth of gold was not truly his Meredith. Her hands slipped beneath the fall of her hair, lifting it briefly, then letting it fall loose like a black silk cloak over the rainbow shades of embroidered flowers and birds scattered over her gown. Even the thin gold circlet she wore was as he remembered it.

His breath caught as the song ended on a fading note. She raised her arms high. The long, trailing sleeves fell back to bare her slender arms as she spun around and around, with laughter so joyous spilling from her lips that he doubly feared to break the spell she had woven. Her slippers crushed tiny plants of thyme, mint and rosemary, so that the wild scents perfumed the air. He saw that her eyes were closed. The delicate arch of her brows and the thick fringe of her lashes were black in contrast to the paleness of her skin. A slow smile curved her lips—a woman's secret smile, as if she hugged some delicious knowledge to herself.

His own lips broke into a smile. She enchanted him. And he thought he would never tire of seeing all the faces of woman that she brought to life for him.

She tilted her head to the side, then cast a glance over her shoulder. "I knew you would come," she said in a voice as sweet and silken as her melody.

"Thou art witch to draw me here with your magic."

She tossed her head and laughed. "Aye, some men would so name me. But not you, Davey. You know me as I am. You always have."

"Aye, and would know you again," he said softly as he walked to her. "I would know you in all the ways a man can know the other half of himself. I would know you for all my days. Tell me," he said, standing before her, "has the time come for me to know all things?"

"Do you know this place we stand in?"

"I have seen it a time or two. I dream of it and what I found here."

"'Tis a place of magic, Davey. A place where dreams for those who are favored by the gods are blessed with the truth of them."

"I already know the truth of my dream."

"Do you?" She searched each feature that was dear to her. Her fingertips traced his strong jaw, lingering a moment longer at the cleft in his chin. Her hand dropped to her side. "I wish I could be as sure as you."

"Meredith—"

"Wait. There is a thing you must do. Alawn," she called.

Davey did not turn or show any sign of surprise that the old priest was here with them.

He came from somewhere behind Davey and moved to stand beside them. He held the Cup of Truth filled with wine.

"Meredith asked for you both to drink. She has something to ask you, and I admit, I would know the answer as well."

Davey looked from one to the other. Both pairs of eyes regarded him so seriously that he felt a prickle of fear. But he did not hesitate to take the cup and drink deeply of the wine. He held it out to Meredith. Her hand was not as steady when she took the cup from him to drink. There was a little left when she handed the cup back to Alawn and he, too, drank, until the cup was dry.

"Go on, my child. 'Tis time now to tell him."

"Davey," she began in a low voice, toying with her linked belt. "If I agree to wed you and leave this place, I will be as any other woman. Whatever powers and gifts were mine will be forfeit. Can you accept me thus?"

Anger bubbled and he swallowed it. He thought about what she said and what it meant. Not to him, but to her.

"I warned you—" Meredith started to say, but Alawn motioned her to silence.

"Can you not see and know that he does not delay to answer for himself? For shame, Meredith. I taught you to be wise in the ways of men. He thinks not of the meaning of this to him, but to you, daughter of my heart. And he proves himself wise to consider the loss of what has always been yours."

Davey took hold of her hands to lift them to his lips. He kissed the palms of each, his gaze all the while filled with aching tenderness.

"Listen to your wise elder, love. What Alawn said is true. None here can lie to the other. The drink from the cup prevents that. Can you live with giving up what has been a part of you far longer than I? These gentle hands impart a healing by their touch and naught else. Thy lips offer sweet sighs that is music enough for this man. Your courage is of the inner woman. We have no need of more, *a ghraidh mo chridhe,* aye, love of my heart. Och, lass, you must know as only a woman can that there is more magic in the love we share—''

He never finished. He could not, for his lips were silenced under the sweet, heady touch of her mouth, which offered him heaven with her kiss.

''Blessings upon you both,'' Alawn whispered beside them. He touched Meredith's shoulder, then Davey's back. ''What was lost long, long ago, is now found. Rejoice in your love, which is greater for the harsh testing and parting you have endured.'' He placed his boney hand on Meredith's head. ''As gifts are given, so let them be taken.'' He looked to Davey, and smiled as he touched him. ''Gifts you have brought back to us, and gifts we give you in return. Long life to you and those you love. The wisdom to bring peace to your many sons. Go forth in your new-found love. Go, I say, the halves are now whole.''

Davey heard Alawn's parting words, but he had a few of his own to speak. The very moment he tired of kissing his soon to be bride. Wife, he amended, for he liked the bond implied by the word. Not that he would be marrying a docile woman. She would never be that. The thought of wedding, then bedding his Cymry maid with all the ceremony and celebration his clan could offer helped him to temper the passionate fire she stoked to life.

He eased his lips free with tiny teasing kisses, and found there was no reluctance within himself for patience to wait.

Meredith searched his eyes for signs of any regret. She could no longer *know* what was in his mind. ''Are you sure?'' she whispered.

"Aye. Did I not tell you from the first that I would have you? 'Tis time for us to go home, love."

"*Home*. 'Tis a beautiful word on your lips."

With his hands on her slender waist he lifted her, their joyous laughter filling the silence. As he turned with her, a mist rose from the still pond, and they both became aware of the eloquent, seductive melody of harp song.

"Davey, 'tis a magic place. When we leave here 'twill be gone from our memories."

He lowered her to stand, then cradled her face within his hands. "What need have I of this place? I hold you in my arms. There's magic enough for this man."

"Aye, 'tis more than enough for this woman, too."

* * * * *

Enchanted by England?

Take a journey through the British Isles with Harlequin Historicals

ON SALE JULY 2001

THE PROPER WIFE
by **Julia Justiss**
Sequel to **THE WEDDING GAMBLE**
(England, 1814)

MAGIC AND MIST
by **Theresa Michaels**
Book three in the Clan Gunn series
(Scotland & Wales, 1384)

MY LORD SAVAGE
by **Elizabeth Lane**
(England, 1580s)

ON SALE AUGUST 2001

CELTIC BRIDE
by **Margo Maguire**
(England, 1428)

LADY POLLY
by **Nicola Cornick**
Sequel to **THE VIRTUOUS CYPRIAN**
(England, 1817)

HARLEQUIN®
Makes any time special ®

HHMED19

If you enjoyed what you just read,
then we've got an offer you can't resist!

Take 2 bestselling love stories FREE!

Plus get a FREE surprise gift!

▬▬▬▬▬▬▬▬▬▬▬▬▬▬▬▬▬▬▬▬▬

Clip this page and mail it to Harlequin Reader Service®

YES! Please send me 2 free Harlequin Historical® novels and my free surprise gift. After receiving them, if I don't wish to receive anymore, I can return the shipping statement marked cancel. If I don't cancel, I will receive 6 brand-new novels every month, before they're available in stores! In the U.S.A., bill me at the bargain price of $4.05 plus 25¢ shipping and handling per book and applicable sales tax, if any*. In Canada, bill me at the bargain price of $4.46 plus 25¢ shipping and handling per book and applicable taxes**. That's the complete price and a savings of over 10% off the cover prices—what a great deal! I understand that accepting the 2 free books and gift places me under no obligation ever to buy any books. I can always return a shipment and cancel at any time. Even if I never buy another book from Harlequin, the 2 free books and gift are mine to keep forever.

246 HEN DC7M
349 HEN DC7N

_____
Name   (PLEASE PRINT)

_____
Address   Apt.#

_____
City   State/Prov.   Zip/Postal Code

* Terms and prices subject to change without notice. Sales tax applicable in N.Y.
** Canadian residents will be charged applicable provincial taxes and GST.
  All orders subject to approval. Offer limited to one per household and not valid to
  current Harlequin Historical® subscribers.
  ® are registered trademarks of Harlequin Enterprises Limited.

HIST01   ©1998 Harlequin Enterprises Limited

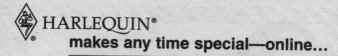